NOT

YOUR

#LOVESTORY

NOT YOUR

#LOVESTORY

SONIA HARTL

PAGE STREET
PUBLISHING CO.

PAGE STREET
PUBLISHING CO.

For Rebecca Podos, who always believed in me,
even when I'd forgotten how to believe in myself.

CHAPTER
ONE

I SPENT SIX MONTHS planning for the Kansas City Royals game—quietly hoarding a few dollars each week, going behind my mom's back to arrange the day off, finally getting my license so I could drive. She'd been a Royals fan since Gramps took her to a game for her fifth birthday, and she hadn't been back to one since. Everything had to be perfect.

When I handed the tickets to the man behind the booth at Gate D, he tipped his hat to me. "I hope you and your sister enjoy the game."

"Thanks." He wasn't trying to flatter us, and I didn't bother to correct him. Trying to explain how my thirty-five-year-old mom had an eighteen-year-old daughter took a lot more energy than I was willing to expend on strangers. I'd learned that lesson a long time ago.

Mom practically bounced on her toes as we stepped through the gates of Kauffman Stadium, into a sea of blue and white and the kind of buzz TV couldn't capture. I didn't have a Royals jersey, so I'd settled for the white peasant top embroidered with little blue seashells Gram had made for me to celebrate uploading my first YouTube video. Dozens of people milled around the food stands and carts selling hats and giant foam fingers. The scent of popcorn and fried bread made my mouth water. It had been a long drive from Honeyfield, and I hadn't eaten breakfast.

"Macy, I don't know what to say. I can't believe you did this for me." Mom's eyes shone in the bright sun. I didn't want her to ruin her makeup.

"Hey." I handed her a napkin. "'There's no crying in baseball,' remember?"

"Right." She sniffed, as if trying to will her precarious tears back in. "You're right, as usual. What should we do first? Grab our seats?"

"Food." I took her arm and dragged her to the nearest hot dog stand.

Once we loaded up with eats, drinks, and souvenirs, we headed down to Section 316, Row C. My hat didn't fit properly thanks to my curly pigtails, and my blond hair wasn't long enough to pull into a ponytail. Oh well. I mashed it down on my head anyway. Even in the shaded section, the plastic seat warmed my legs. Little kids with sticky cotton candy fingers toddled up the stairs with their families, while vendors tried to stay out of the way.

The stadium filled up quickly while I took several photos of me and Mom with the field as our backdrop. I flicked through them, trying out different filters and found the best one to post on Instagram. The whole baseball vibe made me want to do a Royals theme for my next YouTube video. Maybe a group of Kevin Costner films? I shook my head. Fear of mentioning the White Sox under our roof, let alone crafting a uniform for *Field of Dreams*'s signature team, had kept me away from that particular review for years. I'd have to think of something else.

A shadow fell over us. Mom groaned as a guy who had to be near seven feet tall took the seat right in front of her, practically blocking the prime view that had eaten up half my savings to secure.

"Trade seats with me," I said.

She leaned from side to side, trying to see around the guy. "Are you sure?"

"This is your day." Plus, I wasn't nearly the fan she was, much to her disappointment. "You know I'm going to get bored by the second inning and just start playing on my phone."

"I don't know." The worry line between her eyebrows appeared, though a faint outline had started to take up permanent residence on her face.

"It's fine. Honestly. Come on." I stood, balancing my Coke and hot dog in one hand while I pulled her up with the other.

I turned to my seat a little too fast, just as a guy was coming down the other side of the aisle. I stumbled, somehow managed to stay on my feet, but my Coke and hot dog were goners. Unfortunately, they'd gone all over the guy's shirt.

"Shi—" I glanced at my mom. She didn't get after me for cussing at home, but she hated when I did it in public. "Shoot. I'm so sorry." I picked up a few scattered napkins and dabbed at the *KC* on his shirt. He looked to be about my age. "I wasn't paying attention."

"No big deal." He pulled the cotton T-shirt over his head and draped it over the back of his chair. "See?"

"I do see." I nodded slowly, trying to figure out a discreet way of checking to see if my jaw was still attached, or if it had come unhinged and fallen to the ground.

The guy had abs, like body-spray-commercial abs. The kind of abs that created shadows in the ridges of his muscles. I had a strange urge to poke him in the stomach to see if it felt as hard as it looked. A woman in the row behind me had an enormous pink bow tying her hair in a half ponytail, and she giggled as she caught my eye and winked.

"Looks like we're going to be seatmates for the next few hours, so no point in getting hung up over an accident. I'm Eric, by the way. This is my buddy Rod." He stuck his thumb out to the shorter guy behind him I'd just noticed.

"I'm . . ." What was my name again? "Macy. Evans. The Third." I wasn't the third of anything. Why did I just say that? Did the glare coming off his abs fry the portion of my brain that controlled coherent thought?

"Cool. You look familiar, Macy Evans the Third. Liberty High?"

I shook my head.

"Eric Dufrane." He pointed at himself. "I just graduated from there yesterday." He sat, spreading his legs out until they spilled over into my seating area, which made him at least 40 percent less attractive. Bummer.

"I just graduated too, from Honeyfield High, up north. I drove down here so I could surprise my mom for her birthday."

She bent forward and gave a little wave. "Sorry my daughter is a klutz."

"No problem, Mrs. Evans the Second." He flashed a Colgate-worthy smile, but she'd already abandoned her chair to chase down the guy selling foam fingers in the aisle.

Eric settled into his seat, taking up even more room. "Wow, your mom is hot."

Gross. What a waste of perfectly good abs.

After the anthem, the opening pitch, and that mortifying moment where Mom tried to get everyone to do the wave, which petered out after five people, I opened my YouTube app. I tried to watch the game. Honestly. But between tall guy and the manspreader with abs, I had zero chance of enjoying the experience.

The John Hughes/Molly Ringwald review I'd uploaded a few weeks ago of *Sixteen Candles*, *Pretty in Pink*, and *The Breakfast Club* had topped out at twenty thousand views, better than my other videos, which had barely gotten over ten thousand. A respectable number, but not enough. I needed at least a million to attract sponsors and start making real money. I already dressed like characters from the films I reviewed, but I needed to do something more to stand out.

Two days ago, I'd uploaded my take on late-nineties rom-coms: *She's All That*, *10 Things I Hate About You*, and *Never Been Kissed*. The white feathered top Drew Barrymore wore in *Never Been Kissed* had been a nightmare to construct, and *10 Things* was the only movie that really held up. My comments section agreed. It had also been my best editing job to date. I had high hopes, but the ticker moved slow. Three thousand views so far. Only 997,000 to go.

I wasn't even alive when most movies I reviewed were made, but thanks to my job, I had access to the best and worst of the VHS world. And if Hollywood ever stumbled upon my YouTube channel, they'd have a whole road map for how to remake those films, especially if they wanted to do better by women.

Treating us like human beings instead of objects would be step one.

"What are you looking at there?" Eric leaned over. He smelled like beer cheese and bug spray. "My little sister is into those old movies. I watch them with her sometimes on Netflix."

I soften at the mention of his little sister. Nice abs and an appreciation for the VHS era was a formidable weakness. "I review them on YouTube."

"No way. If my sister isn't on Netflix, she's on YouTube." He sounded genuinely impressed, which gave me a little bubbly feeling in my stomach, even if I still thought he was kind of a douche. "Maybe I've seen one of yours."

"I doubt it." I wasn't well-known. Not yet anyway. But one day I'd take Misty Morning, the persona I'd created to host R3ntal Wor1d, all the way to the top of the YouTube food chain. I tucked those thoughts away, though, reminding myself it would take time to build my audience. "I just uploaded one a few days ago. Do you want to see?"

"Yeah, why not?" His arm brushed mine as he tried to

get a better view of my phone. All my nerves prickled with awareness. "Why are you calling yourself Misty?"

"It's like a stage name." I had Instagram and Twitter accounts under my real name, but those were just for me. Misty Morning and R3ntal Wor1d were for something more.

I watched him watching my video. It was a weird experience to be sitting next to someone while one of them played. I didn't even let my friends watch while I was in the room. I thought it would be easier with a stranger, since strangers watched me every week, but nope. Every tic or movement on his face threw me into overanalyzing. Was he drawing his eyebrows together because he didn't get my viewpoint? Or was he just concentrating extra hard? Did the pulse in his jaw mean he was working up the courage to tell me it sucked? Or was that just his regular pulse? Did he think it was silly and immature? So many questions rolled around in my head, I nearly shut off my phone mid-review.

After it ended, I pulled my phone back and sucked in a deep breath. "What did you think? It's okay if you think it sucked. I'm still new at this. I'm sorry it wasn't good."

"Slow down. Breathe." He laughed, which made me want to shrivel up and roll away. "You have some good thoughts. Really good. What's your channel called? I'll tell my sister to look for you." He took out his phone and opened his Notes app.

"It's R3ntal Wor1d." I had to explain that I needed the *3* in *Rental* and the *1* in *World* because Rental World was already taken. At which point it occurred to me that

I could've offered to text it to him. A perfectly reasonable excuse to get his number, but he'd already taken it down and now it would just be awkward.

I literally had no game.

I'd just pulled up my John Hughes/Molly Ringwald review when Mondesí hit a line drive down the middle. Eric launched out of his seat, screaming and hollering with the rest of the crowd as the Tigers shortstop missed the catch and sent Merrifield home. Mom grabbed my arm, cutting off my blood supply as she jumped up and down. The overwhelming presence of the shirtless wonder almost made me forget why I'd come here.

Mom didn't get a lot of breaks. As a full-time waitress at the diner, this was the first Saturday she'd had off in over two years. She'd gone to night school when I was a toddler, and even got an associate degree in business, but there weren't a lot of jobs in Honeyfield. We couldn't afford to move somewhere else. So she stayed at the diner.

She never wanted that to be me, to barely get by, soaking my feet in salt water and trying to fight lines around my eyes in my twenties. Though here in Kauffman Stadium, she looked younger and happier than I'd seen her since the Royals went to the World Series. It made all the saving and planning worth it. I tucked my phone into my back pocket, vowing to get more into the game and really make this a day she would remember forever.

I put Eric out of my mind—okay, to the side of my mind—and focused on trying to get the crowd hyped to do another wave. Because it was goofy and made my mom smile. I grabbed another round of Cokes, and somewhere around the fifth inning, I really had to go to the bathroom. I shifted in my seat, not wanting to get up. I had a serious aversion to public restrooms. But after five straight minutes of squirming, I finally stood.

"Where's the bathroom?" I asked Mom.

"Somewhere over there." She pointed toward the food stands. So helpful.

The lady with the enormous pink bow behind me tapped Eric on the shoulder. "You've been here loads of times, right? Why don't you be a dear and show this young lady where the restrooms are?" She gave me a conspiratorial look that made me vaguely uncomfortable.

"No, it's fine," I said. "I'm sure I can find it."

"Oh, hey. No worries." Eric jumped up. "I've got to go too."

Before I could protest, he shuffled me past an aisle of spectators until we reached the stairs. I walked beside him, and he put his hand on the small of my back, steering me into the short hall that led to the bathrooms. I took a careful step to the side to shift away from him.

His arm skimmed my shoulder as he pointed to the women's room, like I could miss the giant stick figure in a dress, and I didn't know if he was trying to flirt or if he really thought I was that helpless. I looked up at him. "Are you going to help me pee, too?"

"Only if you want me to." He gave me the kind of grin

only a boy cocky enough to know how good he looked could give. Like he'd spent his whole life getting whatever he wanted with just a few smiles.

"I'm fine, thanks." I pushed open the bathroom door and an uneasy feeling hovered over me. As if I'd just walked into a room and everyone stopped talking.

When I came out of the bathroom, I was surprised to find him waiting for me. At my questioning look, he said, "Just in case you couldn't find your way back."

"Thanks?" If he was flirting, he really sucked at it. Maybe he'd never had to hone that particular skill, since his strong jawline and ridiculous abs did all the work for him.

This time, I walked ahead of him. We passed a popcorn stand, and I made a mental note to pick some up on the way home. We headed back to our seats, and had just reached our row when the crowd got to their feet. A middle-aged man nearly hit me in the face as he stretched his arms, and I turned in time to see a baseball headed right for me.

Instinct had me whipping my hat off. I stretched my arm, reaching as my pulse hummed. The crowd, the movement, the noise around me faded to a blur. My vision narrowed on that single white speck in the sky. As if I could mentally coax it closer. Someone tried shoving me to the side, but I kept my feet planted, my eye on the ball.

And I caught it.

The swelling crowd jostled me around, and I stumbled, cradling my hat with the ball in it against my chest. Eric kept me upright and grabbed my hand, thrusting it into the air as he screamed with the rest of the crowd. We appeared on the jumbotron and my head went light. I'd never had a rush like that in my life.

People patted me on the back as I made my way to Mom, who was bawling. The "no crying in baseball rule" went out the window when it came to fly balls. I handed it to her, and she hugged me so hard, my back cracked. Best birthday ever.

The lady with the pink bow gave me a satisfied nod. "Good timing."

"The best." My smile practically touched my ears.

"Nice of you to be there with the assist," she said to Eric.

He blushed, which was cute enough to make me forget my earlier annoyance with him. Besides, he had kept me from face-planting on the jumbotron. "She made a great catch."

Mom passed the ball over to me so I could let Eric get a closer look. He took a selfie with it, the field behind him, and handed it back to me. Then I took a similar selfie and handed it back to Mom so I could get a shot of the two of us and the ball.

The lady with the pink bow raised her phone and sort of pointed it toward me, but when I caught her eye, she quickly lowered it and whispered to the man next to her. Weird. The hairs on the back of my neck stood up for a second, but she was probably just taking a picture of the players on the field, like everyone else. I dismissed that feeling as adrenaline, and I turned back to my mom.

This would definitely be a day we'd remember forever.

CHAPTER
TWO

THE NEXT DAY, AFTER I rolled out of bed and got ready for work, I curled up on the sagging recliner in the living room. We had a couch and a love seat in pristine condition, but because Gram refused to take the plastic off, I never wanted to sit on them. I unlocked my phone to check my YouTube channel. My latest upload had five thousand views. Not bad. I was already set to outpace my John Hughes/Molly Ringwald video, and if I could hit a hundred thousand, maybe I'd be able to buy more fabric instead of relying on leftovers from the Bees.

I counted my Goodbye Honeyfield stash this morning, the bills I kept carefully tucked in my underwear drawer next to the package of condoms I sadly hadn't needed to open in months. I only had a few hundred dollars, and it had taken me nearly a year to save that. The Royals game bit into my savings, but if my viewership kept growing at this rate, I'd be able to put away a little more than fifty dollars a month.

At first, I'd wanted to go to LA, to get as close as I could to the movies, but that felt too far away. I still wanted to visit Mom and Gram whenever I had a full tank of gas, so my plans shifted to Chicago. Eventually I wanted to expand my YouTube channel into live coverage of independent film festivals along with reviews, and Chicago had dozens of festivals every year. Not to mention, thousands of jobs that paid more than minimum wage. Just looking through Indeed had my fingers itching to apply. Not yet though. I promised myself I'd stay in Honeyfield a full year after graduation to save money. I'd start my new life off right, which included being able to afford a roof over my head.

After we got home from the game, I spent some time in my room sketching baseball jerseys. No White Sox, definitely no Tigers, but I could do baseball movies as a theme. Maybe all the reasons why *A League of Their Own* was the superior movie, even if it went out of its way to hide the queer history behind the true story. Part of me wanted to rush it, just throw something together and put it up while the nineties rom-coms had so much traction, but that wouldn't help my long game. Quality over quantity.

I had a magic number I wanted to hit. A million views. Then I'd feel legit, like I'd actually made it. When I hit a million, I'd do my *Say Anything* review. I was holding on to it because it meant the most. It had started everything.

A lot of people thought *Say Anything* was just a romance movie from the eighties, but it was so much more than that. It was about a girl named Diane Court who'd been sheltered by her father, had her life planned out for her, until she met a guy named Lloyd Dobler, who had nothing planned. He showed her what it felt like to be free, while she showed him what it meant to have a future. They worked because they gave each other something the other needed.

While most kids got the Talk in middle school, Gram and Mom sat me down to watch *Say Anything*, and when it was over, they talked to me not just about condoms and consent (though they'd covered those, too), but about female sexuality in general. How cis-men would try to control it or shame us for it or shove us into boxes where we couldn't be smart and funny and sexual all at the same time. They made sure I knew that who I wanted to be was my choice, not the choice of a man who marked boxes for me. I grew up watching eighties and nineties movies because they were Mom and Gram's common ground. They disagreed on nearly everything, except movies and the kinds of messages they sent to girls.

While I'd found the entire thing mortifying back then, it was also the first time I really understood that movies were magic. Not special effects and explosions, but they could speak to your soul, start conversations, reflect the things you needed to say. It was the whole reason why I'd started doing reviews. To dig into what others considered mindless entertainment, and pull out those nuggets of truth. To look at the way people connected to certain stories in a way that made us real and human. It was all I ever wanted to do for the rest of my life.

"Morning." Mom drifted down the hall, rubbing sleep out of her eyes.

"Someone call a reporter," I said. "Gracie Evans, sleeping past nine. Which means pigs are taking flight and they're building an ice rink in Hell as we speak."

"Har." She ran a hand over my hair, which had started to resemble an unruly dandelion once the summer humidity hit. "I like Charlie's new look."

Charlie, the ceramic parrot Gram had won on *Wheel of Fortune* in 1984, back when there was still a shopping round, sat directly in front of the window, his place of honor since Gram had brought him home before Mom was even born. I'd put the KC hat on him. Sometimes he wore Santa hats or Uncle Sam hats, and I figured catching a fly ball was as good as a holiday.

"We should make a Royals outfit for one of the Vannas," I said.

Mom stuck out her tongue. "Now you're going too far."

The Vannas were Gram's collection of Vanna White dolls. She displayed them above the fireplace, and other than the light layer of nicotine-stained dust, they remained in their boxes and in mint condition. They gave me nightmares as a child.

I followed Mom into the kitchen, where Gram and Peg had their quilting patterns spread out on the dining room table. It was that time of year again.

"You two got in late last night," Gram said. "How was the game?"

"I'm still wondering how I got so lucky in the daughter department. Macy caught a fly ball." Mom gave me a knowing look over her coffee mug. "And a boy."

"What's this about a boy?" Gram lit a cigarette and fixed

her steely gaze on me. She barely cleared five feet but had a way of making everyone else around her feel smaller.

"It's nothing." I shot Mom the stink eye. "I didn't even get his number."

"For Heaven's sake, why not?" Peg crossed her arms. She lived down the street, but ever since Gramps died, she spent all her time here. She'd probably move in if we had an extra room to spare. "This is what we old people mean when we say youth is wasted on the young."

Desperate for a subject change, I picked up one of the quilting patterns. "What are the Bees thinking their theme will be this year?"

"We're debating that now," Gram said. "Peg doesn't like First Love."

The Bees were the queens of the Shelby County Fair quilt show. They had most of the main quilt done already, but every year they picked a theme and hand-embroidered the squares before piecing them together on a giant frame that took the place of the dining room table while they worked. None of the other quilting bees in the county could compete. Most of them embroidered on machines and picked basic designs from a book. They treated it like a hobby.

The Bees made it their reason for living.

"Because it's boring," Peg said. "What else have you got?"

"You're just saying that because you've never been in love," I said, taking a seat in Iris's old chair. RIP. I wished I could say I missed her, but she was a mean old biddy who used to poke my hand with her needle. Not entirely on accident, either.

Peg smacked the back of my head. "And what do you know about love, wise one, when you can't even get a phone number from a boy?"

"Love is overrated," I said.

"All right, no one here likes love." Gram threw the pattern into the tulip-shaped waste basket by her feet. "What about something to commemorate Iris?"

"Lordy, that would be the ugliest damned quilt." Peg winked at me. "I'm not sure how well the Satan theme would go over with the judges."

"That's not very nice." Gram sniffed. Even if she agreed, she'd handpicked all the Bees, and acted personally responsible for keeping their hive harmonious.

"Come off it. You know as well as I do she was a miserable bitch." Peg reached over to Gram's lap and took a few sheets of patterns to look through. "You've got some good ones in here. Donna will lose her mind over this flower power one." Peg leaned closer to me. "That one peaked in high school. Make sure you don't get too attached to this time in your life."

"Yes, ma'am." That wouldn't be a problem for me. I couldn't think of anything I was less attached to than the high school experience.

Gram snapped her fingers. "How about we do Defining Moments in History?"

Peg tapped a finger to her papery lips. "I like it, but we have a more pressing problem. Our pattern is going to be off without Iris."

"We could put out a call in the paper," Gram said. "Or

put it on that one list a gentleman named Craig owns? Little Larry suggested that when I needed to sell my old snowblower."

Little Larry lived two streets over, a forty-five-year-old pediatrician who worked in the next town. Due to being named after his father, he'd been Little Larry since they'd brought him home from the hospital, and no amount of aging or professionalism would change that.

"You mean the Craigslist," Peg said. "I learned about it on the World Wide Web. You don't want to put an ad on there."

"Why not?" I asked, though I wasn't sure if I wanted to hear the answer.

"That's where people go to buy sex." Peg gave a curt nod as if that settled the matter.

I rubbed my hands over my cheeks. Some questions were better left unasked.

"Well. We certainly don't need any more of *that* business around here." Gram glanced at Mom—because she really didn't know when to let things go—and pulled out a packet of envelopes tied with paisley-print ribbon. Her filing system on prospective future Bees. "Iris has been gone six months now—I don't suppose it would be disrespectful to give her spot to someone else. Or do you think we need a full year for mourning?"

"You were mourning?" I asked.

Peg chuckled into her sun tea, which she turned into a cough when Gram gave her a stern glare. Patting her chest, Peg straightened up, but the ghost of a smile remained.

"I don't think Iris needs a full year. If she knew we were preserving her spot out of some sentimental obligation, she'd admonish us all for partaking in fanciful wish-wash."

Gram sighed and spread the envelopes out in front of her. "Maybe we should look at someone new. What about Glenn Harris?"

"Dead," Peg said.

"Oh my. I guess we waited a bit too long on that one." Gram frowned as she pulled out another envelope. "Sylvia Clair?"

"Just married," Peg said. "So as good as dead."

Gram went through more envelopes, looking for a decent candidate. "One more dead, and another moved away. I really should cull this list more often. Or see if there is anyone new in town we haven't met yet."

"I doubt there is," Mom said. And she had a good point. People didn't really come to Honeyfield. It was more the kind of place people drove away from, tires squealing, their rearview mirrors ripped off.

Peg clutched Gram's hand. "Why don't we put this away for now? Hearing about our dead contemporaries isn't how I'd like to spend this morning."

The doorbell rang and I jumped. "That's Elise. Gotta run."

"You didn't even have breakfast." Mom frowned. On her list of transgressions, not eating breakfast was right up there with reading CliffsNotes instead of the assigned book, swearing in public, and wearing pajamas to the store.

I grabbed my lunch and a generic toaster pastry off the

counter, and dashed out the door. Elise's truck rumbled in the driveway. The rusty hinges creaked when I got in, and I offered her the toaster pastry. I wasn't that hungry.

Elise flipped her long braid over her shoulder and ripped off the cellophane. She had a sweet tooth and a weakness for anything strawberry flavored. "Momma said you caught a fly ball. And a boy."

I rolled my eyes. By noon the whole damn town would be talking about this boy I'd supposedly caught. Gossip was its own form of currency in Honeyfield. A juicy enough story earned lunch invitations for a week straight.

Of course my mom had to tell Momma Gomez about Eric, who I'd never see again. Our moms had been close since the toddler park days. It didn't surprise me that Elise already knew about the fly ball, even though I hadn't yet posted that picture to Instagram.

"My mom overexaggerated," I said. "I just happened to sit next to a guy who was sort of a tool, but cute. I didn't even get his number, so whatever. But I did catch that ball."

"Why didn't you get his number?"

It's not like I couldn't ask for a guy's number. I dated. It was a thing I'd done. But he lived in Kansas City and I lived two hours north, and why couldn't I just be awkward and weird and call it flirting with a cute stranger and leave it there? My mom was a hopeless romantic, and she ended up pregnant at sixteen and stuck in a dead-end job with no hope of escape. I wasn't anti-love, but I had other things I wanted more.

I hunched down in my seat. "You sound like Peg."

"Peg has seen some shit." Elise shuddered. "She knows."

I snorted. Peg had seen about as much as the rest of us who lived in this town, which wasn't a whole lot more than miles of corn and cows. Unless Elise counted that one time the septic system broke down. Then we'd all seen some shit.

Elise parked behind Honeyfield Video and Repair, where I worked on the video side and she worked on the repair side. The front window display had a washer and dryer with VHS tapes and DVDs stacked on top, in case anyone got confused over exactly what we offered. Dishwasher break down? Stop on in and let us know, and pick up a movie from 1978 while you're at it.

"Ready for another exciting day at work?" I asked.

"Nope." Elise got out of her truck and grabbed her toolbox from the back.

She always took tools home with her because she picked up side jobs around town with her dad. By next year, she hoped she'd have enough saved to put a down payment on her own repair shop, I'd grow my YouTube viewership, and we'd be on our way to Chicago. Some people took a gap year after high school. We were taking a gap life. Neither of us had plans for college. In my house, college just meant taking on a bunch more debt only to end up waiting tables until your feet fell off.

Elise went around the back, where someone had dropped off a leaky refrigerator. They'd found it on the side of the road and wanted it repaired so they could flip it. I went through the front door and waved at Mr. Nobel and

Mr. Crouch—two old men who spent their summers camped out on the bench in front of the store. They didn't wave back, too distracted by their daily debate over the best war movies. A bell above the door dinged to announce my arrival back from my first Saturday off in over a month. I gave a little twirl and a bow at the entrance.

"Who missed me?" I said to the nearly empty store. We wouldn't pick up until lunchtime, when everyone with nothing better to do would come in and pretend to browse movies while hoping to pick up on some gossip to get them through the rest of the day.

Midnight, the shift supervisor (a title she'd given herself), pushed a VHS tape into the rewinder. She scratched her eye, smudging the thick black liner she wore like armor. "I missed having someone here yesterday to rewind these tapes. New guy will be here any minute."

We usually took on an extra person in the summer due to the pass-through traffic we got from people on their way to better places. They were our biggest source of revenue. We kept a hundred working VCRs—that stayed working thanks to the repair shop—and tourists had no problem dropping twenty dollars on the "VCR plus two movies" rental deal so they could experience the marvels of VHS. DVD rentals kept us current, but Gen X nostalgia was our biggest draw.

"Cool." I tossed my backpack with my lunch into the tiny closet we called a break room. "You can show him how to rewind the tapes."

She gave me her "I'd rather be at Hot Topic" look.

Which was both true and depressing, since there wasn't a mall within a hundred miles of Honeyfield. Thankfully for her, and her discount goth look, they were willing to ship to the middle of nowhere. She'd graduated last year, but not from my school. At least, I think so. I couldn't remember ever passing her in the halls, and she was someone I'd definitely remember. She didn't talk about herself all that much. I didn't even know if she lived in Honeyfield. The only thing I did know was that Midnight wasn't her real name, but I had no idea what it was. I'd never bothered to ask, and she'd never bothered to supply it, so we called her what she wanted.

Butch, the fifty-year-old ex-Marine, who was technically the manager, slept off a hangover in his office on the repair side. Though it was a shock that he showed up at all. Usually he left us to our own devices and only came in when his wife kicked him out of the house again and he needed a place to crash for a little while.

I uploaded the picture of me and Mom with the fly ball to Instagram while Midnight put out the popcorn on the counter. Our employer didn't provide snacks for sale, or much of anything really, so Midnight bought popcorn and candy from the grocery store and sold the packages individually. A somewhat lucrative side hustle I was mad I hadn't thought of first.

The entrance bell dinged and a huge Asian guy with a soft face took up the entrance. I recognized him from school. He seemed a little lost, and did that thing with his hands where he'd clasp them together then put them back at his sides because he wasn't sure what to do with them. I connected with his general discomfort on a visceral level.

"You must be Brady." Midnight used her (self-appointed) shift supervisor voice. The all-business tone, short spiked black hair, and heavy eyeliner were an intimidating effect. Brady took a full step back. "Macy is going to train you while I do paperwork in the back."

His dad owned the pharmacy, which made his appearance a little surprising. I didn't think the rich kids had to work like the rest of us. Or at least the kids who were as rich as anyone could be in Honeyfield.

I hooked my arm through Brady's. "You're one of us now," I said.

"Okay," Brady's voice cracked, and his cheeks pinkened as he cleared his throat.

"What made you get a job here anyway? I'm not trying to be rude, but I know I wouldn't be here if I didn't have to be."

"My dad said I couldn't spend all summer playing video games. He wants me to show initiative and responsibility or something. So here I am."

"Here you are." I pulled him toward the back of the store. "I'll give you the grand tour. Should take all of five seconds."

I pointed out where the thin carpeting met the concrete floor, to differentiate the video store from the repair shop. After I showed Brady how the Action, Drama, Comedy, and Children's sections were divided by rows and kept in alphabetical order, I brought him over to the spinning DVD racks. We had way more DVDs than VHS tapes, but they took up a fraction of the space, since whoever owned this place put more emphasis on saving wall space for the tapes in the summer. The Tuesday after Labor Day, we closed the store and moved the tapes to the racks and the DVDs to the walls, since most of our winter business came from local farms too remote to get any decent streaming services.

A narrow wall by the register held our staff picks. We each got to choose five movies and write up an index card with a short description. "The top row is mine," I said.

Brady pursed his lips as he read my index card for *Toy Story*. "'Middle-aged cowboy has existential crisis over emerging technology'?"

"Tell me a more accurate description." When he remained silent, I moved on. "This dark and gloomy tomb of classics is Midnight's. She thinks black-and-white films add to her whole noir persona, but I happen to know her actual favorite movie is *Bring It On*."

Brady cracked a smile for the first time since he'd walked into the store. He touched the index card for *Citizen Kane*. "'Despite infamous wealth and fame, man's greatest regret is that one time he didn't make it with a sled.'"

"Paxton wrote that one. You probably know him from school. Graduated this year? Tall guy? Big ears? Bigger smile? Anyway, he works over on the repair side. We swapped it out with the description Midnight wrote two weeks ago and she still hasn't noticed."

"Midnight is kind of . . ." Brady gulped.

"Scary?" When he nodded, I nudged him. "Will it help to know her real name is Sunshine?" Probably not true, but he didn't need to know that. "Don't tell her I told you though, or she will literally sacrifice me to the blood moon."

"Don't worry, it'll be our secret." He grinned and I had a strong urge to hug him and protect him from all harm for life. Even though he was three times my size.

I almost felt bad about sticking him on rewind duty, but better him than me.

CHAPTER THREE

THE BELL ABOVE THE door dinged and I hopped off my stool, expecting a customer. Instead Paxton Croft strolled in through the front entrance. His soft brown hair curled around his ears, which stuck out in an elfish way, and he was wearing . . . Oh my God. Was that a giant bunny sewn across the chest of his T-shirt?

Midnight poked her head out of the closet/break room and smirked. Elise dropped her wrench on the concrete floor and wandered over with her hands in her pockets. The image of a snake slithering up on a mouse popped into my head. Poor Brady kept sneaking glances at Paxton, like he wasn't sure if he was supposed to laugh or not.

"I know what you're all probably thinking." Paxton's hazel eyes sparkled as he gestured to the bunny on his shirt, as if any of us could look away from it. "Let's just get it out of the way so we can all get back to work. Go ahead. Give me your best shot."

"Someone forgot to tell you that you're too old for Baby Gap," Elise said.

"You're the reason why swipe left was invented," Midnight said.

"You look like you failed first grade for the twelfth year in a row," I said.

"Seriously?" Paxton leaned against the wall with a bored expression. "I told you to give me your best shot and that's all you could come up with? Pathetic."

Elise screwed up her face. Challenge accepted. "You're like a human version of the free box at a garage sale."

"You look like you collect two-dollar bills," Midnight said.

"Like you're auditioning for the part of 'sassy old lady' in a Hallmark movie," I said.

"All right. That's enough." Paxton gave us a slow clap. "Everyone, back to work."

"Excuse me." Midnight held up a hand. "I believe I'm the shift supervisor here, and I'll tell everyone when it's time to get back to work."

"I believe you gave that title to yourself, and no one cares."

She flipped up her middle finger and went back to her paperwork. Now that the show was over, Elise got bored and resumed working on the almond-colored refrigerator that probably wouldn't be worth the price to fix it for a flip anyway. Paxton grinned at me. We'd been friends (and occasional coconspirators) since we'd started working here at the same time—me on the video side and him on the repair side—but most people thought he worked on the video side of the store since he spent so much time over here.

"Macy Mae, back from the big city." He reached up, fingers skimming the ends of my short hair. I'd cut it the day before the game, not having the patience to grow it past my chin. "I bet your mom was one of those obnoxious fans who tried to get everyone to do the wave."

"Correct. What's all this about?" I pointed to the comically large shirt bunny.

"Gigi made it for me, and you know I can't tell her no."

"Ah. Say no more."

Gigi had been a Bee for the last two years, and she was also the wife of Paxton's grandma Lisbeth. Everyone loved Gigi, but Paxton loved her best. Even though Gigi and Lisbeth had been married since they were legally allowed, a lot of people in town still acted like they were similar to Gram and Peg. Just gals being pals. The VHS rental store wasn't the only thing ass-backward about Honeyfield.

Paxton and Gigi raised rabbits together for the county fair competitions and he always said it was the thing that saved him, though he never elaborated beyond that. Most everyone assumed it had to do with his parents. They spoke about it in whispers around town. Like there was a car accident and they died, but he survived, and that was why he lived with his grandma and never learned how to drive. No one wanted to ask him directly in case it was a sore subject.

Paxton made his introductions to Brady like we didn't all go to the same school that had less than a hundred students. Total. Paxton clapped a hand on Brady's shoulder. "Don't let the girls take advantage and stick you on rewind duty all day."

"I don't mind doing it." Brady's voice was featherlight.

29

Paxton raised his eyebrows at me, and I stifled the urge to laugh. No one wanted to be on rewind duty. Literally no one. But if Brady didn't mind . . .

"Leave him be," I said to Paxton. "If he likes to rewind, let him rewind."

"See how they pretend to be friendly?" Paxton asked Brady, winking at me. "Are we doing movie on the lake tonight?"

"I'm in. I'm sure Elise is too. Do you want to come, Brady?" I asked. "It's a lot of fun."

"Sure." Brady hunched his shoulders, like being addressed directly made him squirm. "I'm not sure what movie on the lake is, but I guess I'm one of you now."

"You have to experience it to really know," Paxton said.

Movie on the lake was a lot less glamourous than we made it sound. Mostly it involved Paxton breaking into the park's storage unit and snagging two paddleboats, tying them together, and sitting in the middle of the lake with his laptop. But since our rental store was the hub of entertainment in this town, we had to make our own fun.

I called toward the closet/break room. "Midnight, you in for movie on the lake?"

She came out of her hovel and shrugged, a gesture that for Midnight was practically akin to jumping up and down with excitement.

"What's tonight's feature going to be?" I asked. "And don't say *Jaws*." Paxton had this weird obsession with watching tragic water movies on the water. He said it gave

30

the experience atmosphere. We'd already run through the first three *Jaws* movies.

He frowned. "What's wrong with *Jaws*?"

"I'm all *Jaws*'d out. And Midnight is too." She gave a noncommittal grunt, which I took as a sign of agreement. "Pick something else."

"Joke's on you, because I already picked something else—*The Perfect Storm*."

Midnight and I groaned in unison, but we'd go, because what else were we going to do? I hopped on the stool by the register, letting my feet dangle just above the floor. I spun the stool side to side while I opened the YouTube app. Just one more check, then I'd put it away for at least an hour.

Paxton wandered around the counter, close enough for his T-shirt to be a whisper on my shoulder. "How's the register running? Midnight said it was acting up last night."

"I don't know. I guess we'll have to wait for the lunch rush to find out." I set my phone aside. "Hey, Elise." She popped her head up from the refrigerator. "Want to rent a DVD and spare us all from *The Perfect Storm* tonight?"

"Please, yes." She came over to spin the rack and smacked her gum, scanning the titles as if she didn't already have them memorized by heart. "Are you ever going to get DVD copies of the movies you have on VHS?"

"Probably not."

The guy who owned this place didn't bother with doubling up on movies. He didn't even live in town. He likely had a private jet and permanent home-plate seats at

Kauffman Stadium and so many businesses that he forgot this one existed. We didn't even know his name. None of us could read the signature on our paychecks. Occasionally we'd get a movie back where the tape had worn thin, broken, or made static lines appear on TV screens, and Midnight always fired off an email using the only contact address we had, asking for a replacement, and a week later a DVD of that title would show up. It was a weird system, but at least we had jobs.

Elise eventually decided on *Dirty Dancing*. "It has a lake scene—don't bitch," she said to Paxton. He poked her on the nose, and she batted his hand away, laughing. While I rang her up, she blew a bubble the size of her head and stuck a hole in it with her tongue, coating her lips in sticky pink goo.

The register popped open after a few bumps with my fist. I spun my stool toward Paxton, my knees gliding across his waist. I hadn't realized how close he'd been standing. "It's working fine. Midnight just doesn't have the touch."

I picked up my phone again, unlocked the screen, and nearly dropped it.

"What happened?" Paxton put a hand on my shoulder as he leaned over me.

My breath whooshed out. Somehow my rom-com review had hit one hundred thousand views. In an hour. I thumbed through my other videos. The most recent ones had gone over the fifty thousand mark. What? How?

Brady stopped rewinding and looked over his shoulder as Elise rushed around the counter. I must've looked like my soul had unhooked from my body and gone floating into the ether, because that was just about how I felt.

My fingers and toes tingled as I handed my phone to Elise. "I . . . uh . . ."

"Holy fuck. Our girl Misty Morning is Internet famous." Elise let out a whooping laugh. She grabbed Brady's hands, and he froze while she attempted a little spinning dance with him. "Her latest video hit one hundred thousand, baby."

"Congrats," Paxton said, like he didn't really mean it. He had an aversion to all things social media. He went online to get movies, and nothing more.

"I can't believe this is happening." My voice came out breathy and light.

I felt weightless and terrified all at the same time. This was everything I'd been dreaming of and working toward. That moment when I could start earning an income stream from my videos. It was something I brushed off to my friends, and never said out loud, in case I couldn't do it. In case I failed. I just said I did them for fun, and I did, but I also really, really wanted to make it. To call myself a YouTuber and mean it.

But I had no idea what prompted the sudden surge in my views. I hadn't expected to get close for another year. Maybe two. My heart soared as I turned back to my phone and started scrolling through the comments. Maybe I'd find some clue in there to explain my left-field success, something that flipped the switch so I could repeat it.

I flicked to the first comment. *DISGUSTING*, bold and

capitalized. Yikes. And okay, I made Molly Ringwald's hair out of some red Vanna's Choice yarn that Gram had lying around, but we couldn't all afford real wigs, Sharon. All the big videos had nasty comments though; maybe that meant I had arrived. I deleted Sharon's comment and moved on.

Except the next few comments were some variation of questioning my morals, my upbringing, my looks. All the sound around me washed out. I could only hear my pulse pounding blood into my brain. I scrolled until I landed on one that said, *a quickie at kauffman stadium? shame on you. my kids go there.*

"Everything okay?" Elise stopped celebrating and rested her chin on my head. "Jesus, those comments are vile. The Internet is full of trash people. Ignore them."

I couldn't though. My tongue stuck to the roof of my dry mouth as I opened my other apps. I hadn't hooked up with anyone, but I'd definitely been at Kauffman Stadium. How did they know that? I posted all my videos as Misty Morning under R3ntal Wor1d.

My Instagram had much of the same, but I used my real name there. How did they link that to my YouTube? I kept them separate on purpose. I quickly made my account private and went over to my Twitter. At some point between flipping through apps, Elise or Paxton had gone to get Midnight. They huddled around me like a protective shield, not daring to speak while I tried to find the source of this nightmare.

After scrolling through my clogged-up mentions, I found it. Dozens of pictures of me at Kauffman Stadium.

Sort of blurred out, but not enough. Anyone who knew me, who knew I was going to the game (which was everyone in town), would've been able to identify me. Or at least identify the seashell shirt Gram had made for me. Not to mention all the unblurred pictures I'd posted myself to Instagram. The images appeared to be taken from the row of seats behind me. I clicked on the picture of the person who had started a hundred-thread tweet about my supposed romance at the ball game, and vomit rose up in my throat.

She didn't have her pink bow on in her picture, but I still recognized Jessica Banks as the woman who'd sat behind me. Who had encouraged Eric to escort me to the bathrooms. Who dropped her phone as soon as I looked at her, but I thought she'd been taking pictures of the field. She hadn't. She'd been taking pictures of me.

I scrolled to the top of the thread, and the photo was one of me trying to awkwardly wipe ketchup off Eric's shirt. She'd captioned it: *this is how meet-cutes happen in the movies, y'all.* She followed it up with heart-eye emojis around Eric's shirtless picture. Ew. He had to be young enough to be her son.

A whole series of our every move followed, all of them captioned with exclamations to make it seem like there was more going on than what had actually happened. Every time his arm brushed mine (did people know how small those seats were?), every time I looked over at his bare chest, and when I showed him my rom-com video. At least that answered how everyone had found my YouTube channel. She didn't bother to blur out my phone screen.

She even rewrote the whole fly ball catch. She took a picture of Eric with the ball, and then him handing it to me, with the caption, *he gave her the fly ball. now that's love.* That pissed me off more than anything. I'd caught the ball on my own, thank you very much.

The worst one, the most damning picture, had been taken of me and Eric walking down the short hall toward the bathrooms. When he had his hand on the small of my back. The picture had been cut off from just the right angle, so it looked like the hall only led to the women's room. The shot came from directly behind us, by the popcorn cart. Jessica must've followed us there. She'd captioned the picture, *They're going to the bathroom. TOGETHER. OH EM GEEEE!!!* It had over 900,000 likes and 300,000 retweets. Followed by a picture of me and Eric leaving the bathrooms.

I couldn't have been in there for longer than five minutes, and even though I was aware of how quickies worked, no way could anyone believe we'd had sex in the time it had taken me to pee and wash my hands. I checked the time stamp on the one of us walking away from the bathrooms. She'd held on to that picture for twenty minutes before posting it. Plenty of time. She knew exactly what she'd been doing.

I searched for Eric Dufrane, just to see if he'd been identified yet. If not, at least I could warn him so he wouldn't get the shock of his life. I searched for him on Twitter, and what I found turned my blood to ice. He had forty thousand Twitter followers under the handle @baseballbabe2020. His bio had one sentence: *catching fly balls and feelings.*

And he'd retweeted Jessica's thread.

I wanted to scream or throw up or disappear or all of the above at the same time. My phone had become this living being trying to choke the life out of me. I threw it against the wall, cracking the screen. I might've started crying, or not. I had no clue. I couldn't feel my face.

"Take the rest of the day off. I'll cover you." Midnight gave me an awkward shoulder bump. She was definitely not the hugging type, but she was trying. It offered me no comfort.

"I . . . I'm sorry. So sorry." Paxton held my gaze as devastation and something darker replaced his normally gentle humor.

His arms came around me and I stiffened to keep from curling into him, from letting go and completely losing it right there in the middle of the store. He immediately dropped his arms and stepped back. Not in a mad way, but like he sensed I needed the space to hold it together.

"I'm taking her home," Elise said. It wasn't a request. She led me out to her truck and opened the door, depositing me in the front seat like I was an injured kitten she'd rescued from the side of the road. "Your mom will know what to do."

No, she wouldn't. This was beyond her. Beyond any of us. In a matter of hours, amateur Internet sleuths had dug up my real name, my YouTube channel, and all my social media accounts. Every time someone googled my name, that was what they'd see.

And I couldn't do a thing to stop it.

CHAPTER
FOUR

ELISE STOPPED SO ABRUPTLY in my driveway, I lurched forward on the seat. I clenched my hands together, like they were my sole reminder to keep breathing in, breathing out. Everything I'd built, worked for, swept away within hours. Elise moved to get out of the truck.

"Wait." I gripped her arm. "I don't want to tell my mom. Not yet."

We'd just had one of the best days, and I couldn't let her see what had come of it. Not when she'd had her first weekend off in years. It's not like she could go on the Internet and personally scream down everyone who'd mentioned my name, though I wouldn't put it past her to try. I still shuddered whenever I thought about the time she'd unleashed herself on the parents of three boys who'd stolen my doll and drowned it in the lake during one of our park days. She put momma grizzly bears to shame.

"Okay." Elise waited. I didn't need to explain anything to her; we'd had an innate understanding of each other since we were toddlers. "You can't keep it from her forever though. People in town are going to talk."

"I know. Just . . ." I stared at my house and swallowed.

"Just give me a day."

"I have to get back to work." Elise squeezed my hand. "If you need anything, don't even hesitate. I'll have my phone on me all day."

"Thanks." I straightened my spine as I slid out of the front seat.

As soon as Elise drove away, I pulled out my phone and cursed the cracked screen. I opened Twitter. Before I faced the Bees and Mom, I wanted to see how involved Eric was— had he just retweeted Jessica, or had he been in on it from the beginning? The thought made my pulse pound in my ears again.

I scrolled through his timeline. He'd retweeted Jessica's thread, but he didn't comment on it like he knew it had been happening. So that was something. Still, he replied to people bombarding his mentions with a whole "Aww, shucks" demeanor I found disingenuous. And he lied about catching the fly ball. A ridiculous lie. If anyone had gotten a picture of me catching it, it would blow up with a quickness. He'd only posted one update since the night before.

@baseballbabe2020: Dreamed about a cute blonde and seashells last night. I hope she's real. #baseballbabe

Barf. If he'd really been that into me, he would've gotten my number instead of acting like a lovesick puppy on Twitter. But texting me didn't get him likes and retweets. Posting that he'd been dreaming about me did. A lot of likes and retweets. Over fifty thousand.

Still, I followed him. I needed access to his direct

messages. There was no way I'd question him out in the open, not when my mentions were already a mess. He didn't follow me back, and I closed the app before I threw my phone again and damaged it for good.

The chatter from the dining room halted as soon as the screen door slapped shut behind me. Usually the Bees were so elbow-deep in old lady gossip, they rarely noticed whether I came or went, but the silence that followed my footsteps had my gut twisting. Maybe they already knew. Maybe they'd found out from the web of information that spread across this town faster than it took for Wi-Fi to catch up. If I didn't get to tell them myself, their reactions would be ten times worse. Gram would rage, Mom would worry. A roaring fire erupted between my temples. I'd burn the entire Internet down and feast on the smoldering bones left in its ashes.

Donna looked up at me as I entered the room. A woven leather headband circled her head, flattening her flowing gray hair. She'd never left her hippie days behind. Gigi gave me a little wave, and Paxton's bunny shirt flashed in my mind. I had to choke down the laugh, for fear that if I let it go, it would become hysterical and never stop.

"Heard you caught a boy at the game." Donna's bright eyes twinkled. No doubt remembering all the boys she'd "caught" during the era of free love.

The muscles in my back stiffened. "What else did you hear?"

For the first time, I dared to slide a glance at Gram. If she'd found out from anyone other than me, I'd see it simmering within her like the tip of her cigarette. She looked me over and gestured for me to take a seat. My knees cracked as I slowly, so slowly, lowered myself to the wobbly chair next to Peg. Gram generally had more bark than bite, and most days I didn't have a problem with testing her, but this was not most days.

The ceiling fan whirred above our heads, twisting the sticky paper that hung from it, littered with dead flies. I kept my gaze on the pear-and-apple design of the plastic tablecloth as Gram's gaze pierced a hole in the side of my head, as if she could empty the thoughts in there from sheer will alone.

I turned, and Gram's sharp gaze narrowed. "Why aren't you at work?"

Gigi stared between the two of us, as if she'd be willing to throw herself in as a buffer if the interrogation got to be too much. Gram meant well. Underneath her scaly layers—deep underneath—beat the heart of a softie who would claw apart the world for her family. Even if those claws were sometimes directed at us and what she deemed as our shortcomings.

I sucked in a deep breath. "Butch hired a new guy, and he's never had a job before, so I let him take my hours for extra training."

Gram sniffed like she could scent the lie on my tongue. "That was nice of you," she said, as if she meant the exact opposite. "And how are you going to make up those lost wages?"

Of course I had to get the lost wages lecture on the worst day of my life. Because no one could take a day off around Bizzy Evans unless you were sick, and at that point you better just die, because you could've powered through it otherwise. Mom had taken four days off for strep throat three years ago and Gram still brought it up whenever she was in a mood.

"I could try selling sex on the Craigslist," I said just to annoy her.

Peg let out a cackling laugh. "Nobody wants what you're selling, girl."

"I haven't seen any boys sniffing around the back door in ages," Gram said.

"Thanks, you two. Really." I crossed my arms. "I was just thinking the other day I had way too much self-esteem, and I've been looking for a way to get rid of some."

"That's the problem with your generation." Gram put out her cigarette in an overflowing ashtray. She'd burn the house down one day. "You get your participation trophies and slack off at work, and then you're left with all this time on your hands to think about self-esteem."

Gram was truly a relic from another era.

The Bees went back to sorting through their quilting patterns, trying to come up with a new design to account for Iris's untimely absence. Gram probably thought I'd wormed my way out of work because I was tired from the game. Which was fine. She could think whatever she wanted, as long as I had a full day to process how I'd break the news of my sudden notoriety. I needed to protect the good memories of the game for Mom, while keeping Gram's already less-than-warm feelings about the Internet in check. If I had a Magic 8 Ball, I was pretty sure it'd tell me *Outlook not so good.*

"If you're done giving her the third degree"—Donna nudged Gram, a sparkling laugh quirking the corners of her full mouth—"I'd like to hear more about this boy from the game."

Just the mention of Eric made me seethe. The way he was preening away on Twitter, acting like he'd caught the fly ball and given it to me. And for what? What did he stand to gain from all this? I had no doubt this was all some kind of grand ruse. Either to stretch out the fifteen minutes of fame he seemed to bask in, or because the pull of approval was too strong.

I understood that pull. That spark I'd get in my chest whenever I got a thumbs-up on one of my reviews. The way it felt to see my number of views steadily rising. The want and need to be successful, to earn a proper income stream from YouTube. To get out of Honeyfield. Maybe Eric had similar dreams. Maybe he was just making the best of a shitty situation.

"Don't bother." Peg gave me a wink. "Macy didn't even get his number."

I hunched my shoulders. "Thanks for the reminder." If I had gotten his number, I'd be using it right now to call him up and ask for an explanation. "If you're all done picking over my non-love life, am I excused?"

Gram waved me away. "Fine. Go on out back with the other layabout."

I ground my teeth. One weekend. Mom takes one

weekend off in two years, and Gram was suddenly acting like she'd been freeloading since I was born. Never mind that we all pitched in to keep our heads above water. Gram's social security checks barely covered the taxes on the house, her smokes, medical insurance, and quilting supplies for the Bees.

Mom and I took care of the rest.

I pushed open the screen door on the porch to find Mom laid out on an old beach recliner. Strips of the plastic had broken away and they dragged along the near-dead lawn. She had one foot dipped in the kiddie pool beside her with a glass of lemonade in one hand and a worn copy of a Nora Roberts novel in the other. She looked up from her book and smiled, and I wanted to keep that image forever. She looked so relaxed. Happy. I made the right call on putting off telling her about Eric and Jessica Banks.

"Permission to enter the Hamptons?" I asked.

Mom stood and gave me a grandiose bow. "Permission granted."

I kicked off my shoes and stepped into the kiddie pool. The cool water lapped at my ankles, taking off some of the burn still rolling around inside me. "Butch let me take today off work too, so now Gram thinks we're both sponges on society."

Mom splashed a little water at me with her foot. "She's just mad because I won't let her into the Hamptons with that gnarly toe of hers."

Raptor foot. Gram had an enormous toenail that had gone bad, and instead of having it removed like a normal person, she'd let that hard, crusty thing grow. Sometimes clicking it on the kitchen floor at us whenever she wanted to be truly evil. Nothing got us to clear a room faster than the sound of that nail on linoleum.

I made a retching noise. "Please don't make me vomit. I didn't even eat lunch yet."

"I was just about to go over to Fanny's for some eggs." Mom pointed to the basket of cucumbers she'd picked from our garden to barter. In the summer, most of our food came from trading with others in town. It's how we all got by. "Do you want to come?"

"Nah, someone needs to keep an eye on the Bees during their time of need." I'd no sooner said the words when a shriek came from the dining room, then all four voices raised at once. Getting them to agree on the theme for their most important quilt of the year hadn't yet ended in bloodshed, but it had come close.

Mom left with her cucumbers to trade for eggs, and loaded up last year's winning Bees quilt to trade for a half a cow at the Jackson farm, which would pack our garage freezer and give us enough beef until next summer. It was the way we'd always done things, and likely always would, unless I got my YouTube channel off the ground.

That wide-open pit of fear, of never having enough, opened before me again. Things had been going along fine until Jessica Banks. Even if she had boosted my views and likely thought she'd done me a favor, I didn't want this. Not this way. R3ntal Wor1d was supposed to be my way out.

Something I could build and call my own without having to give away pieces of myself just to survive.

Even though Gram never said it, I knew it killed her to trade those quilts for beef. Just like it killed Mom to wait on those people she went to high school with, who only came back to town to visit family, and who smirked at the sorry life of the pregnant cheerleader. Gram and Mom did what they had to do, and I was proud of where I came from, but I wanted options. The chance to fail or succeed outside of what this town expected of an Evans. I'd created Misty Morning to keep my real life separate. I'd never given anything away, never mentioned my real name on R3ntal Wor1d, but with one series of misconstrued events, Jessica Banks had torn the doors off everything I'd wanted to keep locked away.

I thumbed open YouTube. My phone took a sizable chunk of the two hundred dollars a month I'd been earning from my reviews, but I'd told myself it had been worth it, it would all be worth it. Someday. I again swore at the cracked screen I'd eventually have to pull together enough money to replace, and flipped over to my channel to see if I could deal with what strangers were saying about me—not Misty, but Macy Evans and who I was as a person. The one thing I swore I'd never barter or trade.

GinaLaCross: *How can you talk about feminism in your videos and then let some guy treat you like a truck stop glory hole? Hypocrite.*

Nope. Too soon. I closed YouTube and opened Twitter. Eric had finally followed me back, and I had a new DM in my inbox. It could only be from him. I'd long ago set options to only allow those I followed to DM me, thanks to one too many dick pics sent by random sickos. As much as I wanted to figure out what kind of game he was playing, I didn't click on the message right away. DMing him put me at risk of screenshots. It would be so easy to twist my words with a well-placed photo chop. I knew how Twitter worked. I'd seen both the rise and fallout of viral fame, with popcorn in hand, for years. Never thinking I'd one day be weighing my every word and wondering which ones could be used against me.

The preview of his message showed: *We should talk*. My finger shook as I moved to tap the message. I desperately needed answers, and this was the only way I'd get them. Sucking in a deep breath, I clicked.

Eric (Baseball Babe) Dufrane: *We should talk. I think this situation could benefit us both. Feel free to FaceTime me.*

I stared at his phone number. Talking face-to-face made me more comfortable than DMing. I wouldn't have the time or space to weigh my words properly, but at least I could avoid the threat of screenshots. I started typing, deleted, typed again, still unsure of how I'd answer him. His profile picture appeared in a little bubble in the DM with three dots.

Eric (Baseball Babe) Dufrane: *Hi.*

This was too much. I closed Twitter and headed inside to break up another fight between the Bees. I'd figure out what to do about Eric and his DM tomorrow.

CHAPTER
FIVE

AFTER DONNA AND GIGI went home, I headed into the kitchen and poured myself some sun tea. Condensation beaded along the faded daisy print on the glass, and I rested it against my cheek. It had been so hot today. The window air-conditioning unit above the sink barely had enough power to cool half the room. The cross-breeze Gram tried to create by leaving the doors open on either end of the house didn't do a lot when there wasn't any breeze to begin with.

Peg came into the kitchen, thrumming her nails on the peeling yellow countertops that hadn't been changed since Gram bought this house forty years ago. "We can handle ourselves, you know. You don't have to throw yourself into every squabble."

I smirked. "Is that why Donna looked about two seconds away from ripping out your throat with her teeth?"

"I make one joke about a pro–Vietnam War theme and she loses it." Peg's lip curled. "Peace and love, my ass."

The front screen door slammed shut, and I patted Peg's arm as I passed, laughing at the snarl still etched into the lines around her mouth. Mom carried in a basket of brown eggs, a loaf of freshly baked bread resting on top of them. I raised my eyebrows in question.

"I caught Fanny on baking day." Mom nodded to the bread. "I offered her some peppers from the garden, but she said she already had more veggies than she could eat in a week."

"Nice." I'd give Fanny a free rental next time she came by on my shift. I took the basket from Mom and she followed me into the kitchen. We had chili mac baking in the oven, and the homey scent made my stomach rumble. "I'm so hungry, I could eat that whole loaf myself."

"Me too." Mom ruffled my short hair.

I hadn't managed to eat lunch, my stomach still too sick to handle food. Instead I spent hours on Twitter, using my mobile browser in incognito mode instead of the app. It didn't do anything except keep my searches out of my history, but it made me feel better. Like if it wasn't in my history, I didn't really look it up. I stayed glued to my phone until the battery dwindled to 1 percent.

I read full threads calling out voyeurism and asking people to respect my privacy. I read comments questioning whether I was pretty enough for the stunning male specimen that was the Baseball Babe. I read a handful of people wondering if I got paid to have sex with Eric in the bathroom, because my Instagram pictures showed I was clearly in need of money. I'd locked my Instagram hours ago, but not before plenty of people had gotten screenshots. Someone set up a GoFundMe for my lawyer fees, for when they expected I'd inevitably sue Jessica Banks. A roaring headache pounded in the bridge of my nose and went all the way down to my neck.

Jessica fielded questions like a pro. It was like she'd been given the lead role in the summer's biggest blockbuster, and she was milking it for all it was worth. I had no idea what she wanted from all this, but she bathed in the attention, tagging every media outlet on the planet, making it very clear how willing she'd be to give even more details on air. Stuff she said she hadn't yet posted to Twitter. Like the whole lie she created about Eric screwing me in a public bathroom wasn't enough.

When I'd had about all I could take of Twitter, I flipped to my email. I had no clue how my email address had gotten out there, but I read three offers to star in a porno movie and five rants about how "girls like me" were single-handedly responsible for all the filth and corruption in the world before I shut that down too. I still had over fifteen hundred unread messages in my inbox. How could I act normal enough to choke down dinner?

Mom went to work cutting up vegetables for our salad while I set the table. We fell into the easy rhythm of Sunday dinner prep. Even with the sweltering heat, I lived for summer nights like this. Current situation notwithstanding. After dinner we typically humored Gram and Peg by pretending to watch the evening news while they took bets on which anchor would be the first to keel over from a heart attack. Old people and their morbid games. Then Peg would go home, Gram would go to bed, and Mom would slip out to the Hamptons to enjoy a glass of tea and her romance novels until the sun set. I still had movie and lake plans, as far as I knew. No one had texted me to say otherwise.

Elise had touched base with me a few times to see how I was holding up, and to fill me in on all the ways Midnight was terrorizing Brady on his first day. Aside from sticking him on rewind duty, Midnight had him go through the store to make sure everything was still in alphabetical order. She also quizzed him on various movies he'd probably never heard of, let alone seen, so he could make appropriate recommendations. And of course she looked down her nose at him for not knowing any of the VHS movies. He didn't even need to know old movies to rewind and run the register; she just liked to play boss.

Peg had gone around back to help Gram unload the half cow from the car. She'd bring some of it to Gigi—and Donna, once they were on speaking terms again—since their efforts had helped purchase the beef. We gathered around the table, conversation flowing easily enough between Mom, Gram, and Peg that no one noticed how I picked at my dinner. I was starving, but my mind drifted back to Twitter, Eric, and Jessica.

"Next time you're at work, can you bring home *Big Business*?" Peg asked me. We were one of a handful of homes in Honeyfield that still had a working VCR. The perks of living with an old lady who refused to throw anything away. "I sure do like that Bette Midler, and it's been ages since I've seen that movie."

"No problem." I tried to smile, but it took more effort than it was worth. This might be the last family dinner we had together before I told them what happened. And once I did, everything would certainly go to hell.

Mom kept shooting me worried glances, that line between her eyebrows deepening, like she knew I was wrestling with something, trying to find the right words to voice it. She'd always let me have my space to work things out, and wouldn't question me within Gram's sharp hearing range. But she worried.

We cleaned up dinner as Peg and Gram headed into the living room. Once they left the kitchen, Mom turned to me. "Is everything okay?"

I'd probably been acting as twitchy as she had when she had to tell Gram she was pregnant. Which no doubt activated her greatest fear. The fear I'd come home one day and announce the same. Mom didn't set down a lot of rules, but she'd been very firm on three: No Sex before College (already broke that one), Never Chase a Dream Over a Paycheck (on my way to breaking that fully with my YouTube aspirations), and Never Date Your Coworkers (the only one I hadn't managed to break yet). She didn't have a problem with me dating, so long as I followed the rules, which I swore up and down I did.

I'd never tell her I already lost my virginity. She'd probably march out into the streets and try to find it again. It scared her bad. The handful of times Lance and I had had sex, we'd been careful. We broke up months ago and I hadn't been with anyone since.

"I'm fine." I gave her a fake grin, which was probably

more of a grimace judging by the way my lips stretched tightly over my teeth. "Peg and Donna got into a pretty ugly fight, and I'm still on edge from it."

Lies. Lies. Lies. I hated lying to Mom. It curled around my heart like poison. I just wanted her to have one good weekend without stress. My drama would still be there tomorrow.

From her pinched brows and ever-present worry line I could tell she didn't buy it, but whatever she saw in me, it wasn't a bun in the oven. As far as she was concerned, everything else was manageable. "If you need to talk later, let me know."

I nodded, and I would. Eventually. When the timing was right.

After loading the dishwasher, we went into the living room, where Peg and Gram already sat on either end of the couch. The only ones who didn't mind the plastic covering crackling beneath their seats. Mom took the recliner, and I sat on the floor at her feet near Charlie, still in his Royals cap, as the evening news filled the fuzzy TV screen in front of us.

I plugged my phone charger into the wall, opened my texts, and choked on a laugh. Elise had sent me a picture of Paxton putting a hand on Midnight's shoulder, but underneath his hand was a Post-it note with a tiny tombstone drawn on it. She had five of them sticking to her back. A new record. The last time Paxton and I had played that game, we got to four before she caught us. As retaliation, she'd let all the air out of Elise's tires, knowing we'd be stuck pushing her truck over to the gas station down the street to refill them. That was how Midnight operated. If you broke her pinkie, she'd cut off your leg.

I focused in on that picture of Paxton, the way his soft hair curled around his ears, which stuck out even from his side profile. The laugh that made his whole face light up. Something in my stomach fluttered, dangerous enough to make me lock my phone. It wouldn't do me any good to think about Paxton in fluttery ways. We were friends. Coworkers.

Mom had gotten tangled up with a cashier at Wilson's Grocery, a college guy home for the summer, while she'd been a sixteen-year-old bagger. Their breakup had been ugly. She threw a whole dozen eggs at his head in checkout lane three. It had taken her nearly a year to find another job. He'd long since disappeared and she was left alone with me.

That was why she'd set down the Three Rules before I'd even been born, and I'd grown up in the shadow of them. I understood why. Even if I bent and broke the first two, she hammered the coworkers one home hardest. That year she'd been without a job had left scars that still lingered. The two months she and Gram had gone without electricity, when they'd gone weeks at a time without eating any meat because it cost too much, not having a car or a phone or those everyday conveniences most people took for granted.

Because I was raised on those stories, and because I needed my job in the worst way if I ever planned to get out of Honeyfield, I didn't think about Paxton like that. Except that one time . . . Not entirely my fault. We'd been texting before I went to bed, and my dreams took an interesting turn. I took care of myself while I imagined him putting his mouth where I placed my fingers.

My breath caught, and I pushed that memory away, even as my blush lingered.

The news anchor's monotone voice droned on through the TV. A wrinkled old wisp of a man whose name I couldn't remember, but Gram had twenty on him being the first to die. "Tonight we bring you a lighter story . . . ," he began.

My heart stopped as one of my Instagram pictures filled the screen. I couldn't hear anything outside the roaring in my ears. I dove for the TV, gripping the edge as I reached for the power button to shut it off. I could barely move after that initial surge. My fingers felt as if I'd dragged them through mud, and the news anchor kept going on and on while my picture faded, only to be replaced by Eric's. I couldn't breathe. My lungs were too tight, my shaking fingers utterly useless. Finally, finally, I got a solid grip on myself and slammed my hand against the power button. Silence cut across the room, closed in on me, as I hunched my shoulders up to my ears and turned around to face my family.

I couldn't stand to look at Peg or Gram. My gaze shot right to Mom. Her pale complexion squeezed my chest. She raised a hand to her throat. I dropped to the ground, wrapping my arms around my knees, and let myself fall apart.

A shadow dropped over me, but I didn't want to leave the comfort of my knees. I floated on a scrap of wind. Like I'd left my body, and the shell of me became a sobbing, screaming mess. Mom enfolded me in her arms, and the light scent of her apple shampoo surrounded me. I sobbed harder.

"Baby girl." She stroked my back, letting the tears shudder through me. "It's okay. You're going to be okay. We're here. We'll figure this out."

"I'm sorry I didn't tell you." My voice cracked over every syllable. "I was going to tomorrow. I didn't . . ." I didn't want to ruin her perfect weekend.

She knew what I was going to say, even if I couldn't form the words. She pulled back, lifting my face with gentle hands. Hands that worked too hard, never got breaks, never got to have a fancy office with a view or cocktails with interesting men who had artful beards, and all those things she still quietly wished for. She wiped away my tears.

Gram made a sound low in her throat, like a lion about to roar. She crossed her arms as her gaze blazed into me. "What, exactly, happened?"

Gathering the bits of unyielding willpower I'd inherited from her, I pulled myself together and launched into the story. At least what I knew of it. Mom's face tightened when I mentioned that Jessica Banks had been the lady with the pink bow sitting behind us. I still didn't know her exact motives. From the way Jessica acted online, I had to assume she was desperate for attention, and I knew the kind of high that sort of attention could generate. The first time one of my reviews had gone over a thousand views, I strutted around the house like the Queen of England for a week. Those likes and thumbs-up were intoxicating.

It excused nothing though. I reviewed movies. Jessica had taken pictures of strangers, created a fantasy that never happened, and rolled it all out on Twitter without asking me or Eric how we'd feel about it. There was a world of difference between me and Jessica Banks.

When I finished, Gram stuck out her hand. "Your phone."

"Mom. This isn't her fault," my mom said from beside me.

Gram's eyes had become molten lava, and even Peg trembled on the other side of the couch. I physically felt Mom shrinking beside me. She might as well have been sixteen again, telling Gram she was pregnant and alone. Gram's hand stiffened. She wouldn't ask again. Slowly, I pulled my phone out of my back pocket and handed it to her.

Goodbye, YouTube and Twitter. Goodbye, freedom.

Gram's lips thinned as she looked at my cracked screen. The lecture about taking care of my belongings wouldn't be far behind. She barely managed to open it with my birth date, and practically hissed at all the apps that came up. "How do you make the Google appear?"

If the situation weren't so serious, Mom and I would've shared a quiet chuckle over "the Google," but we just looked at each other with confusion.

"Do you, or do you not, have the Google on this contraption?" Gram asked.

"W-why?" I asked, barely daring to breathe.

"Because." Gram lifted her gaze to mine. "I'm going to find this Jessica Banks, then I'm going to peel her skin off in layers, feed it to a pack of wild dogs, and light the rest on fire."

All the tension flooded out of the room. Peg sagged a bit on the couch. She hadn't offered any commentary while I spoke, which was so unusual for her, I knew she'd been genuinely concerned. Peg spent more time online than the other Bees, she had a mean Pinterest addiction, and she understood a lot better than Gram the kind of shit I was in.

"Jesus Christ, Mom. That's next level. Even for you." My mom paused. "But if that's the plan, then I call shotgun."

I let out a shaky laugh and took my phone back. "As appealing as murder sounds, I'm pretty fond of you both and wouldn't want to see either of you go to jail."

I could only imagine Gram in prison. I'd give the inmates a week before they tried to tunnel through the walls, just to escape her.

"I locked most of my social media," I said. "But I can't . . ." I sucked in a deep breath, preparing to battle. "I can't shut down my YouTube channel. Please don't ask me to do that."

Gram lit a cigarette and waved to the Vanna dolls gracing the fireplace. "When that piece of shit Hugh Hefner ran photos of the Queen in *Playboy* without her consent, do you think she buried her head in the sand? Quit her job?"

I shook my head.

Gram held my gaze through a trail of smoke. "You're an Evans. We're forged of fire and steel, and when the world tries to shove us down, we don't bend. For anyone. Keep your YouTube, do whatever it is you had been doing. This will pass, but until it does, do not bend."

"Yes, ma'am." I had a strong urge to give her a salute. The general of our tiny troop.

I should've known Gram would be on my side. No one messed with her family. No one. She scared half the town, but I wondered if they were afraid because they could see that fire and steel in her. That refusal to bend. When others left to escape the stifling poverty that had a fist around this entire town, Gram dug in her raptor toe and refused to break.

We survived because anything else would be inexcusable.

CHAPTER
SIX

PEG HAD GONE HOME, giving my shoulder a pat before she left. With Gram tucked into bed, and Mom tucked into the Hamptons with her book (after a million reassurances that I was fine), I waited until the sun began to dip below the tree line, then set out for the lake on foot. We only had one car, and despite Gram's support, I didn't want to push my luck by asking for the keys. The lake wasn't that far anyway.

Cicadas hummed in the distant trees as the air cooled. Fireflies sent off little sparks of light over the long grass bordering the sidewalk. I turned down two streets, the scent of summer-warmed pavement and overgrown wildflowers trailing my every step. The walk helped clear my head. While I still didn't know what to do, I kept reminding myself not to bend.

My phone buzzed in my back pocket. I flicked the screen, groaning when I read the text from Elise: *Me and Midnight are out. Will explain tomorrow.*

I sincerely hoped they weren't hooking up again. Elise and Midnight had a want/hate relationship. Like they hated how much they wanted each other. It had been months since they'd last been together, all anger and passion that burned bright and fast, but after the last time, Elise swore no more. Not after the anger had burned out of her and she wanted more than tangled limbs in the alley behind the store on breaks. Midnight was not the candlelight-dinners-and-holding-hands-at-the-movies type, and it ended up hurting them both.

I could go back home. And deal with Mom hovering, trying *not* to ask me how I was doing, while we both danced around my guilt and her worry. My phone buzzed, startling me enough to make me yelp. A text from Paxton: *I'm already here.*

I thumbed open the group text: *Almost there.*

Paxton and I had never been alone for movie on the lake. We'd never been alone outside of work at all. Maybe we wouldn't be alone if Brady showed up though. Three dots appeared on my phone, disappeared, appeared, and finally: *See you soon.*

I walked over a small hill. The sun had fully set, and the lake waited at the bottom. The public park was on the other side, where I'd spent most of my summers as a toddler while my mom and Momma Gomez formed an unbreakable friendship, and Elise became the closest thing I'd ever have to a sister. The ancient swings swayed in the gentle breeze—the place where I'd kicked Lance Harrington in the shins after he pushed Elise into the wood chips. Who knew he'd be the one to take my virginity ten years later? Not me, that's for sure. Lance had been nice, a little awkward, but nice. I didn't have any hard feelings against him, or him against me. We were just . . . nice. Okay. Fine. And that wasn't what either of us had wanted in the end.

Paxton came around from the other side of the community storage shed as I approached.

"No Brady?" I looked around like I'd really expected him to show up.

Paxton chuckled. "After dealing with Midnight all day, did you think he'd willingly spend time in her company off the clock?"

"That bad, huh?" Even though I already knew, thanks to Elise's updates.

"The rewinder ate *Interview with the Vampire* under his watch."

Poor Brady.

The silence settled over us, not uncomfortable—we weren't ever really uncomfortable around each other—but we always had Midnight or Elise around. I tucked my hands into my pockets, mainly because I didn't know what else to do with them.

Paxton cleared his throat. "Did you still want to watch the movie?"

"Do you even have the movie?" Elise had been the one who rented it.

"No." He grinned at me. "But I did go to all that trouble breaking into the shed." He gestured to a boat resting on the sandy shore near the "beach" part of the lake.

I toed at the pebbles lining the path around the park, trying to keep my voice light and casual. "It would be a shame to waste your efforts."

We left his laptop and our phones on the grass near the

shed. Once I settled into my seat, he pushed the boat off the shore, climbing in from behind. Our knees touched as we faced each other. Water lapped at the sides of the boat as he rowed, and I did *not* notice the way his biceps flexed under his T-shirt from the movement. A firefly skimmed the surface of the lake, then took off into the night. Crickets chirped from the cattails lining the opposite shore. Without the movie to provide the usual distraction, I felt like I'd fallen into a scene from one of my mom's books. Except this wasn't a romance. Just a late-night boat ride between friends.

We reached the center of the lake, and Paxton stopped rowing, letting the oars rest in their metal holders. "I'm really glad you came out tonight."

The full moon offered enough light for me to note the concern. I tried to gather that Evans steel, but something in his expression brought all my fears and insecurities bubbling to the surface. Not just his concern, but it almost looked like he understood. As if he knew exactly how I felt, which was ridiculous. He wasn't anywhere online. I'd already tried to google him months ago, and other than becoming an inadvertent expert in all things Bill Paxton, it had been a complete waste of my time. Paxton had no idea how I felt. But with all of it reflecting back at me nonetheless, a fresh wave of pain rolled in.

"I don't want to talk about the game." I swallowed. "Or anything that happened after."

"What do you want to talk about, Macy Mae?" He rested his arms on his knees and leaned forward. "Tell me something about you no one knows."

No one knew I thought about him while I took care of myself one night, but I'd be keeping that particular moment to myself. Forever. "When I was a little kid, I used to think Gram's Vanna White dolls were going to eat me in my sleep for not playing with them."

"Morbid." He thrummed his fingers against his leg. "What's your favorite color?"

"What is this? Twenty questions?"

"It can be. Depends on how many questions it takes, I suppose."

"How many questions it takes for what?" I gave him a wary look. If he was trying to work around to asking me about Eric and Jessica, I wasn't interested.

"For me to get to know you better." He ran a hand through his hair. In the moonlight, his hazel eyes looked more soft bronze than green. "We never hang out alone outside of work, and we should, because I only like work when you're there. But I don't even know what your favorite color is, and that is a very basic thing to know about someone."

"All right." What did he mean when he said he only liked work when I was there? Why was I even thinking that? It had to be the moonlight putting weird ideas into my head. Hopefully these ones would stay out of my dreams this time. "My favorite color is blue."

"What kind of blue? Navy? Aquamarine? Sky? Robin's egg? Turquoise? I'm going to need you to be more specific here."

"The blue of our kiddie pool when it's filled with water and my mom is dipping her toes in while she reads a romance novel and is totally relaxed and happy. And the kind of blue the sky turns right before a spring storm, when it has just a touch of gray. The blue of Gram's favorite Vanna's Choice yarn when she's creating for her own pleasure and not for competition. Those kinds of blues."

Paxton's face lit up. "Now that's an answer."

"What about you? What's your favorite color?"

"Chartreuse," he said with absolute sincerity.

I snorted. "No one's favorite color is chartreuse."

"It's mine, though my reason is significantly less poetic than yours. For the longest time I thought chartreuse was a shade of maroon, and when I found out it was actually yellow-green, it was like knowing a secret. Half the people in the world have no idea what color it really is."

"You are such a dork." I smiled, a real smile, for the first time since finding out what Jessica had done to me. "What's your favorite movie?" The repair side didn't get to put their favorite movies up on the wall.

"*Say Anything*."

I narrowed my eyes. "Are you just picking a movie from my favorites on the wall?"

"It's one of your favorites too? I had no idea." He gave me a slow grin. The liar. "'I gave her my heart and she gave me a pen' is the most quotable line, and that scene where Lloyd stands outside Diane's window with the boom box is an important moment in cinematic history."

"Anyone could figure that out from a Google search. That's not what makes a movie great. If it's really your favorite, you're going to have to do better than that."

"Okay." He rubbed his chin. "I don't proclaim to be an expert on reviews, but I think people might see Lloyd as pushy, calling Diane eight times, standing outside her window after she ended things, and maybe he is, but I see it another way too."

"Oh?" I sat up a little straighter. I saw it another way too, and I'd only ever had Gram and Mom to talk to about this movie. Everyone else thought it was too old or irrelevant, not really understanding how it was ahead of its time.

"I think with Lloyd, Diane finally had the freedom to be who she wanted to be, not who her dad expected her to be, and he knew that." Paxton's cheeks flushed.

"Keep going." I nudged his knee with mine. "This is good stuff."

"Take Diane's dad for example." He cleared his throat. "He only had a real problem with Lloyd, enough to want her to end things, after she admitted to having sex. And she was the one who initiated it. Like, I don't know, like she no longer fit this box he tried to shove her into."

"Exactly. That is exactly it." My pulse picked up, the way it always did whenever I dug into the deeper meaning of movies. Especially my favorite movie. "Her dad expected his version of perfection from his daughter at the cost of her own happiness."

"And Lloyd is, like, the opposite of her dad." Paxton's voice had become just as animated as mine. "All his friends are women, he lives with his sister, who is a single mom. It's, like, the people he surrounded himself with taught him how to be better."

"And that one time he tried to be a dude-bro and hang out with the other dude-bros, he saw what a bunch of shits they were, how he would never be like them or fit in with them."

"Yep." Paxton leaned in closer, like he was drawn to our minds melding or something. "Diane never wanted to give him that pen and end things."

"It was all her dad trying to manipulate her, the way he manipulated those old people out of their money. And Lloyd knew that because he was the only person who ever bothered to get to know the real Diane."

"Yeah." Paxton sat back, as if suddenly realizing how small the boat was and how much we'd tilted toward each other. "Anyway. I like movies that say something. That are more than what people expect them to be. That's why it's my favorite."

"That's why it's my favorite too." I didn't know if Paxton had purposely tried to distract me from everything going on, but I finally felt normal again. Like I could talk about Jessica without breaking down. I bit my lip to keep it from trembling. "It was on the evening news tonight. That's how my mom and Gram found out."

Paxton swore under his breath. "How did Bizzy take it?"

Gram knew more about Paxton's history before Honeyfield than anyone else because of Gigi. I once asked Gram why he moved here, and she yelled at me for trying to gossip, even though the Bees were the worst gossips in town. But she wouldn't speak of it, and I knew better than to bug her for information she didn't want to share.

"She threatened to peel the skin off the woman who took my pictures and feed her to wild dogs. So." I shrugged. "I'd say she took it pretty well."

He laughed, and that warm, rich sound made my toes tingle. "I always did like your grandma, even if she still terrifies the shit out of me."

"That makes two of us." Though, truth be told, I was more afraid for anyone who messed with me or my mom. A lifetime of living under Gram's roof taught me how to weather her storms. I picked a piece of lint off my shirt and flicked it into the water. "She doesn't want me to shut down any of my accounts. She thinks I should just keep posting like normal."

Paxton stiffened. "Why?"

"I don't know." I let out a breath. "She filled my head with a bunch of war talk and not hiding and brought Vanna White and *Playboy* into it. It was a whole thing. And I sort of agree with her. I don't want to give people online the satisfaction of chasing me away."

"But sometimes stepping back is the only way to keep them from eating you alive." The invisible, yet palpable, shadows gathering around him let me know he wasn't just talking about me anymore, but he didn't offer up any more information.

For the millionth time in the last year, I wanted to ask him what had happened. How did he come to live with his grandma? Why wouldn't he learn how to drive or use the Internet beyond Amazon? But he wouldn't appreciate me poking at his demons, and he hadn't pushed me when I didn't want to talk about mine, so I tilted my head back until I couldn't see anything other than the endless night sky. "Do you believe in aliens?"

"Wow. You're really bad at casually trying to change the subject."

"Shut up." I gave him a light shove, but the motion rocked the boat, sending me sprawling into him and nearly dumping us both overboard.

That easy amusement he always seemed to carry in my presence danced in the air between us as he held my arms to help me up. My hands rested against his chest, so close I could feel his breath sweep across my lips. Neither of us moved. The humor on his face faded. Slowly, his fingers trailed down my arms, a gentle caress, bringing out goose bumps that had nothing to do with the chilly lake air. My gaze drifted to his mouth.

I could've kissed him. I could've . . .

Then Eric, Jessica, everything I'd read about myself on Twitter blasted through my brain. I scrambled back. Too fast. With too much force. The boat rocked the opposite way and I flipped right over the edge and into the water.

Paxton's deep laugh rang out over the lake as I sputtered and choked my way to the surface. It was too early in the summer for the lake to properly warm, and my tennis shoes pulled at my feet like anchors. The small waves I'd created rippled against the side of the boat. I pushed my hair out of my face as I treaded water and glared at him.

He'd leaned over the side of the boat, resting his dry arms on the ledge, like he didn't have a care in the world. "If you say please, I might help you up."

I ground my chattering teeth together. "Please."

He held out his hand, and I latched on a second before he saw the flash in my eyes and tried to let go. Too late. I had a firm grip, and I tugged. Hard. He went crashing into the water.

He broke the surface and shook his wet head, which sent droplets flying toward me. "You are so in for it now."

I yelped and swam away from him, but he caught me around the waist and I was laughing so hard, I swallowed a mouthful of water and choked. He held me above the surface while I coughed until I could breathe again. He still held my waist when I put my arms around his neck. To stay afloat. My light pink tank top might as well have been white once I hit the water, which made my red bra completely visible, even in the dark.

Paxton glanced down. "I think my new favorite color is red."

"Hey. Eyes up here, perv."

"Sorry. Your bra is just . . . there." He paused and turned his head. Our boat had drifted forty feet away. "We lost our boat."

I laughed and took in another mouthful of the lake.

"Okay. You clearly can't be trusted around water." Paxton held me tight as he swam for the shore. I crawled up onto the grass, coughing a few times before I collapsed onto my stomach.

He lay next to me on his back, hands tucked behind his head. "You know, as soon as you're done dying, you have to retrieve our boat."

I leaned up enough to shove him, then fell back onto the grass. The soft blades tickled my cheek and hid my smile. I didn't turn toward him though. If I did, I knew I'd want to finish what I'd considered on the boat before I flipped into the water. Then I'd be doing a different sort of drowning. But I couldn't, under any circumstance, kiss him. Not when my life was already a complete mess.

By the time I got back home Gram and Mom had gone to bed, so it was like I had the house to myself. For once. I still had too much nervous energy bouncing around inside me to sleep, so I put on the TV. I had the recliner fully extended out in the living room, my quilt pulled up to my chin. The Bees had made this one for me and I'd had it for years. Pretty floral fabrics blended together in a burst of rainbow and life. *Ferris Bueller's Day Off* had just started on TBS, and I decided to watch even though I'd rented it fifty million times already.

My phone buzzed, and my pulse quickened at the text from Paxton: *Whatcha doin?*

Me: *Watching Ferris Burlesque*

Paxton: *Kinky*

Me: *Bueller, not burlesque asdfghjkl autocorrect*

Paxton: *Rental or TV?*

Me: *TV, TBS*

Paxton: *Now I'm watching too. I'd forgotten what a dick Ferris was to Cameron*

Me: *Total dick.* Type, delete, type, delete. *It's late.*

Paxton: *Can't sleep, so I'm watching Ferris Burlesque with you*

What was going on? He usually went to bed way early in the summer so he could tend to the rabbits in the morning. Why couldn't he sleep? I knew why I couldn't sleep. I couldn't stop thinking about how close I'd come to kissing him tonight. His mouth would've grazed mine, soft at first. I would've run my hand up his chest, dragging him closer. My lips would've parted and he would've glided his tongue over mine. . . .

My phone buzzed twice in my hand. Two texts from Paxton: *I always thought Ferris's sister was hotter than Sloane.* The next: *You fall asleep on me?*

Me: *I'm here. If you think Jennifer Grey is so hot, you should have no problem with watching* Dirty Dancing *for the next movie on the lake.*

Paxton: *You say that like I don't already own the collector's edition*

Because I couldn't stand it anymore. Me: *Why are you really awake?*

Paxton: *Nosy*

Me: *Bunnies throwing a wild party in the backyard? Too much noise?*

Paxton: *Funny, but no. I'm just thinking about something from tonight.*

Me: *Which part?*

He waited so long to respond, I thought he'd fallen asleep. I put my phone on the arm of the recliner and snuggled back into my quilt. Ferris had just declared himself the Sausage King of Chicago when Paxton finally texted me back: *The part right before you flipped into the water.*

My face heated. Me: *Oh*

Paxton: *Night, Macy Mae*

I didn't text him back.

CHAPTER

I AWOKE WITH A start and rolled over to check the time on my phone. Just after two in the morning. I groaned and stared at the ceiling as the horror of my nightmare lingered over me. I'd dreamed that I really had gone into that bathroom with Eric while I wore the Molly Ringwald yarn wig, and I told Jessica she could film it if we split the profits. Ridiculous, but the whole thing left a sheen of cold sweat on my skin.

Since I was awake, I opened Twitter again.

@JohnBClarkwell: I'd do #flyballgirl. #baseballbabe #IonceGotBusyInAburgerKingBathroom

@AbbyAnnaAndrewMommy: I don't get all this #baseballbabe fuss. The girl isn't even that pretty. I don't know whether to laugh or cry every time her pic rolls past my timeline.

@SealedLipsTightShips: Going to a Little League game tonight. I don't even have a kid. I just want to find a #baseballbabe

@JuneDayFashion: New Twitter poll on #flyballgirl fashion. Is it a No, a Hell No, or a Kill It with Fire? #baseballbabe #UglyClothesOfTwitter

@catladyclea: I hope they burn down that bathroom #baseballbabe #crabs

@ChrissyBleeker: This whole #baseballbabe thing isn't a

love story. It's gross and invasive. The comments on here just go to show how vile this whole situation is. 1/25

    @samtravesty: Did you all see how young #flyballgirl's mom is? Do some math on that one. I guess the apple doesn't fall far from the tree. . . . #baseballbabe

    @MargoHeartsDrWho: That #baseballbabe is going to be my new nightly fantasy. Those abs! He could Get. It.

One scroll through, and the sickness crested up in me again. Not just from the slander of my morals and looks, which was enough to make me want to crawl into a hole, but even the majority of well-meaning comments felt like a judgment. Like their approval of me went as far as I was willing to go with Eric.

He got to be a new nighttime fantasy, while I just got to be that girl who screwed a stranger in a public bathroom. All the slut-shaming, and none of the sex. Like that time Elise and I stole a bottle of cheap wine from her parents and didn't even get a buzz off it, but we both had monster headaches the next morning.

Eric played his part to the fullest. I checked his timeline again and he'd posted a YouTube clip of a song called "Love Is Like a Baseball Game" by the Intruders. I still hadn't worked up the nerve to reply to his DM or FaceTime him. I just continued to scroll through Twitter in incognito mode and didn't get back to sleep until after five.

I slammed my fist on the dryer, but no amount of pounding

would make it start again. It was dead, and I'd put off laundry all week. I was down to my last pair of ratty underwear with all the elastic torn out. They kept sliding down my hips under my shorts. It drove me nuts.

"Mom, dryer won't start!" I yelled down the hall.

She came out of her room, tying her hair into a knot on top of her head. The worry line between her eyebrows had deepened and she had dark circles from a sleepless night. If I ever met Jessica Banks in person, I'd pay her back for that alone.

Mom's orthopedic shoes, the kind built for running trays of food for eight hours, swished across the threadbare carpet. She'd cleaned her uniform the night before. An order pad stuck out of the pocket of her apron. If my YouTube channel took off enough to support my family, that apron would be the first thing I'd burn.

"Call Elise. Let your grandma know. I have to go to work." She ran a hand over my hair, pausing to check me over, the question lingering in her downturned mouth.

"I'm okay," I said. Because she needed to hear it.

She nodded, kissed my cheek, and headed out the door.

The truth was, I didn't know if I was okay or not. After my dip in the lake with Paxton the night before, I'd started to feel okay. But I couldn't stay away from Twitter. It was like a compulsion. I didn't want to see what people were saying about me, but I also really, really did. While the bathroom assumptions would damage my future in ways I couldn't begin to process, the comments about how I looked and dressed hit me so much harder. Gram made most of my clothes, including the shirt with the seashells. I loved the feel of the fabric and the way it had been sewn specifically to fit me. Now it made me feel backwoods. Homespun. Trash.

Maybe Paxton was right about stepping away. From all of it. Gram wanted me to do what I had been doing, to keep my head high, to not bend, but how far could a person push back from bending before they snapped in half? I'd scrolled through Twitter until I'd passed out, and woke up again when I'd hit myself on the forehead with my phone. And with each tweet, each time I'd come across my name, the hole in my heart expanded. Until it became this void. This empty place where the person I had been went into that black hole and didn't come out again. If I waded into the fray, I wondered if that hole would seal permanently, or if it would just shatter me completely.

I trudged into the dining room, where the Bees were already gathered, bickering over their quilt theme. If they didn't get it together soon, they wouldn't even have a quilt.

"I don't see what your problem is with Defining Moments in History." Peg glared at Donna. "Bizzy likes it. Gigi likes it. I like it. Unless that's your problem."

"I didn't say I liked it," Gigi said, her voice soft and soothing. "I said I didn't have a problem with it. But I also see what Donna is saying. History in general covers a lot of ground. It's not coherent enough."

Peg huffed and crossed her arms.

Gram lit a cigarette. "What if we could make it coherent?

We could make it Defining Moments in Recent History. A few select events that tie together, like the invention of the automobile and the moon landing. The judges like that Americana shit."

"Maybe," Donna said. I could practically see her debating all the events of the sixties she could shuffle through and pick from. "As long as Peg sticks to the theme."

"I've been sticking to the theme since you were still gluing felt flowers to your leather vests." Peg's fingers curled into fists.

Gigi chuckled. "You mean since last week?"

"As much as I hate to break up this wonderous meeting of the minds," I said, plopping into Iris's old chair, "the dryer is broken. Elise will fix it, but I need to go to the laundromat."

Gram flicked her cigarette over the overflowing ashtray. "Ask if her momma needs any sewing done. And bring up a few jars of jam and canned tomatoes from the cellar."

Elise would fix the dryer for free, but Gram would never allow it. We didn't have any money to pay her, so Gram would pay in labor and canned goods. She'd give away everything that wasn't nailed down before she'd accept help. Pride kept her from doing otherwise, and she'd hoard that pride with her dying breath.

In a town like Honeyfield, some people clung to their hate, some clung to a misguided sense of superiority, and some clung to their religion. And then there were the people like Gram, who clung to their pride. Because when you didn't have anything else, you held on to the one thing no one else could take.

The *Today* show came on over the little TV with a coat hanger antenna that Gram had set up in the dining room. Eric's cocky grin flooded the screen and I groaned. It didn't even surprise me to see him, considering the evening news bit. It would only be a matter of time before the other networks followed the story.

He told the anchor how some events had gotten misconstrued, but he still had feelings for me, as he turned all sorrowful. "If you're watching right now, Macy, I really want to see you again."

"We hope you see her again too." The news anchor placed a sympathetic hand on his arm, all smiles for the beautiful, lovesick boy at her side.

I rolled my eyes.

Donna cleared her throat, shooting a tentative glance at Gram. "He certainly is a catch. If I were a few years younger, I'd be tempted to let him feel me up in the back of a van."

"Gross." I threw a balled-up piece of thread at her. "He doesn't even know me."

"There are worse things in life than having a pretty boy trying to win your affections on national TV." Gram waved her hand, causing smoke to dance on the air.

I quirked an eyebrow. "Don't you want to rip off his skin and feed it to wild animals?"

"That woman who took your pictures, yes. But he's just as much a victim as you are and look at that face." Gram turned toward the TV with a soft expression I found deeply unsettling. "He has an honest face. Maybe you should give him a chance."

The most honest faces told the best lies.

I didn't have the energy to point out that he was still lying about the fly ball. At least he'd been nice enough to say we didn't have sex in the bathroom, and that was how far my expectations of human decency had fallen in just a day. I'd become pathetically grateful for him simply telling the truth about one thing.

"I'll think about it," I said.

Peg gave me a smug grin, which I ignored as I texted Elise to let her know what was going on, and went to go dig up enough quarters to finish the laundry. After going through the junk drawers, between the couch cushions, and behind my dresser, I came up with just enough to maybe finish two loads. If I could shove them both into one dryer. I'd bring along four nickels and five pennies, just in case I needed that extra eight minutes of drying time. I loaded up my baskets and soap into Peg's car.

I hated going to the laundromat. It sat right in the center of town, with wide-open windows to reveal all the people who couldn't afford a washer and dryer. Even though paying to do laundry weekly cost so much more money. Being poor was damned expensive.

I pushed the door open with my butt, a basket under each arm, and nodded to Gina, the woman in her late forties who owned the place. Her bangs were teased with so much hair spray, the ozone wept. Monday afternoon meant I had my pick of washers. I threw my dirty clothes into the one in the back, farthest away from the windows, and passed the time doing BuzzFeed quizzes on my phone. I'd finally gotten my fill of Twitter for the day, though I had no doubt I'd be back on there later. Once my clothes finished washing, I hauled them plus the ones I washed at home into a single dryer and fed it every last quarter I had, praying the fifty-six minutes I'd been able to buy would dry two loads.

With two minutes left on the dryer, I opened it up to check on my clothes. Warm steam blasted me in the face as I shoved my hand into the pile. Damn it. I needed more time, and trading my nickels and pennies for a quarter still wouldn't buy me enough. I couldn't bring my clothes home wet. The last time I'd done that, everything I owned had dried stiff and crunchy. I could barely stand to let those clothes touch my skin.

Midnight was at work. She might have a few quarters in the cup holder of her car. If I offered her a few popcorn packets from home, maybe she'd be willing to trade me. Glancing at the dryer still spinning my clothes, I told Gina I'd be back in a few minutes. She ignored me and kept thumbing through the pages of her year-old copy of *People* magazine. Which was whatever. It's not like I had the kind of clothes worth stealing anyway.

I went outside and stopped short. Someone dropped three quarters, and I nearly started crying at the sight of them. Jared—last year's graduate and future Creeper

Feature of the Week in *Mug Shots* magazine—and his buddy Brett hung out in front of the hardware store. Farm boys. They'd been raised on corn and testosterone, and their idea of a fun night consisted of PBR and beating the hell out of each other. Most of us in town avoided them.

I ignored Brett's snickering and dropped to the ground next to a crushed Styrofoam cup, an undecipherable pink puddle, and old cigarette butts. My fingers slipped right over the quarters, and I tried again. They didn't budge. Brett and Jared started laughing. At me. I couldn't grab the quarters because they'd glued them to the sidewalk.

"Problem?" Jared asked with a bite in his tone. A shadow fell over me, and the steel toe of his farm boot stopped right under my line of vision. "Look at the famous Macy Evans, crawling on her hands and knees for a couple of quarters."

Tears gathered under my eyelids as the deeper fire of humiliation burned in my gut. I kept my gaze on the sidewalk, refusing to look up, refusing to give them what they wanted. "Don't you have a sheep you should be fucking right now?"

He placed the tip of his boot under my chin and used it to lift my face. He smirked at me, and it took every ounce of my willpower not to claw his eyes out. I had no doubt he would've been more than happy to stomp that boot against my throat. "There's a bathroom in the hardware store, and I have more quarters in my pocket. Or are you only interested in fly balls?"

I willed the tears back—pushing against that voice in

my head that told me I'd never get out of this town and away from these people. I'd never escape this life. *Don't cry, don't cry, don't cry.* "Fuck you."

Jared bent down, beer already on his breath, even though it was just past noon. "I was willing to be a gentleman. But now—"

"Hey. What are you doing?" Brady marched up the sidewalk from the pharmacy and shoved Jared. "Leave her the hell alone."

Jared sized up Brady, the sheer mass of him, and I had a brief glimmer of satisfaction as Jared backed up a step. Brett had disappeared into the hardware store, no doubt worried about the handful of people who had stopped to gawk. Not to do anything or help me in any way, but to watch it all go down.

Jared shook his head. "Forget it, man. We were just having a little fun."

Brady stood next to me, staring Jared down. With a last sneer, Jared turned around and went back into the hardware store.

"Thank you," I said, too quietly.

"No problem. I can't stand those guys." Brady held out his hand to help me up, and as much as I hated every second of crouching on the ground, I needed those goddamned quarters. I pulled my phone out and slammed it against the glue holding them to the sidewalk, breaking them free so I'd have just enough money to finish my laundry.

I put the quarters in the dryer and found the darkest corner in the laundromat to curl up against.

I loaded the rest of my clothes into my laundry baskets as soon as the buzzer went off. Somehow I managed to get out of there without making eye contact with anyone who passed me on the sidewalk. As soon as I got home, I dragged the laundry through my front door and then checked YouTube. All of my videos had now gone over a hundred thousand views. Depending on how many clicked the ads, the two hundred dollars I'd been earning would increase to somewhere around three thousand. In a month.

I bit down on my fist. I'd never had that kind of money in my life. For the first time I'd be able to open an actual savings account without paying fees, instead of using my dresser. I'd be able to afford the rent in Chicago. I'd never have to scrape another quarter off the sidewalk again. All because a stranger had wanted to tweet about a meet-cute so bad, she invented one where it didn't exist.

I opened my DMs. Sucking in a deep breath, I pulled out my phone and FaceTimed Eric.

CHAPTER
EIGHT

ERIC'S FACE FILLED THE screen, just as chiseled and perfect as it had been at the game and on TV. The snake. "Macy." He said my name with the kind of awe reserved for the church we never bothered attending. "I'm so glad you called."

"Why? Because you're hungry to extend your fifteen minutes?" He came off as all sad and sincere, but I wouldn't bend. Not on this.

"It got a little out of control, but I really did want to see you again. I missed you."

"You don't even know me." Or maybe he did? My stomach rolled at all the pictures I'd put on Instagram and personal details I'd shared on Twitter, thinking no one would care because I'd kept them separate from R3ntal Wor1d and my Misty Morning persona. "Were you in on it?"

"No." He put enough bite in the word to have me considering. "I had no idea Jessica was taking our pictures or that it would go viral, or any of it. I swear."

"But you had no problem playing along." My voice was like ice, and I didn't care. I wasn't going to be the stumbling and awkward girl he'd met at the game, or whoever he expected me to be after he'd rifled through the images of my life online. I was an Evans. I came from Gram. Fire and steel. And today I'd let Eric see that the monster crawling within her heart also lived and breathed within mine.

"Didn't you also play along by following me on Twitter?" A careful smile, like he was teasing me. "Jessica isn't a bad person. We've sort of become friends through all this, and she had no idea it would go viral either. She's catching a lot of shit for it."

"Boo-fucking-hoo." I had zero sympathy for Jessica. She'd fully brought the shit she caught on herself when she'd decided to make a sideshow attraction out of two strangers. "People in my hometown are talking about me." Just thinking about Jared and his quarters again made my hands shake. Eric's face went temporarily blurry. "Everyone thinks I had sex with you in a public bathroom. Thanks for not setting the record straight on Twitter, by the way."

"I said we didn't have sex on *Today*." He frowned. "I'll fix that. Right now. Hold on." His face paused, then a moment later he was back. "Done."

I opened Twitter, which paused FaceTime on my end.

@baseballbabe2020: Talking to @MacyAtTheMovies and need to say again that we did NOT have sex at the Royals game. Carry on. #baseballbabe #flyballgirl

I closed Twitter. "Okay. Good."

"It's been wild." He continued on like he hadn't even heard me. "Me and Jessica have both gone on *Today*; we're scheduled to go on *Entertainment Tonight*. I think if you agree, the two of us together could get a spot on *The Tonight Show*."

"Why? What's in this for you?"

He went somewhere faraway in his mind, taking on the dreamy expression that had sent the Internet swooning over this pretty, sun-kissed boy. "I want to be a sports reporter."

Whatever I had been expecting him to say, that hadn't been it. "Go to college. Major in journalism or something. You don't need to be famous to do that."

The dreamy expression vanished. "I have a blog. I had a handful of hits before this whole thing took off, but now I'm competing with guys who have been doing this for years. As for college, I'm already going. I have a baseball scholarship, full-ride at Mizzou."

"And?" It's not like he'd shown off his reporting skills with all the strutting he'd been doing on various TV circuits, but at least that explained why he hadn't told the truth about the fly ball. The type of people who followed a sports blogger with a baseball scholarship probably wouldn't be impressed that I'd caught that ball right out from under him.

"Don't you get it?" He leaned in so close to his phone, for a moment he just became a single deep brown eyeball. "With my recent numbers I can get more access, locker room interviews. Thousands of people go into journalism, but only a few make it. This is how I'll stand out. It's the edge I need."

No wonder he had no problem telling everyone we didn't have sex. He needed to stay in my good graces. One post from me would cause enough doubt to ruin his chances. And here I thought he was just being a decent human being. Silly rabbit.

"And you need me too," he said.

"W-what do you mean?" I stumbled over my words, knowing exactly what he meant.

"Your YouTube channel. I know you've seen your numbers. Imagine how high they could go. Imagine if you didn't have to work at the rental store anymore or live in that shithole town. You think I don't know you're scraping by? That the whole damn Internet doesn't know, with all those pictures you've posted on Instagram? They're dying to crown you and make you a queen. They want your Cinderella story."

It was like he'd sliced me open and looked directly into my soul. All of my hopes and wants and fears spread out before him like a buffet to pick over, to decide which ones he could use to manipulate me. But at the same time . . .

He wasn't wrong. I wanted that picture he'd painted. I wanted it so bad, it was like a living thing inside me. A twin I'd absorbed in the womb. The kind that still had its teeth, gently chewing away at those useless things like pride and honesty. The things that hadn't gotten me anywhere except a dead-end job in a dead-end town with a future so eerily like my mom's. A future of working until every muscle in my body ached, and it never being enough. Of always being one emergency away from utter despair. Of not even getting the peace of living paycheck to paycheck because those never stretched as far as they needed.

"What, exactly, are you suggesting I do?" Every word on my tongue tasted like the bitter aspirin my mom had never quite been able to mask with syrup. From the gleam in his eye, he knew he had me. And I'd never hated myself more.

"We should make a public appearance. Nothing too obvious, but I know the perfect place. We could meet halfway on Wednesday or Thursday. I'll handle the reservations."

"You want to pretend we're dating?" I shook my head. Too far. This was going too far. It was one thing to tweet and play coy on the Internet. That wasn't really real. Seeing him in person though. Driving to see him. That was completely different territory, and not one I was equipped to navigate.

"It doesn't have to be fake." His voice softened. "I really do think you're cute, and I'm sorry I didn't get your number."

"Yeah. Why is that?" I gave him a coltish bat of my lashes. He thought he was running this game, but I knew how to play too.

"I'm—" He scratched the back of his neck. "I'm not so good at talking to cute girls. My buddy Rod called me a dumbass the whole way home, and I felt like it too. I was so scared you'd say no that I left before I could ask you."

What an absolute load of bullshit. I'd seen his Instagram. He had no problem in the confidence department, nor did he appear to have trouble talking to cute girls. Unless he had a lot of cousins who he routinely took shirtless pictures with.

"Even if this isn't the way we expected things to go, I'm really glad I got to see you again. I mean that." Nothing but sincerity in Eric's voice, and I . . . just didn't buy it. He was too good. Too smooth. It set off all the warning bells in my head, even if he was dateable on paper and tried very hard to seem like he was into me.

But he was right about one thing. We needed each other. If Jessica's thread got me over a hundred thousand views on my videos, I couldn't imagine how many I'd get if I let this fauxmance play out online. Half the Internet was rooting for us to get together. Granted, the other half thought I had crabs, but I wouldn't think about them.

"You have my number now," I said. "I have to work on Thursday, but I have Wednesday off if you want to make reservations. Just let me know where, and I'll be there."

"Sounds good. See you, Macy."

His face faded from the screen and I sat down hard on my bed. On a scale of one to ten, I had no idea how gross this made me. We were lying. For clicks and retweets and blog hits and subscribers. The whole thing was deeply disturbing. But Eric and I both had things we wanted, and could maybe get with whatever happened between us.

Thanks to Jessica, I had nothing left to lose, and I was tired of letting her and Eric reap all the viral benefits. They got spots on the *Today* show, while I spent my nights in an anxiety-soaked black hole, scrolling through Twitter in incognito mode and absorbing every nasty comment.

I was so done with that.

After I tossed my phone on my bed, I put on a blue shirt to complement my eyes—light enough to bring out the glow of my summer tan, plain enough to avoid ending up on any more Ugly Clothes of Twitter lists. I took an hour getting ready, fixing my hair until soft blond curls framed my face, then did my makeup. Smoky eye shadow and bright red lips.

I could've been a darling or a demon, and I honestly didn't care either way.

In front of my green wall, I smiled at my phone, already recording from my makeshift pedestal. A smile big enough to show all my teeth. "I've been thinking about you for days, Eric. Can't wait to see you soon."

I adjusted the graphics, double-checked to make sure all of my videos were monetized, uploaded it onto YouTube, and then flipped back over to Twitter.

@baseballbabe2020: Making dinner plans for me and a beautiful lady ;) #baseballbabe #flyballgirl #datenight

I clicked on the link to tweet. Even if my real name and real life were out there, playing this game with Eric wasn't a whole lot different from donning my Misty Morning persona. This was just a different type of wig, a different costume.

@MacyAtTheMovies: Can't wait to find out what @baseballbabe2020 has planned for Wednesday <3 #DateNight #FlyBallGirl #BaseballBabe

I linked the YouTube video in my tweet, and then pulled my quilt over my head.

What the hell had I just gotten myself into?

CHAPTER
NINE

THE COMMENTS I'D SCROLLED through in the middle of the night still crawled beneath my skin, but I wouldn't allow myself to be vulnerable again. I wouldn't let another Jared put me down. Never again would I scrape quarters off the sidewalk or watch the Bees sell a piece of their soul for beef or see my mom soaking her feet in salt water after working a double just to keep the lights on. I'd been given a way out, and I was going to make the most of it.

@MacyAtTheMovies: BTW, I saw your @TODAYshow interview, @baseballbabe2020, and you looked just as cute as you did at the game #BaseballBabe

I closed Twitter, then went down to the basement. We still had a broken dryer, and the money from my latest views wouldn't come in for another month. I'd just brought up the jams and canned tomatoes to bring over to Elise's, when there was a knock. We weren't expecting company.

I opened the door and a squat man with wire-rimmed glasses shoved his phone at me. "Fly Ball Girl, what's the status on your relationship with Baseball Babe? Did you contact him because you saw him on TV? Are you really planning a date together?"

Panic seized my lungs. I slammed the door and locked it. And leaned against it for extra reinforcement. I couldn't remember the last time we'd locked our door. He knocked again, and the sound pounded between my temples. How did he find out where I lived? I never posted my address online. Not even on the accounts I'd kept separate from R3ntal Wor1d.

I looked out the peephole. He wasn't from around here. I would've recognized his face. He didn't look like a reporter, and there was no news van, no real camera. He just had his shitty phone. A random stranger. Who showed up at my house because of Jessica Banks.

"Macy, what's going on?" Gram came down the hall, holding an electric flyswatter.

"There's a man at the door." I could hardly talk, hardly draw a breath. "I don't know him. He recorded me and asked me questions."

"Step aside." Her voice reminded me of thunder, the way clouds would boil and roll before unleashing cracks of lightning. Her expression pinched tight, deepening the lines in her face.

"What are you going to do?"

"Don't you mind." I'd never seen Gram so mad, and her mood was permanently set on mad. If yesterday's evening news story was a six, she was now at an eleven. "Go on back to the dining room with the Bees."

I would do no such thing. "You're not going out there."

"This is my property and I'm a grown woman. I'll do

what I want." Before I could grab her arm, she flung open the door and marched outside.

The man had his phone raised, like he was taking pictures of our house. As soon as he caught sight of Gram, he turned his phone on her, and she swung the flyswatter right at his face. His scream split the air, and I winced at the angry crisscross pattern already taking shape on his right cheek from the electric shock.

"Get off my lawn." Gram hit him with the flyswatter. "Get out of my town." He tried to block her, and got another shock as the flyswatter zapped his hands. "And don't you dare come near my granddaughter again." The man ran, and Gram chased him all the way to the end of the driveway, hitting him on the back of the head. The electric flyswatter zinged as it singed his hair.

"What the hell?" Paxton stopped a few feet from the edge of our property. Quilting patterns fell from his arms and crinkled like autumn leaves across our dead lawn.

"Um. Small issue. No big deal." I glanced from him to Gram, who was still after the stranger with her flyswatter. To my horror, I noticed a second person with the guy—a woman who had recorded the entire incident.

She swung her phone toward me. Paxton froze. All the color drained from his face, his lips turning to a chalky blush. He shook so hard, the single quilting pattern he'd held on to rattled like a flag in a windstorm. I blocked her view of Paxton and charged. Her eyes widened as her phone arm dropped. Both the man and woman dashed into a car parked on the other side of the street. Their tires squealed against the pavement as they drove away.

I turned around to check in with Paxton, and only caught sight of his back as he ran for the cover of the trees. He tripped over a root and went sprawling across the leafy wooded floor. Before I could take a single step forward to ask if he was okay, he was on his feet again and gone through a thick cluster of brush.

Gram chuckled as she scooped quilting patterns off our yard. "You sure can send them running. Still want to put that sex ad on the Craigslist?"

"Har, har." I helped her gather up the rest of the scattered papers. "Was the flyswatter really necessary?"

Gram straightened her blouse, swept back her short gray hair, and gave me a grim nod as she headed into the house. "They need to learn they can't invade other people's privacy."

I followed her in, shutting and locking the door behind me. "Did you see that woman with him? She was recording too. They're going to post that video all over the Internet."

"Good," Gram said. "Let it be a warning for anyone else who wants to show up here."

I had no response for that. Gram didn't go online. She had no idea what she'd just unleashed. I followed her back to the dining room. Gram had literally fried a guy's face for me, which was why I couldn't tell her that she'd likely made things worse.

The phone rang and Gram yanked the cord out of

the wall. "Those damned reporters have been nonstop all morning. I'm calling the phone company."

"I'm sorry." Useless words.

"This isn't your fault." Gram lit a cigarette and blew smoke at the fan. "We'll change our number and get on with it. Bad timing with the fair coming up and all." She patted my cheek. "Get those canned goods over to Elise's momma."

I put the boxes in Peg's car, and Gram stood by the front door with her flyswatter in hand the entire time, but no one else came around. She said she'd use my cell phone later to get our number changed. If only I hadn't sat next to Eric or ogled his abs so openly or let him walk me to the bathroom or a hundred other things Jessica had used to craft her story. It wasn't my fault, and I'd keep telling myself that until I believed it, but I couldn't deny this whole mess had upended our entire world.

I drove to Elise's, Paxton's reaction running through my mind the entire time. I'd never seen anyone so terrified in their life, including the time Elise's pants got caught on Grumpy Gill's barbed-wire fence when we'd cut through his farm behind her house for the first and last time. The scene outside my house was chaos, but Paxton acted like those people were coming after *him* with a chainsaw instead of Gram going after *them* with a flyswatter.

I pulled into Elise's driveway and texted Paxton: *Are you okay?*

Paxton: *Fine*

Okay . . . Me: *It just looked like something was going on there*

Paxton: *I'll see you at work.*

Cool. I could tell when I was getting the brush-off. No need to spell it out.

I sat in Peg's car, scrolling through Twitter. The woman who recorded Gram taking a flyswatter to her boyfriend didn't waste any time trying to collect a piece of that viral fame. She'd posted it about ten minutes after pulling away from my house.

@EmilyPayneBlogLife: Check out #FlyBallGirl's crazy grandma. I'd be careful if I were you #baseballbabe #flyswatter #fuckinginsane

@torontoraptors4life Replying to @EmilyPayneBlogLife: HOLY SHIT!!!

@MinaWillis Replying to @EmilyPayneBlogLife: I hope you're filing charges.

@dogsbiteback22 Replying to @EmilyPayneBlogLife: Damnnnnnn, that old lady fucked him up. how embarrassing for your boy.

@trinanotnina Replying to @EmilyPayneBlogLife: How is no one talking about the slippers yet?

@fruitbythefoottt Replying to @EmilyPayneBlogLife @trinanotnina : Didn't you hear? Dirty slippers are in this year #TrailerParkChic

Rage spotted my vision, pulsed in my veins, gnashed its teeth inside me. It was one thing to tear me apart and judge the Instagram pictures I'd willingly posted online, but Gram wasn't even on Twitter to defend herself. She'd only been protecting me. They didn't know her; they didn't know a single thing about me and my family. I responded with shaking fingers.

@MacyAtTheMovies Replying to @EmilyPayneBlogLife: Maybe you should've stayed home then. Come to my house again and you'll get worse than a flyswatter to the face.

Then I rolled down my window to get some air so I wouldn't puke all over Peg's dashboard. Gram's pink quilting slippers were nearly as old as me, and more gray than pink now, but it's not like she wore them to a fancy dinner party. She was at home. Minding her own business. Like Emily Payne Blog Life and her boyfriend should've been doing.

Elise tapped on the roof of the car, and I jumped. My phone flew out of my hand and landed at my feet. "Why are you sitting out here like a weirdo?" she asked.

"No reason. Gram wanted me to bring the jam and tomatoes for fixing our dryer, and she asked if your mom needs any sewing done." I opened the door and got out. As I reached for my phone, Elise snatched it first.

"Are you on Twitter? No one goes on there anymore." She scrolled through the thread I still had open. "Your grandma burned a dude with an electric flyswatter?"

"Yeah. That woman and her boyfriend showed up at the house this morning. I think they're amateur journalists or bloggers or something. Gram chased them away."

"Bizzy Evans is a motherfucking legend. Please, God, let me be that awesome when I'm old." She closed the app before handing my phone back to me. "Stay off Twitter. No good will come of looking at those threads."

"I know." But I still couldn't stay away. It had become an addiction. "Paxton brought over some of Gigi's patterns while those bloggers were there. He seemed super freaked out."

"Don't stress over it—he's just a really private dude. I have to get to work, but I'll be by your place tomorrow with my tools and get that dryer fixed," Elise said. "Momma's inside. Just bring the box in to her."

As soon as Elise drove away, I got back into the car and scrolled through Twitter again.

CHAPTER
TEN

AFTER MOMMA GOMEZ DECLARED me too thin and loaded me up on roasted chicken and rice, she let me leave. Elise had forgotten her lunch, so she sent me over to the Video and Repair to bring it to her.

The bell above the door dinged, and Lance Harrington walked in behind me. His light brown hair turned sandy in the summer and he already had a deep tan from helping out at his parents' farm. He was only a few inches taller than me, but Harrington boys managed to fill out just fine. Elise pinched his cheeks like she used to when I was dating him—he really did have the most pinchable cheeks—and went to let Midnight know she had a customer.

"I'm not here to rent a movie," he said. "I was hoping you'd be working."

"I'm not actually working." On a scale of one to ten, how sad did hanging out at work off the clock make me look? "I'm running errands. And stopped in to say hi."

"Okay." He didn't look like he cared either way. Coincidently, the same look he'd had when I'd told him I wanted to break up. "I just wanted to let you know I've been contacted by a couple of reporters and bloggers."

"What?" I swayed a bit to the side, and Lance put a hand on my arm to steady me. "Why? What did they want?"

"I think . . ." He bit his lip and looked at the ground. "I think they saw pictures of us on your Instagram before you went private. They wanted to know if we were still together, if you broke my heart, if I knew Baseball Babe."

"Oh God. I'm so sorry. I don't even know what's happening." First Gram and now Lance. How far into my personal life would this poison spread?

"It's so bizarre. Momma had a fit when she found out you were Fly Ball Girl. She was following the story, all into it, and then, well . . ."

I could only imagine what Lance's good Christian momma thought about that bathroom picture. The chicken and rice I had for lunch threatened to make an appearance all over his shoes. "So, should I change my identity now or . . . ?"

"Don't worry about it." He waved my question away, even though I was dying of humiliation all over again. "She thought for a second that one shot of you going into the bathroom was pretty bad, but I told her to think real hard about that. She knows you."

I didn't know which made me feel worse, the fact that Lance's mom so easily believed I'd have a quickie in public with a guy I'd just met, or that it was only because of Lance that she no longer believed it. How many people in town had seen those pictures? How many of them knew me from a distance, but not the way the Harringtons did? If Lance's mom could buy into Jessica's lie, I had no doubt most of the town thought I'd done it. Why wouldn't they? Weren't pictures supposed to be worth a thousand words? And even if I had, wouldn't that have been my business? How was this any different from Peeping Toms who ran through towns at night, looking in people's windows to see if they were getting it on or not?

"Anyway." Lance scratched his shoulder blade. "I didn't tell anyone who called about you or us, and I won't either. I just wanted to give you a heads-up. They're sniffing around."

Lance was a good one, and that was why I wouldn't ever regret him being my first. I hugged him. "Thank you. I mean it."

Elise gave me a catlike grin when he left. "I forgot to ask you earlier how it went last night with Pax . . . ton?" She drew out his name as if it were two words, and the look she gave me had me backing up a step. As if she knew what I'd debated doing before I came to my senses and flung myself into the lake.

"It went fine." I shrugged. "We went swimming."

"Really?" Her grin stretched wider.

"Yes, really. Why are you looking at me like that?"

Elise wound the end of her long braid around her finger. "I asked him about last night, and you should've seen his smile."

"Is he here? Did he say anything about the bloggers?"

"He's out on call, and why would I bring that up when I wanted to get the goods on the lake date?"

He and Elise took turns being on call, where one of them would stay at the shop and fix the smaller items that could be brought in, and the other would head out to fix larger things, like appliances. Since Paxton didn't drive, Elise took more of the appliances, but on the days when it was his turn, Gigi would drive him where he needed to go.

"It wasn't a date. Nothing happened." Or would ever happen. I'd just gotten carried away by the romance novel setting and my steady diet of rom-com movies. "And speaking of which, where were you?" The words *I could've used a buffer last night* hung unspoken between us.

She blushed, actually blushed. Oh no. "Me and Midnight . . ."

"Seriously? Again?"

Things had been tense when they broke up, or stopped hooking up or whatever they were, and had just started getting back to normal. Another reminder of why I needed to stick to the No Coworkers Rule. Elise had almost quit last time, and if she hadn't been able to go fully on call for that first month, she would've. I couldn't afford that kind of a breakup.

Elise glanced at the storage room, where Midnight was holed up doing paperwork. Or more likely, pressing her ear against the door to listen in on this conversation. "Don't say anything. I'm not sure where this is going to go, but I want to keep it quiet for now."

"I'll tell you where this should go." I pointed to the garbage can by the door. I hadn't forgotten how thoroughly my best friend had been shredded the last time. No way would I let that tiny gothic terror hurt her again.

"It's different this time." Elise pressed her lips together. "Don't mother hen me, okay? There's a lot going on with her that isn't my place to share, and just trust me. It's different."

I held her gaze. "Fine." It was her life. "But she's on probation."

Elise snorted. "So nothing will change."

I left and went back out to Peg's car. My shift started in a few hours. I'd be working with Midnight and Paxton, who both had double shifts with two breaks in between. Would Paxton be as curt with me tonight as he'd been in his texts? Ugh. That moment I'd almost kissed him hung over me like a wet wool blanket. Maybe he'd told Elise. Probably, judging from the way she'd circled me like a vulture over a corpse. I didn't have time to think about it though. I had to run peppers, cucumbers, and tomatoes from our garden over to the Brewster farm in exchange for milk, the Neilson farm in exchange for honey, and the Jackson farm in exchange for a chicken, help Gram get dinner in the oven, and get back here for my shift.

Because I still needed to do my part to keep our home running. I still needed the paychecks I got from the Video and Repair. Going viral didn't do anything to help me get dinner prepared. And rumors whispered about me in town wouldn't deliver the vegetables waiting for me in Peg's car.

After I finished up our barters, and a wily chicken at the Jackson farm nearly pecked off my big toe when I got too close to her eggs, I had a few hours before I had to get to work. While my current videos were still doing well, I needed to build on this momentum. Thanks to my deal with Eric, I had the kind of spotlight I'd been working toward for over a year, and I didn't intend to waste even a second of my fifteen minutes.

I'd planned on uploading a baseball video next, but with Gram in full fair mode, she wouldn't have time to help me with the costumes. Plus, a romance would've been better. Something I could suggestively tag Eric in. The feel of Paxton's hands around my waist in the lake floated through my mind, and I rummaged around in my closet until I found a white button-down I could tie into a knot above my stomach. It wasn't Jennifer Grey's wispy pink lift dress, but I had to improvise on short notice.

Dirty Dancing was right up there with *Say Anything* as a most watched movie in our house. Mom could (and often did) quote every line. The aftermath of the abortion scene was where I'd learned about reproductive rights, Baby standing up to her father was where I learned how some will stop seeing you as a person once you shatter the illusions of who they want you to be, and the way her father treated Johnny didn't give me my first lesson in classism (life had done that), but it was an easy way for Mom and Gram to segue into the discussion. I had enough talking points to fill three videos. I didn't touch any of them. Not when I didn't have time for my usual routine of handwritten cue cards and hours of research.

Instead I burned one of my favorite movies on hashtag clickbait.

I'd always planned to have my *Dirty Dancing* video dig into the topics that had shaped my entire worldview, making me a baby feminist at the age of nine. Instead I took ten minutes to wax poetic about the romance between Baby and Johnny. The romance was great, no doubt, but that wasn't what set *Dirty Dancing* apart. That wasn't what made it magic to me. But that was the angle I needed to work Eric into the video.

As I added the graphics to the background, an invisible hand pressed down on my chest. That pressure grew when I uploaded the video. And when I tweeted the link with *this one's for you #BaseballBabe*, my palms sweat and the pressure on my chest became heavy enough to make me light-headed. But this was what I wanted. This would get me the views and clicks and a big enough paycheck at the end of the month to leave it all behind.

And if I had to leave pieces of myself behind too, so be it.

CHAPTER
ELEVEN

I'D BLOCKED EMILY PAYNE Blog Life, but that hadn't stopped the comments from rolling into my mentions like a tidal wave. Before Baseball Babe, I had 59 followers. I was lucky if I got one like a month. Now I had so much junk to scroll through, I hadn't even gotten a chance to peek at how many retweets the link to my video had gotten before I had to leave for work.

Elise's shift ended and she had to do repair errands with her dad, so I had no ride. Gram said Mom had called dibs on the car after her shift. For what, I had no idea. So I got stuck walking. Gram didn't want me wandering the streets alone after that guy had shown up at our house, but I assured her I'd take the back way and get a ride home. She didn't want to keep me from work, and I had my cell phone.

It didn't stop me from looking over my shoulder the whole way, my pulse jumping every time a twig snapped in the woods. I'd always felt safe in town. Until now. I hadn't been totally honest with Gram about the ride home, but I could always call Elise if it came down to it.

I made it to the end of the trail behind our house and cut across the nicer neighborhood on my way to Main

Street. Nicer in this town meant splurging for a sprinkler so the grass wouldn't die and keeping up with the siding and shutters if paint started to chip. We didn't have mansions in Honeyfield. We had a handful of middle class, the working class who thought they were middle class, and the rest of us, who had no such delusions.

The bell to the Video and Repair chimed above my head as I entered. Brady stood at the register, his whole face pinched, like he couldn't stand another second of this place. He really hated the customer part of the customer service job.

"You're free," I said.

He unclenched and his expression became softer. "Are you doing okay?"

"As well as I can be, I guess. Thanks again. For earlier."

"No problem. I owe Jared worse than a shove, but that wasn't the time or place." His lips thinned and I wondered what kind of run-in he'd had with the town asshole.

I opened my mouth to ask him and shut it again when Midnight came out of the closet/break room and looked me up and down, spending extra time evaluating my hair and makeup. Like it was an armor she knew well. "You're late."

"Good thing you're not my boss then." I tossed the backpack holding my dinner into the room behind her and cleaned out the return box to start rewinding.

Brady took that as his cue to leave, and I'd never seen anyone run so fast. I didn't even get a chance to utter the word *goodbye* before he was gone.

Midnight leaned against the doorjamb. "What crawled up your ass and died?"

"Nothing." After my morning with Jared, my deal with Eric, the bloggers, and my subpar upload, I was on the edge and it wouldn't take a whole lot more to push me over. I slammed VHS tapes on the counter, picturing Jared's and Emily Payne Blog Life's faces on each of them, until one of the cases cracked. I yanked the cover and tape out and then threw it on the floor and stomped on it until the plastic broke and shattered beneath my foot.

Midnight's nostrils flared as she looked between me and the ruined case. "If I were you, I'd save that rage for the next time you see Jared, rather than burn it out on this bullshit."

Air got stuck in my throat, making it hard to breathe. I wanted to scream and tear something apart with my bare hands, rip its head off with my teeth. My anger was a starved and injured beast, and I wanted nothing more than to let it out of its cage. "Who told you?"

"Who didn't tell me would be a shorter list."

My gaze snapped up the street to the diner, where my mom was still on her shift. If Midnight knew, they'd be talking about it there, too. All the fire died out of me. Replaced by a layer of shame that coated me like an oily second skin. Mom would worry, customers would pity her, and she'd try to keep it from showing, even as her back and feet ached and she'd still feel like it wasn't enough. That it was her fault. That if she'd only smiled a bit brighter or hustled a bit faster on the drink refills, there would've been enough quarters to spare me from Jared.

"I hate people," I said.

Midnight gave me a considering look. "Welcome to the dark side. We have popcorn." She tossed me an individually wrapped movie butter and I put it in with the rest of her display.

Two guys wearing skinny jeans, tight striped V-necks, and knitted hats walked into the store, and me and Midnight glanced at each other. While the steady stream of tourists passing through were our lifeblood in the summer, we also got a number of hipsters, who we didn't quite welcome with the same open arms. They generally reeked of gourmet coffee and trying too hard, and the worst part was that they didn't spend money. They came here for one reason only: to gawk. Having one of the few remaining VHS rental stores in the Midwest had made us an oddity of sorts. A pit stop on a retro road trip. And sure, we played up the trendy museum angle as much as we could to move twenty-dollar VCR rentals, but this was also a place where real people lived and worked. The hipsters treated us like modern-day freak shows. Apparently, the last gasping breath of a town on the brink of collapse made for compelling Instagram moments.

"I told you this place was like a time capsule." The guy wearing chunky black geek glasses nudged his companion, who then went and posed beside the action movies while his friend took his picture with his phone.

"Rent something or get out," Midnight said.

The guy with the chunky glasses just turned his phone to Midnight and snapped her picture. She snarled, leaping over the counter so fast, I didn't have time to grab her, even if

I'd wanted. Which I most definitely did not. Feral Midnight was my favorite show.

The shock on their faces as she barreled toward them, a tiny tornado of spiked black hair and fury, froze them in place. She yanked the phone away from the glasses guy, smashing it on the concrete floor of the repair side. His friend ran out the door, no doubt wanting to protect his own phone. I grabbed a wrench we kept under the counter for when the register acted up. I kept an eye on the guy with glasses, hitting the wrench against my open palm. He grabbed his smashed phone and backed away toward the door.

"You're crazy. Both of you." But he froze as he looked at me, recognition flickering in his eyes. "Hey, aren't you that girl from the baseball game?"

"Get out." Midnight launched herself at him, shoving him out the door with the kind of strength generally reserved for panicked mothers lifting whole cars off their babies.

After she threw him out onto the sidewalk with so much force his knees buckled, she leaned against the frame to catch her breath. She took one look at me still holding the wrench before a smile split her usual dark and morose features.

"What?" I asked.

"You—" A laugh rasped out of her, then a louder one. I'd never heard Midnight laugh out loud like that before. It kind of freaked me out. Within seconds she was holding her sides, laughing uncontrollably. "Were you going to hit him with that wrench?"

"I don't know. Maybe."

She paused, looked at me, and started laughing again. I couldn't help myself; I grinned back at her as she wiped at her smudged eyeliner. The door opened, and she nearly fell over backward, but Paxton caught her by the shoulders.

"I saw two hipsters leaving with their tails between their legs." Paxton glanced at the wrench still in my hand. "Did I miss the fun?"

I searched his face for the fear I'd seen at my house, but I only saw regular Paxton. Loose limbs and easy smile. The smile I'd very nearly kissed the night before. My toes tingled and I shook my foot. Lingering adrenaline from the hipster encounter must've been doing funny things to my body.

"We handled it." I tucked the wrench back under the register.

Paxton leaned against the counter with a half grin. "Who knew you were such a badass?"

"Midnight's the badass." I jerked my chin to her. "I'm just her menacing backup."

"Sorry I missed it again." His gaze swept over my lips, which I'd painted bright red again after making my video, and my cheeks heated. "I should get to work." He pushed off from the counter and went over to the repair side.

I stared at the worktable on the other half of the store. The point above his head. The wood counter with years of dents and scratches worn in. Midnight gave me a knowing look, like she could tell how hard I tried *not* to stare at his backside as he walked away. I flipped her off and she blew me a kiss. Business as usual.

She went back to the closet/break room, and I had the front of the store to myself. Butch stumbled in, gave me a sloppy wave, and went back to his office. He booted up the computer and at least pretended to work. That was new.

Paxton looked up from the vacuum he'd just taken apart and raised his eyebrows at me. I shrugged in return. Whatever our so-called manager did or didn't do while he was here mattered very little to us. As long as the owner of this place kept cutting the paychecks.

Monday nights tended to be slower than other days, but we still stayed pretty steady, renting out ten VCRs and twenty DVDs. After the seven o'clock rush, I opened up my phone. The pressure on my chest returned instantly. I knew what I'd been doing, why I did it, and if throwing a few tweets and videos out there meant I'd never crawl for quarters again, I'd do it. But it also felt so permanent. In the way things on the Internet tended to be forever. If I ever had a change of heart, it would be too late to take it back.

I opened Twitter first, completely ignoring the mess of my mentions. Those I'd save for the middle of the night, when I couldn't sleep and I was really in the mood to hate myself. Eric had retweeted my video five minutes ago.

@baseballbabe2020: If @MacyAtTheMovies wants to dance, I'd be a fool to turn her down. #baseballbabe #flyballgirl

@MacyAtTheMovies Replying to @baseballbabe2020: Yeah, you would. #FlyBallGirl #BaseballBabe

Let people pick that apart for a while, as long as they kept clicking on that video. My first message to Eric had reached thirty thousand within the first hour, more views than my first year as a reviewer combined. I flipped back over to the hashtag to check the responses.

"What are you doing?" Paxton asked.

I dropped my phone like I'd been caught with my hand in the cookie jar, except these cookies were laced with arsenic and would make me sick before ultimately ending me, but I couldn't stop eating them. "Nothing."

"How many hours have you spent doing nothing today?"

A lot. Too many. "Like, maybe ten minutes."

He rested his arms on the counter. "When you lie, the left side of your mouth quirks up just a little bit higher than your right."

"I'm so glad you've spent enough time looking at my mouth to notice."

His whole face lit up. "Not a lie."

"Oh my God." I shoved his arms off the counter. "I'm never talking to you again."

"Lie."

I covered my mouth with my hands. "Aren't you on the clock? Go fix something."

"I have all night to fix stuff." He paused. "But to make us even, I'll tell you something that isn't a lie." He reached up, his fingers grazing the ends of my curls. "You look really pretty today. And I've spent the last hour trying to work up the nerve to tell you that."

I blushed all the way down to my toes. Those new feelings I'd been keeping in check burst open again. I wished we could've gone to the lake last week, before Baseball Babe, when I could've just flirted and had fun and not worried about my every move being watched.

Which was why I couldn't respond to Paxton. The entire Internet, which also included a gross number of Honeyfield residents, thought I was dating Eric. I needed to stay focused. The money from my YouTube channel was the one thing I could count on to get set up in Chicago. I'd have plenty of time to consider flirting and feelings that weren't part of some game after I earned a steady income from my reviews.

I was saved from having to respond by Butch throwing open the door to his office. He looked between me and Paxton, his eyes slightly glazed, as if trying to place our names to our faces and coming up empty. "I've just gone over the yearly budget."

What budget? I mouthed to Paxton. He looked as clueless as me.

At the sound of Butch's booming voice, Midnight poked her head out of the closet.

"You." Butch waved a hand at her. "Unholy Mistress."

Paxton coughed, loud enough to barely cover his laugh. Midnight stiffened, shooting a glare at me and Paxton, daring us to call her that from now on. I was pretty certain the look we'd given each other already had her plotting our very messy deaths.

Butch rambled on, unaware or uncaring of the silent back-and-forth going on around him. "You get money for snacks and popcorn. Why don't we have more candy by the register? People love that stuff. Order whatever you want. You. Repair guy." He pointed at Paxton, and Midnight looked positively murderous that Butch hadn't bestowed him with a nickname of equal annoyance. "Buy some tools or whatever this place needs."

"Where is this coming from?" I asked.

He gave me a look that suggested *I* was the one who spent my days either passed out in the office or not bothering to show up at all. "We do this every year."

I glanced at the counter, stocked with movie snacks Midnight had bought and sold on the side. Paxton gave me a subtle jerk of his chin. A warning to let it go. Likely because Butch would go back to his office, pass out, and forget this conversation had ever happened.

"Right," I said. "Last year. I remember now."

Lie, Paxton mouthed to me. I bit the inside of my cheek to keep from laughing.

Butch gave us a satisfied nod and went back to his office. He propped his feet up on the desk and promptly fell asleep. That whole hour of work he'd done must've completely drained him.

Midnight pulled up Amazon on her phone.

"What are you doing?" I asked. "If you're ordering snacks in bulk, I'd hold off on that. There's a good chance Butch won't remember this so-called budget in the morning."

"If he forgets, I'll just take the income from them for myself," she said.

Midnight went back to her snack ordering and Paxton

went back to the vacuum he'd taken apart earlier, like he hadn't just called me pretty. Which was fine. For the best, really.

Without the distraction, I opened up YouTube. My *Dirty Dancing* video had twenty thousand views already, and I'd gone up to fifty thousand subscribers. Actual subscribers to my channel who wanted to be notified of future content. Before all this had started, I had twenty-five hundred. These Twitter games were already starting to pay off.

I had a suspicious number of thumbs-downs, but I didn't dare wander into the comments. People were clicking; that's all the advertisers cared about. After I closed YouTube, I went over to Twitter.

@MacyAtTheMovies: Thank you all so much for the support you've given my videos. It really feels like a fairy tale come true #blessed

Yuck. I'd officially become one of those people who hashtagged *blessed.* I wanted to punch myself in the face. But if this got me more subscribers, then fine. I'd do whatever it took to get to Chicago, even if I had to #bless my ass across the Internet.

CHAPTER
TWELVE

AFTER THE LAST RUSH of locals had left, gossiping about me in the Comedy aisle like I couldn't hear them right there at the counter, a shadow fell over me. I glanced up to find Paxton's mouth set in a grim line. I locked my phone and placed it on the counter. Even though I hadn't been doing anything wrong, a snaking line of guilt curled around my stomach.

"You're tweeting," he said. Not a question. He'd seen my fingers tapping against my screen.

His flat tone had me straightening my spine. "So?"

"Why are you getting involved?" He words were laced with simmering anger, not at me, but at my phone resting on the counter. "Did you like strangers showing up at your house? Do you enjoy being torn apart for sport?"

"What do you know about it?" My voice quiet. A gentle, probing question. The closest I'd ever come to pushing him or asking him about why he avoided social media.

The light that always seemed to surround him died out, taking him someplace else. And that place wasn't kind. "I know more than you can imagine." I had a snapping retort on the tip of my tongue, but he continued before I could speak. "I'm not trying to be a bossy asshole or tell you what to do. I'm trying to warn you."

I lifted my chin. "I don't need saving."

"I never said you did." He gave me a half grin, nodding to the counter, directly above the shelf where we kept the wrench. "Just . . . be careful about how much you give them."

"I always am." Until now. Until Jessica Banks had made it impossible for me to separate myself from Misty Morning and R3ntal Wor1d.

Paxton went back across the store and I reopened my Twitter app. The bell dinged above the door, and Fanny Vanderlugt walked in smelling like cinnamon and sugar toast and waved at me. She picked up *Die Hard* for her husband and *Die Hard 2* for herself, bringing them both to the register. As one of the handful of people in town who still had a VCR, she always grumbled in the summer when tourists took all the good movies.

"That'll be five dollars even," I said.

She tilted her head. "You sure about that? I got two movies there."

"I know. Second one is on the house." I winked at her. "Thanks for the bread the other day. It was delicious. We ate the whole loaf in one sitting."

"You're a good girl." She patted my hand. "Beatrice Combs was clucking her chicken-shaped head off about that baseball business the other day, but I told her to shut it. I told her there is no way Gracie Evans's daughter would ever disgrace her like that." She gave me a look that suggested it was more of a question than a statement.

"No, ma'am," I said to the floor. "I didn't go into the bathroom with that boy."

"I knew you wouldn't." I tried to ignore the way her entire body relaxed, like she'd believed it. Whether or not she'd wanted to, whether or not she'd told Beatrice Combs to shut her mouth, she had believed I'd gone into that bathroom with Eric.

Speculation would only increase with our upcoming date. It also kept the clicks coming. I couldn't have it both ways, and I'd chosen my path, but it still hurt.

After Fanny left with her movies, I rested my chin in my hands. We only had another hour until close, but that last hour of work was like three. I swiveled my stool back and forth. The bell dinged, and Elise came in.

"Hey, loser," I said. "Don't people usually spend their off shifts away from work?"

"Hey, hypocrite. You're just mad I'm not here to see you," Elise said. "Momma wanted me to drop off Midnight's tamale order, then I'll be on my way." Momma Gomez ran a second business selling tamales out of her kitchen, the only plus of living in a town that was basically a corn ocean. She had back orders for weeks. She and Gram had a long-standing barter arrangement going back before Elise and I were born, and tamales accounted for a tenth of our diets. No complaints.

As soon as Elise disappeared into the closet/break room, Paxton wandered back over to my counter. "I noticed we both have Wednesday off," he said.

"We do." I had a date with Eric that night. Our first public appearance as an—air quotes—couple. "Have any plans?"

He shuffled his feet, not meeting my gaze. "I was kind of hoping we could hang out."

"You want to hang out with me?" Date. Date. Date with Eric. My boyfriend for all intents and purposes, if those intents and purposes included helping ourselves to blog hits and subscribers. "Why do you want to hang out with me?" I squeaked as Elise came out of Midnight's office and looked us both over with a slow grin.

"A day without my favorite cashier is like a day without magic." Paxton gave me a half smile, that gentle humor I adored radiating from him like unfiltered sunshine.

I rested my elbows on the counter and cupped my face with my hands. "A day without my favorite repair guy is like a day I'm forced to switch bodies with my mom to learn the true meaning of selfless love."

He leaned against the register. "A day without you is like a day I'm forced to hang out in the ice-cold Atlantic because someone is too greedy to share that big-ass door."

My cheeks hurt from grinning so hard as I spun my stool from side to side.

Elise threw her hands up. "Would you two just get a room already?"

"What room?" Paxton looked around and pointed at the floor. "This room?"

"This room is nice," I said.

"Forget it," Elise grumbled, and stomped toward the exit.

"Is this not a good room?" The pure innocence in Paxton's tone had me stifling a laugh. "Do you want to help us pick out a better room?"

"I hate you both!" Elise yelled on her way out.

"She'll be fuming all day tomorrow," I said.

"Good." The mischief in Paxton's eyes dimmed as he ran his finger over a small dent in the counter. "So, uh, do you want to? Hang out?"

"Oh. Um." I did. I really did. But Eric. Future. Subscribers. Ugh. "Normally, yes. But I kind of have a thing. A previous obligation." Was I supposed to tell him about my not-date? It wouldn't exactly be a secret, but I didn't want to get into it. "It's hard to explain."

"Sure, no problem." Paxton pushed off from the counter like everything was fine, but the light in his eyes had dimmed. "Maybe some other time."

I knew how those "other times" usually went. Might as well have been code for "never." Little prickles of regret poked at my heart, but I hardened myself against them. This thing I was doing with Eric was bigger than a date. Everything I'd been working toward depended on the believability of our ruse.

Midnight came out of the break room, grinning while she tapped away on her phone. She must've been texting Elise. On anyone else that freshly-in-love smile might've been endearing. On Midnight, it looked like a murder clown in a Stephen King fun house.

"Isn't cell phone usage against company policy?" I asked.

Midnight glared at me. "You're one to talk. I'm surprised

your skin hasn't molded to your phone case yet."

"Fair point, but then again, I don't claim to be the shift supervisor. I just thought you'd hold yourself to a higher standard than the rest of us lowly employees."

"Fuck off." She grabbed the zipper bag holding last night's credit card receipts and slammed the door to the office behind her.

"That went well," Paxton said, not looking up from his vacuum.

"She's talking to Elise. I don't like it."

"I know you don't." His slightly mocking tone had me gritting my teeth. He rested his arms on the table and leveled his gaze at me. "But it's not your call to make."

"They're making a mistake."

Paxton gave me a blank stare and went back to focusing on the vacuum. "No matter what you think, they might live happily ever after or they might destroy each other. Who knows? It's their choice. And maybe for them it's a risk worth taking."

I didn't even know who he was talking about anymore. "Are you talking about Midnight and Elise? Or someone else?"

He looked at me with the kind of intensity that made me feel more exposed than the night my red bra had shown through my wet tank top. "Who do *you* think I'm talking about?"

Tension snapped in the air between the video and the repair side. Like we both had mental swords drawn and were perched on the opposite ends of a sparring ring. It left me feeling . . . unbalanced. "Why are you being weird? Are you mad I have plans on Wednesday? Because I really do want to hang out. It's just—"

"You don't owe me an explanation. It's really not a big deal." He shook his head and grabbed his backpack, full of whatever odds and ends he'd brought to work. He hefted it over his shoulder. "See you later, Macy Mae."

He walked out of the store without a backward glance.

Who do you *think I'm talking about?*

His question lingered in the air, around the store, in my brain. It was a question I couldn't let myself think about. Not when I had plans for my future already in motion while I waded into these viral waters to see just how far I could go.

With fifteen minutes left before we closed, Midnight joined me to start closing duties. She held two thin strips of paper. "We draw for who wakes up Butch."

"As much as I love playing your games, Unholy Mistress"—I gave her a sweet smile as she gnashed her teeth—"why not just lock up and let him sleep it off?"

"Because last time he woke up in the middle of the night, he forgot where he was and peed all over the middle row of the Drama section. So, unless you're in the mood to do some cleaning in the morning, draw." She shoved the slips of paper under my nose.

I shuddered and grabbed the paper closest to me. From the way her grip tightened slightly, I knew I had her beat before I pulled it all the way out. She balled up her shorter strip and threw it into the trash, her heavy combat boots stomping across the concrete toward his office.

She didn't bother with nice as she flicked on the lights and yanked his rolling chair back, sending his feet crashing to the ground and almost causing him to face-plant onto the desk. I had a feeling she did it that way for the Unholy Mistress nickname alone, but if he wasn't technically the manager, I had no doubt she would've dumped a cup of scalding coffee over his head.

Butch stood in a daze, as if he had forgotten where he'd fallen asleep. He glanced down at Midnight like he'd never met her before. "What time is it?"

"Closing time." Midnight held his office door open, a not so subtle gesture for him to leave. "I ordered those snacks you told me to. I'll print the receipt tomorrow."

"What snacks?" Butch glanced at the video side of the repair shop and weaved a bit, eventually grasping the door frame and hauling himself out of his office. "I didn't ask you to order any snacks."

Told you, I mouthed to Midnight. She didn't seem like she cared, and she probably didn't if she planned to sell those snacks for her own profit. Butch stumbled toward the front door, which Midnight again held open, as if directing him where to go.

"Is he driving?" I asked.

"Nope." Midnight stuck her head out the door. "He made it as far as the bench in front of the pharmacy. Okay, he's asleep again." She shut the door and locked it.

Sighing, I picked up the phone, called his wife to come get him, and shut down the register to count the till.

Midnight kept throwing me glances as I flicked dollar bills between my thumbs, opening and closing her mouth like she wanted to say something. After the fourth time, I shoved a stack of fives into the night deposit bag and faced her.

"Whatever it is you want to say, just spit it out already." I gave her an overexaggerated bow. "You have my full attention."

She chewed on her thumb as she looked me up and down. "Elise told you. About us."

The semi-argument I'd had with Paxton brushed up against my mind. "Yep."

She raised her eyebrows. "That's all you're going to say?"

"Would it make you feel better if I threatened to hit you with a wrench if you hurt my best friend again?" I gave her a closed-lip grin, but it didn't come close to touching my eyes.

Her gaze darted to the counter where I stood, as if she knew I'd only been half joking. "It's different this time." She let out a breath. "I'm different. And I don't care if you don't believe me, but I do care about Elise and I don't want this to come between you and her or me and her or any of it."

I tilted my head. This certainly didn't sound like Midnight. And I wanted Elise to be happy, of course I did, even if I'd never understand why she'd found that happiness with the Unholy Mistress. "I don't know if I believe you, but I don't not believe you either." Paxton's words rang in my head again. "I'll stay out of it."

"I guess, given our history, that's the best I can ask for." Midnight picked up the night deposit bag, and I brought the register to the safe in back. She unlocked the door to let us out, the ring of keys clinking against the old metal door as she locked it again. "Be careful around Jared. Keep away from him at all costs, until this temporary fame thing goes away and he forgets about you again."

It seemed like everyone and their dog wanted to dish out warnings tonight, but something in her tone made my pulse jump. "Why do you say that?"

Her eyes were nearly as black as her spiked hair as she looked squarely at me. "He learned at his father's knee. Consider yourself very lucky that Brady was there."

The cold rolling off her sliced through my veins and I rubbed my arms, as if I couldn't get enough heat, even on this warm summer night. "What did he learn at his father's knee?"

She just tilted her head toward her car. "Come on. I'll give you a ride home. You shouldn't be walking around alone at night anyway."

CHAPTER
THIRTEEN

THE NEXT MORNING, I woke up way too early. I'd had a nightmare that a nude photo of me had started circulating with all of my Instagram ones. I opened Twitter and double-checked to make sure I hadn't been tagged in anything like that, though I wouldn't have put it past someone to get creative with Photoshop.

I now had thirty thousand followers, while Eric had gone up to fifty thousand. Jessica had followed me, but I wouldn't follow her back. I had nothing to say to her. She retweeted my *Dirty Dancing* video. I'd take the clicks, but I wouldn't take the hand of friendship she kept trying to thrust in my face. Sickness and urgency flooded me again as I compulsively scanned the hashtag.

@HollyYale: did you all see the #todayshow? #baseballbabe even said on here he didn't have sex with #flyballgirl. let it go and leave them alone.

@JimmyEatsYourMom Replying to @HollyYale: sit on my face

@trudylennoxx Replying to @HollyYale: I think #baseballbabe is really in love with #flyballgirl and is afraid he won't be able to bring her home to meet the family if everyone thinks she did him in a public bathroom.

"Trudy, please. You're embarrassing yourself with your bad takes," I mumbled to myself.

@suzy_qrs: I hope #baseballbabe is in the next video #flyballgirl uploads. The movie ones are boring, but I'm obsessed with these two. Please let them have babies.

@helpsmerhonda: sitting here with my popcorn, waiting for #flyballgirl to tweet again. #baseballbabe #lovestory

@pettybettyhatesyou: I'm fucking sick of #baseballbabe, someone send me pictures of cute animals please.

@baseballbabe2020: Guess who I'm talking to tonight? #flyballgirl #excited #beautifulgirl #baseballbabe

We had no plans to talk. It was all part of the game.

@MacyAtTheMovies: Looks like *someone* is as #excited as me for tonight #FlyBallGirl #BaseballBabe

Ugh. I needed to stop. I had to get out of the house or I'd spend my entire morning scrolling through Twitter until my eyes bled. None of it felt good, not even the nice comments. I felt like a runway model wearing six-inch heels. Sure, the shoes were great, but everyone was really just waiting for me to fall on my ass.

Since I didn't work until the afternoon shift, I had time to wander around town. At this point I would've been willing to scrape roadkill off the highway if it meant staying away from Twitter for a few hours. The Bees had finally decided on the Defining Moments in Recent History theme, and no one had lost a limb over it, so they no longer needed a watchdog while they got down to the business of embroidering.

I put on a sundress Gram had made me out of leftover fabric from last year's quilt, and the patchwork of different floral fabrics was my absolute favorite. I'd never post a picture of it online. After the comments about my seashell shirt, I'd likely never take selfies in anything fun or interesting again. Just plain vanilla tops from now on.

My flip-flops smacked against the floor as I entered the dining room. "I'm going out for a little while, but I have my phone on me and I won't talk to strangers."

"Where are you off to at this hour?" Gram asked through a cloud of smoke.

"I don't know." And I truly didn't. Our house felt too small with all the Bees crammed into it, and if I stuck around, Gram would just roll out a list of meaningless tasks for me to do. "I might go down to the lake. It's going to be hot today."

"I bet that boy from the Internet would drive up here to join you," Peg said.

I rolled my eyes. "Maybe if you spent a little more time on your quilting and a lot less time bugging me about my love life, you'd actually finish in time for the fair."

Donna let out a barking laugh. "She's got you there."

Peg flipped her off, and the two of them adjusted their shoulders, ready to set off another round of their perpetual war. Gigi leaned forward between the two of them. "We have our theme, and we're short on time. Save it for after the quilt's done."

Gram sighed and stood. "This is why you can't ever leave us, Gigi."

She went into the kitchen, and glasses rattled around as she put together a tray of sun tea to get them started on the long day of embroidering. They still had patterns spread around, but today they'd fold up the dining room table and bring up the open sewing table for handwork. Even with their various squabbles, the Bees worked as a hive, their strengths blending into perfect cuts of cloth and thread.

"If you're bored, Paxton could probably use a hand before his double shift today," Gigi said. "He's been so busy getting Matilda ready for the fair, he hasn't had time to properly groom the others."

Matilda was his prized lop-eared rabbit. She had the softest fur, thanks to regular grooming, and the sweetest temperament. Paxton practiced posing with her so often, she'd gotten accustomed to doing what he needed to win a ribbon. Part of me wondered if she understood it all, and if those ribbons meant just as much to her as they did her owner. Things had been off with us last night, but if I stopped by today, maybe we could sort out that weird tension before we had another shift together.

"I guess I could go over there," I said casually. Too casually.

Peg and Donna stopped shooting each other death glares long enough to look at me, and a slow smile spread over Peg's thin lips. I knew that look. It made all the muscles in my shoulders bunch up and tighten.

"No wonder you have no interest in the baseball boy," Peg said.

I glanced at Gigi, silently begging her to rescue me, but she did no such thing. She just sat back with her arms crossed, wearing a satisfied grin. Traitor.

"You got a thing for Paxton?" Donna asked.

My face burned so bad, I thought it might catch on fire. "No."

"Liar." Peg's jowls flapped like a turkey's neck as she cackled. "That boy is as sweet as apple pie on a crisp fall day. Can't say I blame you."

"I don't know what you're talking about." I willed the floor to open up and swallow me whole. I didn't want to have this conversation ever, and I definitely didn't want to have it with Gigi in the room. "We're coworkers. Friends. That's it."

Gram pulled her head out of the refrigerator, where she'd been pushing jars around and clicking bottles together trying to get to the sun tea in back. She came out of the kitchen, totally unaware, and stared at me. "What did you all say to make Macy so uncomfortable?"

"Macy has a crush on Paxton." Donna's eyes sparkled.

"I do not," I said, refusing to meet Gram's steely glare.

"Your momma is going to have a heart attack if she finds out," Gram said. "You know how she feels about dating coworkers. I don't mind it myself. You could do a lot worse than Paxton. He's a good-looking boy and a soft one too."

Thank God that Mom had already left for work. If she'd been here, I had no doubt she would've assumed I'd be impregnated by week's end. I stiffened my spine. "I'm not going to date him. Jesus. I didn't even say I liked him. I just said I *might* stop by to help him with the bunnies, and these old gossips ran wild with it."

"If you say so." Gram lit a cigarette and turned back toward the kitchen. "I still wouldn't tell your momma about helping with the bunnies. She worries too much as it is."

"I know." Because it had been ground into me before I'd even made it out of the womb. No coworkers. I wouldn't be surprised if Mom tried to have it tattooed on my forehead one day. "I'm leaving now, and I *am* going to the lake."

"Tell Paxton to get the hamburger out for dinner," Gigi called as the screen door slapped shut behind me. Peg's and Donna's laughter chased me all the way down to the sidewalk.

I wouldn't go see Paxton. The Bees would never leave me alone again. And Gigi, of all people, totally set me up. I would not go there. I'd go to the lake and dip my toes in the cool water, and . . . somehow my feet took me in the wrong direction. Through a break in the woods at the edge of our property. The way to Paxton's house.

Twigs snapped under my feet as I walked, making my heart race. After the bloggers, I couldn't underestimate how exposed I was out here alone. Lisbeth and Gigi had bought a two-bedroom house at the end of a dirt road, set way back near the trees. The earthy scent of the woods fought for dominance with the farm smell of the bunny hutches spread out along the back of the property line. I'd only been here twice before to run patterns and cucumbers over to Gigi for Gram. Paxton didn't like people coming to his house, and after leaving the chattering Bees behind, I was inclined to agree with him about not wanting company. Lisbeth still worked at the nursing home two towns over, and was gone more often than not, so Gigi had mostly raised Paxton.

The gate clinked against the chain-link fence as I shut it behind me. I didn't text before I came over, because then I would've had to admit I was coming over in the first place. According to Gigi, he needed to deal with the other bunnies while getting Matilda ready for the fair. I didn't want to get in the way of that.

Gigi's daffodils swayed in the gentle morning breeze. She loved to garden, but she was best known for her daffodils, which she often clipped and brought to people who were sick or mourning or heartbroken. Paxton got all his softness from Gigi, even if they weren't related by blood. Maybe I'd ask him if I could bring some to my mom before I left. Browning grass crunched under my feet as I stepped around the side of the house, and stopped short.

Paxton held Matilda above his head, her fur gleaming from a recent brushing, and he kissed her wet nose while her little legs kicked the air. "Who's my sweet baby? Who's taking first place this year?" Matilda's legs kicked faster. "That's right. None of the other rabbits can compare. Not against the prettiest bunny in Shelby County."

I put a hand to my chest, just to feel the place where my heart had melted clean away. I'd seen Paxton with his bunnies before, but usually at the fair, or other local competitions, when he was all business and focused on their posing for the judges. Never with this open and tender joy. Like Matilda held his world in her tiny, fast feet. I once asked him why he'd named her Matilda, and he said because she was magic. Seeing them together, I finally got it.

He caught sight of me and grinned. Not a hint of embarrassment over cooing at his rabbit like she was a toddler. He held Matilda against his chest, waving her front paw at me. "Looks like we have a visitor."

"Sorry I didn't text. Gigi sent me over here. She said you needed help with the bunnies before you went to work, and I didn't have anything better to do." Keep it cool. Easy. Like I just stopped over here and offered to help with his bunnies every day.

"Just finishing up." He tucked Matilda back into her hutch, and brushed his hands off on his jeans. "Is that really why you came over?"

"Gigi also said you had to take the hamburger out of the fridge for dinner." My voice got softer, nearly inaudible, as he walked closer and closer.

He stopped inches away from me, close enough for me to smell the soap on his skin. Closer than I'd been to him since the lake. "And you couldn't have texted me that?"

I swallowed, keeping my gaze at his feet, afraid to look up. I didn't have a lake behind me to flip into. "I wanted to make sure we were okay. Last night felt like a fight, but not."

"I think you're mistaking me for the hipsters you chased out of the store with a wrench." The humor in his voice warmed me more than the sun peeking up over the tree line.

His plain blue T-shirt hung right at the waist of his jeans, like it had shrunk or he had grown after he'd gotten dressed that morning. The button of his jeans was half undone. With one finger I'd be able to flick it open, and do what I definitely should *not* have been thinking about doing with my coworker. The material of his shirt stretched over his chest. Not because he was a secret Superman, but because his shirt really was too small. His lips parted slightly. Finally I met his eyes, and they looked the same as they did last night at work. No humor, just a burning intensity that made my pulse quicken.

"You didn't answer my question." My voice cracked and I wanted to kick myself for being so weird, but with him this close, my brain stopped functioning on normal cylinders.

"What question is that?" He'd angled his head so his words were like a kiss of air across my lips. I'd only have to push up onto my toes.

"When you said Midnight and Elise being together was worth the risk. Were you really talking about them?" I swallowed. My muscles gripped my spine so tight, it trembled. "Or someone else?"

"Someone else," he whispered. The distance between our lips narrowed to the point where even a piece of paper wouldn't have been able to slide in, but he waited.

He could've kissed me at any time, and my skin was warm and tingling enough that I would've let him. In fact, he probably could've taken me behind the rabbit hutches and I wouldn't have objected. Everything inside me was screaming to grab his shirt, pull him against me, and kiss him until I forgot all about Jessica and Eric and Twitter.

Except for that small noise in the back of my mind. A clicking. Scarily similar to the sound of a rotten toenail on linoleum. I was sort of dating Eric. Not for real, but no one could know the truth, and I definitely shouldn't be kissing another guy right now.

I put a hand on his chest, and he shuddered, his heart pounding hard against my palm. It matched the beat of my own. I took a step back. "I have to go."

Without giving him a chance to respond, I turned and ran all the way back home.

After dinner, Mom, Gram, Peg, and I sat in the living room to watch *Wheel of Fortune*. I sat at Mom's feet in front of the recliner, and tried to check Twitter again, but Gram yelled at me. It was family time, not phone time.

"That's Vanna's best dress since Beach Week," Peg said. I looked up from spacing out. Vanna White wore a maroon gown with a beaded empire waist and one strap over the shoulder. "She looks good in chartreuse."

"That's not chartreuse," I said. "Chartreuse is a yellow green."

Had I been out on the lake with Paxton only a few days ago? I was a mess. Even though the Baseball Babe stuff had given me the kind of subscribers I'd dreamed about, I hadn't been sleeping well, my anxiety levels had gone through the roof, and my emotions were all over the place. I was in no position to make sound decisions about relationships. I could barely manage my fake one, forget about adding a real one into the mix. Crossing that line with Paxton while I was still trying to figure myself out wouldn't do either of us any favors.

The show ended, and Gram turned her piercing gaze toward my mom. "Are you going out with that Roger again?"

My head whipped around. "Who's Roger?"

"Cradle robber," Gram grumbled.

"Bizzy." Peg's voice was a low warning. "He's a nice boy."

"Boy?" Gram wheezed as she laughed. "He ain't no boy."

"I'm seventy-five years old," Peg said. "Everybody is a boy to me."

"Would you knock it off, Mom? I don't even want to bring Roger around for dinner because of you." My mom glared at Gram. "And yes, we're going out again tonight. The Royals game is playing at a bar in Shelbyville."

"Um." I held up a hand. "Who is Roger and what cradle is he robbing?"

"Roger is someone I've gone on a few dates with. He's very kind and he's a Royals fan." Those two things were pretty much Mom's only requirements in a man. "He lives in Shelbyville, and he happens to be a few years older than me."

Gram snorted.

"How old is a few years older?" I asked.

"Fifty." Mom crossed her arms, daring Gram to start in on him again.

"Ew," I said. "I'm going to have to agree with Gram on

the cradle robbing. Fifty is really old. Like, a-discount-at-the-car-wash old."

"Excuse me?" Peg sputtered.

"Don't worry." I gave Peg my sweetest smile. "I think you're really old too."

Peg held up her fists. "Do you want to take this out back and see what old can do to smart-mouthed teenagers who don't have any respect?"

"Anyway," Gram cut in, trying to bring the conversation back to a serious tone so she could keep harping on Mom. "The cradle robber is also a fancy business owner."

I turned back to my mom. "You're dating a rich cradle robber?"

"He has a name," she said. "And he owns three businesses in broken-down, pass-through towns. I wouldn't exactly call him rich."

"Richer than us," I said.

"Baby girl, if I turned down every man richer than us, I'd never date again."

True, yet depressing, facts. "As long as he's nice to you, I guess that's okay."

Mom quirked her lips. "I'm so glad I have your permission."

"You didn't get mine," Gram said.

I tuned out Mom launching into a rant about how she wasn't sixteen anymore, and scrolled through Twitter. Because I lived there now.

@baseballbabe2020: Can't wait for @Pellegrino's

in St. Joseph for the best food, and even better company #baseballbabe and #flyballgirl #datenight

@MacyAtTheMovies: Looking forward to seeing the sun set on the river in St. Joseph tomorrow night. #FlyBallGirl and #BaseballBabe #DateNight

I should've told Paxton about my date instead of blowing him off with some bullshit excuse. It was like I existed in two realities, only one of them wasn't real. I closed my eyes and whispered, "Fake it for Chicago, fake it for Chicago."

"What's that, Macy?" Mom frowned at me.

"She's in a trance," Peg said. "I've read about those on the World Wide Web. A spirit enters the body and tries to communicate through a living being, but it comes out jumbled on account of them being dead and not remembering how to make words and all."

I shook my head. "You really need to stop believing everything you read on the Internet. I was just talking about my date tomorrow. Which I have. A date. And I need to borrow the car."

Gram narrowed her eyes. "Who you dating?"

"The guy from the baseball game."

I winced as they all started in at once: Gram said she knew it was going to happen the whole time and everyone should've listened to her, Peg told me to run a credit check on him, and Mom sighed and debated wardrobe choices. I really should've told them one at a time. Or just stolen the car for the night and not said anything at all.

"Anyway." I held out my palms to quiet them. "I have

a big day tomorrow and I need to take care of a few things before then." Like see how many retweets our date night hashtag had gotten and if they translated to more clicks on my channel. "But you're all free to continue discussing this without me."

I went to my room and flopped face-first on the mattress. No texts from Paxton. Just a whole bunch of strangers in my mentions who didn't have a clue I was lying to them all.

CHAPTER
FOURTEEN

BEFORE I LEFT FOR my date, Mom gave me all the "don'ts" of a lifetime. Don't leave the restaurant, don't get in a car with Eric, don't even take a walk with him, don't park in a garage, let the valet take it. And my timeless favorite: don't get pregnant.

Turned out, I didn't need to pay the valet to take my car, because it had already been arranged. Maybe Eric did it because he knew it wasn't a good idea to let an eighteen-year-old girl walk through a barely lit parking garage alone after a hundred thousand people liked the tweet stating exactly where she'd be. Or maybe Pellegrino's did it as a thanks for all the free advertising. Either way, I now stood in front of the restaurant.

Potted plants flanked the walkway laid out with gold rope through iron poles. I brushed a hand down the dress my mom had given me to wear tonight, light blue silk with a tight, dipped top adorned with tiny beads that flowed down and flared out, the hemline just above my knees. It was the nicest thing I'd ever worn, and I had no idea where she had hidden it all these years to keep me from stealing it a long time ago. She'd bought it for graduation when she got her associate's degree. Back when she thought she'd be able to afford all the dresses she wanted.

A man in a solid black suit held the door open for me, and I grimaced as I passed. I would've been 1,000 percent more comfortable at Denny's. The inside smelled like warm bread and oregano, and soft candlelight bounced around the dark paneled walls. The seating area was arranged with plush couches in a rich red velvet, and all of my instincts screamed that I didn't belong. An appetizer here probably cost more than a week's worth of groceries.

Eric stood by a trickling fountain formed from marble angels. His broad shoulders filled out his dark gray suit, and when he looked at me, his golden hair caught the reflection of the candlelight. His deep brown eyes traced the lines of my dress as a slow toothpaste-ad smile spread over his lips.

"Macy." He took my hand, his calloused from batting practice. He wanted me completely in his thrall as he linked our arms. "You look great."

I gave him a gentle nudge. "You say that like you expected otherwise."

"I never doubted you," he said. "Ready for a picture?"

He led me to the fountain specifically to pose, like I was one of Paxton's rabbits, but I couldn't even be annoyed about it. I chose this. For my family, I'd be his Fly Ball Girl. Arm candy and bathroom gymnast for the beautiful boy who could do no wrong.

I studied Eric's profile and had a strong urge to muss his hair or draw a mustache under his nose, something to shake up that unnerving perfection.

The host—or maître d' as he was probably called in a place like this—took our picture. I smiled prettily, tilted my head just so, played the part. Eric uploaded it to Twitter before he said another word to me. Part of me thought he'd smack me on the butt and send me out the door now that he'd gotten what he really wanted, but he just took my arm again as we were led to our table. Where more photo opportunities awaited.

Once the waiter, clad in all white, filled our water glasses and left us alone with our menus, I took a sip and surveyed him over my glass. "I draw the line at sharing a plate of spaghetti with you, *Lady and the Tramp* style."

He chuckled. "Sorry about the picture, but you know how it goes."

I certainly did, but we could at least attempt to enjoy the evening by getting to know each other. "Tell me about your blog."

He launched into a monologue about batting averages and pitching speeds, all with a lot of hand motions. I nodded politely, understanding none of it. My mom would appreciate this conversation so much more than me. I rested my chin on my hands while he kept talking. He hardly paused to take a breath, let alone for me to respond. So I kept nodding, while my mind drifted elsewhere. To Paxton. And my silent phone.

I checked again. He hadn't texted me all day. I couldn't think of the last time I'd gone a whole day without talking to him in some capacity. It threw off my whole equilibrium.

I debated texting Elise to see if she'd talked to him today. Though that might've been more desperate than just texting Paxton myself.

"You should've seen the picture I got of that guy's jump. The ball sailed into his glove. I couldn't have planned that hit any better," Eric said.

It took me a few seconds to realize he had stopped talking and now expected me to respond. "Oh. Wow. Cool."

He leaned back in his chair with the kind of smugness that would've ended a regular date for me. "I'm going to be bigger than *Barstool Sports* one day. When Mizzou went to the NCAA Tournament, I . . ."

I tuned him out again and went back to checking my phone. It's not as if he'd stop talking about himself long enough to ask me any questions anyway. Maybe after dinner I'd stop by work to tell Elise what was going on with Eric. I should've told her about it already, but I wasn't in the mood to hear all the reasons why it was a bad idea.

The waiter stopped back to take our order, saving me from trying to pretend like I was listening to the one-sided conversation. "We'll both have the salmon," Eric said.

My back immediately went up. He hadn't bothered to ask if I had an allergy or if I even liked salmon. It was one thing to bore me to tears, and another thing entirely to order for me. Just like he'd put his hand on my back to steer me at the game. A big part of why we were in this mess. As if he didn't think I could do anything on my own. Or maybe he just moved through life like that, thinking he knew best, because the world had always rearranged itself to accommodate the whims of a pretty boy with a perfect smile.

"Excuse me." I held up a finger. "I'll actually have the stuffed chicken."

Eric's lips thinned and I shot him a look that dared him to challenge me. After a beat of uncomfortable silence, the waiter left and Eric took out his phone to check how many retweets we'd gotten on our picture.

"Two thousand RTs and it's only been up for about ten minutes." He turned his phone to me, beaming. "I had a manager for the Royals contact me today. He said he might be able to get me into the locker room for the next game."

"I'm happy for you," I said with all the enthusiasm of getting a root canal.

"Maybe you can drive down next week." He brightened as he sat up straighter. "Hey, you could even take a video and post it to your YouTube channel."

"That's not really my brand."

"What's wrong? You don't seem into this." He set his phone aside. "And you keep looking at your texts. Are you talking to another guy?"

"Would you really care if I were?"

He leaned forward, his voice low as he hovered over the candlelight on our table. "I'm not seeing anyone else right now."

"Are you telling me that we're exclusive?" I laid a hand over my heart and batted my eyelashes. "Will I get to wear your class ring, too?"

He huffed out a breath through his nose. "All I'm saying

is, it wouldn't be a good look if you got caught on camera with another guy."

"Don't worry about it." I rolled my neck, trying to loosen the tension building in there. I motioned to the quiet and stuffy dining room with the fancy wall art and linen tablecloths. "This is a little out of my element."

"Yeah, I know." He frowned at his water glass as he twirled the stem between his thumb and finger. "But it's public enough to be a story, and private enough for us to control it."

For him to control it. I hadn't done anything other than show up. "Do you have a PR person or something? Because it sounds like you're trying to maneuver me."

"I'm not." Eric paused when the waiter brought our drinks and salads. "I thought we'd come to an agreement, that you wanted this too."

"I don't know what I want." The subscribers were nice, but there was a huge difference between sending out some cheesy tweets and meeting this guy in person. Like we'd stepped into something that would eventually pull us under.

"It's not so bad, sharing a meal with me, is it?" He turned on that charming grin, and when he tilted his head, light reflected off his shiny teeth.

"It's still too early to tell." I picked at my salad, which had orange shavings on top that might've been carrot and little boiled eggs that probably belonged to a snooty bird, like a quail or something equally pretentious. "But either way, doesn't this feel kind of gross?"

"Whoa." He sat back in his chair. "I've been called a lot of things. Never that."

"Not you." This guy and his ego. As if all his new Twitter fans didn't coddle him enough. "I mean this thing we're doing. Doesn't it feel like we're being manipulative?"

"I'm on a date with a cute girl—what's manipulative about that?"

I raised an eyebrow.

"Okay, here's the thing." He reached across the table for my hand. "If this hadn't blown up, I still would've wanted to have dinner with you. Maybe not someplace this nice, but I would've wanted to see you again."

But he hadn't. He hadn't texted me, other than to give me the address of this restaurant. He tweeted at me, but he hadn't DM'd me since that first time. He'd had the perfect opportunity to get my number at the game, when we were still unknown strangers who happened to be sitting next to each other. While I probably wasn't any better, especially since I'd spent a good portion of his monologue checking to see if Paxton had texted me, it still made me feel sick.

Sick of Eric, of me, of this entire thing.

He kept his gaze on me, like he was waiting for me to tell him I wanted to see him again too. And maybe I had the morning after the game, but that felt like forever ago. I wasn't even sure if I was still the same person as I was then.

"Have you checked your YouTube numbers since you posted about having dinner with me?" he asked.

"No."

He hadn't given me the address until last night, and after we'd done our hashtag date tweets, I'd spent all night scrolling through the comments. I didn't get out of bed until almost one in the afternoon and had to rush to get our barters done, shower, do my makeup, dress, get a lecture from Mom. All of it had been exhausting.

"I tweeted that we'd be posting a video of us to your channel right before I got here. You're up to two hundred thousand subscribers," he said.

"Fuck." I'd barely whispered it, but a few nearby diners turned to give me dirty looks.

Two hundred thousand subscribers. It was more than I'd expected, more than I'd ever dared to hope for, and the cost . . . Dinner with a good-looking guy who talked about himself too much. I'd had worse dates, with zero return.

Eric leaned across the table. "I like you. I really do. But there are other perks to this thing between us, and not just for me. We've both been given a chance. Shouldn't we take it?"

He knew exactly what to say to get me, and I didn't even mind that much. This *was* my chance. Never again would I have to crawl on the sidewalk for quarters, the Bees could keep their winning quilt this year, Mom could afford to explore job opportunities outside of Honeyfield. It wasn't just about me.

I linked my fingers through Eric's. "I get to post the next picture to my timeline."

He let out a laugh. "That's fair."

Our food arrived, and because Eric was a specific type of

jerk, he wanted a picture of him feeding me a bite of salmon, just to prove it was better than my stuffed chicken. He held the fork to my lips. I shook my head, and he kept pushing the fork at me, to the point where the other diners kept one eye on us as they ate. The waiter shifted his stance while he held my phone, poised to take the picture and clearly hating every second of this. Since we had an audience, I couldn't exactly say no. Not when that picture was going on my timeline.

After I took the bite and the waiter gave me my phone so he could make a quick exit, I held a hand to my throat. I coughed and waved my hands around, opening and closing my mouth like a freshly hooked fish.

"What are you doing?" Eric's eyes widened to the size of our dinner plates.

"Allergic." I feigned a gasp for air. "Salmon."

"Oh God. I didn't know." His gaze darted around the restaurant and I half wondered if he'd just make a run for it and let me choke to death. "Should I call 9-1-1?"

I'd held my breath long enough to make my face turn red. "EpiPen."

"Do you have one with you? Where is it?" He flailed his limbs, and he looked so ridiculous, I nearly lost it. "Tell me what to do!"

"Purse." I pounded the table with my fist and pointed at the ground by my feet, even though I hadn't brought a purse with me.

The other diners weren't even pretending to eat anymore. They full on gaped at the spectacle. Eric leapt to his feet, rocking the table as he dug his fingers into his scalp. The centerpiece candles flickered.

I relaxed my breath, took a bite of chicken, and smiled. "That'll teach you to shove food in a girl's mouth without asking."

The other diners gave me looks of disgust, but I didn't care. A hundred percent worth it.

Eric paled as he sat down with a hard thud. "You're one twisted bitch."

"We're going to have so much fun together." I raised my glass and clinked it against his.

Eric, to his credit, looked like he'd made a deal with the devil. Good. It didn't hurt to keep him on his toes. I knew he'd been manipulating me, especially when he brought up my subscribers after I'd told him I hadn't checked. He thought this small-town backwoods girl would just let him run the show.

He didn't think that anymore.

CHAPTER
FIFTEEN

DURING DINNER ERIC AND I staged a video, with an actual script. We took turns going back and forth over what we'd say, how cutesy to be, and how long we wanted to make it. I let him post the third and final picture to his Twitter timeline: our linked fingers on the white tablecloth next to our shared plate of sugared raspberry cake, which I didn't actually share. We agreed I'd get the video for YouTube. By the end of dinner he'd dropped all pretense of trying to woo me. We had become a business arrangement, and I only briefly wondered how my mom would feel about me having gone on a date with a coworker.

The valet brought my car around. I let Mom know I was on my way home, but I'd be stopping by work first. It was still early, and my not-date had left me feeling as empty and alone as I had on those nights when I scrolled through Twitter. If I were lucky, I'd be able to catch Elise before the end of her shift and see if Paxton had texted her about how I blew him off when he asked me out, and then again when he almost kissed me. That had to have been why he hadn't texted me all day. We'd never gone this long without talking before.

I parked in front of the store fifteen minutes before

close and called Mom to let her know I'd made it back to Honeyfield. As I went inside, Brady passed me on his way out the door. I stopped to say hi, but he looked so uncomfortable, I let him go without a word.

Elise stood at the counter with Midnight. She froze mid-laugh as she turned toward me and crossed her arms. "Look who it is. The girl who used to be my best friend."

Uh-oh.

"I'm just gonna . . ." Midnight pointed at the closet door before disappearing behind it.

"What the hell is that supposed to mean?" I mimicked Elise's defensive posture.

She flipped through the DVD rack. "I don't know. Seems like best friends would talk to each other about upcoming dates."

Damn it. I should've texted her last night. Even if I didn't want to deal with her calling me out, it's not like it could've stayed a secret with the way Eric and I had been playing footsie on Twitter. People in town had nothing better to do than gossip, and our little rental store was the hub of Honeyfield's favorite currency.

"But instead I had to find out about it from people coming in here and telling me to look you up on fucking Twitter. I hate Twitter," she said. Maybe a small part of me had hoped she wouldn't find out right away because she hated Twitter. And Instagram and Snapchat. If it wasn't TikTok, she had no use for it. "Please tell me this is all an elaborate joke and you're not dating a guy who is using you so he can capitalize on hashtagging your public humiliation."

Yeah. Well. He wasn't the only one. "Gram thinks he has an honest face."

"Yes, so honest. Like how he told everyone you really caught the fly ball. Oh wait. He didn't do that, did he? And you're seriously dating him?"

She had the same look on her face as that time in grade school when I'd borrowed a few of her Barbies and painted their outfits green and given them all buzz cuts so they could be my army against Gram's Vannas. Disappointment, annoyance, frustration. Check, check, and check.

"Not seriously." I chewed on my bottom lip.

"Did you at least knee him in the balls and steal his wallet?"

"Ha." If only. I had to tell her the truth. If she somehow found out later, she'd never forgive me. "I'm going to tell you something you're not going to like, but please hold your judgments until the end."

Drawing in a deep breath, I told her the whole story. Why I'd FaceTimed Eric, what he had proposed, what it meant to me in terms of subscribers, how I avoided telling her because I knew she would've given me the verbal ass-kicking I deserved. Everything.

"Let me get this straight. You're only pretending to date him?" She screeched so loud, dogs two blocks away started barking. At this point I didn't know which she'd consider worse: my unholy alliance with Eric or dating him for real. "What the fuck, Macy?"

"I know, I know. It's gross." I didn't need her to put me in the Box of Shame. I already had a standing reservation. "But it's worth it to me. So. Can you put on your supportive best friend hat, and take off the one where you call out my ridiculous shit? Because I need those subscribers if I'm ever going to get out of here."

Midnight poked her head of her office. "You need to tell Paxton."

I glared at her. "Don't you have closing duties to do?"

"We can both pretend like I haven't been pressed against the door listening in the whole time." She shrugged. "Doesn't change that you should still tell him."

"Agreed." Elise traded a look with Midnight. I did not like that look. "He stopped by earlier," Elise said. "I was checking out your date on Twitter and he saw the pictures over my shoulder. I'm sorry."

"Why are you apologizing? You didn't do anything wrong." I did. Because now Paxton knew "the thing" I had to do tonight, and he hadn't heard it from me. "I think I really fucked things up with him."

Midnight gave me the same look she'd given that one customer who'd asked why our DVDs didn't work in his VCR. "You think?"

"Why was he even here?" I asked. "I thought he had the day off."

"If you want to check the trash on the repair side." Elise kept her gaze on her feet. "Um, in there. He was going to leave them on the register for you to find tomorrow."

I approached the metal can on the repair side and lifted the lid. There, buried under a stack of invoices, daffodils from Gigi's garden with a ribbon tied around them. A note hung from the end of the ribbon, and my fingers shook as I turned it over.

I like you, and not just because you're my favorite coworker. I like your passion for old movies and the color blue. I like how your right cheek turns just a little bit pinker than your left when you blush. I like how you wear red lipstick on days when you're mad. I like the way you look when you look at me. I like all of you, YouTube videos and viral fame included, just the way you are.

My heart shattered on the concrete floor. His late-night texts, the way he always touched the ends of my hair, and the way his lips nearly grazed mine all flashed through my mind. Guilt—clawing, persistent guilt—squeezed at my lungs. He'd been making his feelings clear, and while I'd been feeling the same, I kept stepping back.

I put the lid on the trash and tried to will my face into not showing how bad everything hurt as I turned back toward the video side. "Is he mad at me?"

"No," Elise said. "You could probably stab him in the chest and he wouldn't be mad at you. He threw out the flowers after he saw all that staged romantic bullshit on Twitter. He thinks he misinterpreted things between you two, but I've known you my whole life, and I don't think he's misinterpreting anything, is he?"

I shook my head.

My throat tightened, and Elise wrapped her arms

around me before I started to crumple. The last week, my whole life, everything had crashed into me all at once. Like those flowers and that note broke open the dam I'd been keeping sealed up tight. I burrowed against the thick braid slung over her shoulder. She rubbed my back and murmured words of comfort as I held on to the tears that threatened to spill down my cheeks.

I'd made a mess of everything. My business partnership with Eric danced in front of me like a plastic bag on the wind, just as mocking and flimsy. Paxton had been open and honest with me, while I couldn't even be honest with myself. It wasn't just the desire to leave town that had me going all in with the Baseball Babe drama, and it wasn't just the Baseball Babe drama that had kept me from taking that final leap with Paxton.

It was fear.

Stone-cold, bone-deep fear of retracing my mom's history. Of becoming the girl she'd been and waking up as the woman she was now. I loved her, so much that it physically hurt sometimes, but I didn't want a dead-end job in a broken-down town. I didn't want my only escape to be a beach recliner and a kiddie pool and worn copies of romance novels.

"I don't want to be her," I whispered to Elise, hating myself so much more than I had when I'd agreed to playing these stupid Twitter games with Eric.

I'd never said those words out loud to anyone.

"I know." Elise kept stroking my back, not even having to ask who I meant. "I know."

She held me until I stopped trembling, until I could face

what I'd finally voiced. What had always been in my heart. It made me feel sick and dirty. My mom had sacrificed so much to give me the best life possible. She'd raised me so I'd never know a day without love. While I'd gotten my spine and tendency to mouth off from Gram, every scrap of goodness and light I possessed had come from my mom.

Elise pulled back and cupped my cheeks. "It's okay to feel that way. It's okay to want a better life far away from here. She wants that for you too. Why do you think she works so hard and worries so much? She knows you're built for something else."

I knew that in my head, but it didn't stop me from feeling as if I'd betrayed her. Like the sperm donor who'd knocked her up and breezed out of town without a care in the world. And here I was, trying my damnedest to leave too. Trying so hard that I was willing to sell out every decent bone in my body in order to accomplish that goal.

I'd looked up the man I shared DNA with only once. I found him on Facebook. He had a wife and two kids, who I had no desire to meet, and a nice big house in the suburbs of St. Louis. His parents had moved out of Honeyfield when the paper mill shut down, and he hadn't been back since Mom told him she was pregnant.

I hated him. I hated his smile, so similar to my own. I hated his nice house and his new car and his family vacations. I hated that he posted the anniversary of when he and his wife went on their first date. I hated that it was a year before I was born. Most of all, I hated that easy life he got to have. The kind of life that could've, should've, would've been Mom's.

If it hadn't been for me.

Elise held my gaze, as if she could see my every thought. "Stop punishing yourself for the mistakes other people have made."

Because I never talked about my deeper fears, preferring to push them down or handle things on my own, I didn't realize what I'd been doing, and how bad I'd needed to hear those words. The tightness in my chest eased a fraction. "I don't deserve you."

"I am a precious pearl in a sea of clams." Elise grinned.

I grabbed her hand as she turned to finish up her closing duties on the repair side, conveying everything I felt without words. She squeezed my hand in response.

Suddenly a bottle of peach schnapps clunked down in front of me. Midnight had stolen it from Butch's stash for those days when we needed a little pick-me-up. She gave me a tentative smile and nudged the bottle forward.

"I figured you could use a shot," Midnight said.

I unscrewed the cap and took a small sip. It burned my throat and warmed my stomach, and that tightness in my chest eased a bit more. "Thank you."

She shrugged. "It's the least I can do."

CHAPTER
SIXTEEN

I LEFT WORK SO Midnight and Elise could close. If I'd been smart, I would've driven straight home. It was late. Paxton was probably already in bed. Or he was awake and pissed at me. But I hadn't been doing anything smart lately, so why start now? I pulled my car up next to his front yard, shut off the engine, and rested my head on the steering wheel.

If I laid out all my feelings, the way he had done, where would that leave me? What if we eventually broke up? Would I be able to stand working with him? Or what if we didn't break up? What if we had an amazing relationship? Would I still be able to move to Chicago? His refusal to drive pretty much said he'd be staying put, and regardless of my recent revelation, I couldn't do the same. I needed more than this town could offer.

Even with all those questions racing through my mind, I wanted him. I didn't want to be afraid of my own feelings anymore. I didn't want to let my mom's path in life haunt every step of my own. If she hadn't gotten pregnant, she would've gotten out. She would've had her high-rise office and bearded boyfriends. And I could still get out too. Caring about a boy who cared about me wouldn't ruin my future if I didn't let it.

I went through his back gate, prepared to tap on his window. This was a terrible idea. He'd probably yell at me for showing up in the middle of the night, like any normal person would do. I'd have to move to Canada, change my name to Maple, and take up curling.

As I went around the side of the house, I caught sight of a faint glow. Paxton lounged on a lawn chair with Matilda on his lap. His computer sat open on a garden table, with *Say Anything* playing on the screen. He looked at me and jumped up, nearly dropping Matilda, grabbing her scruff at the last second.

"What are you doing here?" His gaze slid over me, to the hemline of my dress, lower, and back up again. He swallowed hard. "I thought you had a date?"

"It ended hours ago." I took a step closer to him. "I'm sorry I didn't tell you, but it wasn't, like, a real date. I didn't even shave above my knees." Oh my God. What was wrong with me? "Not that you asked about my pre-date rituals. Please say something so I'll stop talking."

"Hold on." He put Matilda in her hutch and walked back to me just as Lloyd held the boom box over his head. "It wasn't a date?"

"I don't want to talk about it. It doesn't matter." Maybe it was the dark or what I'd confessed to Elise or most likely the peach schnapps, but I felt bolder than I had in a long time. I took another step, closing the gap between us. "Why haven't you texted me?"

"I thought you wanted space."

"I don't want space." I wrapped my arms around his shoulders and pulled him against me. Here in the dark, surrounded by bunnies and daffodils, with the feel of Paxton's hands on me, I wanted something real. I didn't want to be Fly Ball Girl. I didn't want to be one half of the viral Internet couple. I just wanted to be me.

He cupped my face with one hand, while the other slipped around my waist. His thumb grazed my jawline, and I pushed up on my toes and kissed him. His lips, so soft and careful, pressed against mine. I opened for him and his tongue swept over mine, slowly exploring at first, until I tugged him closer and deepened the kiss. He groaned, and the sound traveled all the way down my spine.

My fingers tangled in his hair as his hands roamed. Up my back, over my stomach, and across my ribs. Everywhere he touched burned, followed by a pleasant shiver that went straight down to my toes. He broke the kiss and his lips brushed my ear, trailed down my neck, then back to my mouth. I couldn't get enough. I rubbed his chest over his shirt, touched his arms, solid from working in the repair shop for the last year.

His breath was warm on my neck as he murmured against it, "You taste like peaches."

"Do you like peaches?" My voice had gone breathless.

He pulled back, his thumbs circling my sides. "I fucking love peaches."

His mouth covered mine again, and I was drowning in the scent and taste and feel of him against me. I wanted more.

I wanted everything. He guided me over to his lawn chair and sat, pulling me with him. I straddled him, grinding against his hips. He was hard beneath me as his fingers dipped under the hemline of my dress. I smacked his hand away and he chuckled in my mouth. The gentle vibration nearly undid me.

"I forgot you didn't shave above your knees." He traced the lines of my calves.

"Believe me, if I'd known I was going to come over, I would've." My hands rested against his chest, and it took all my willpower not to rip off his shirt.

"Why did you come over?" He rubbed my arms. "Not that I'm complaining."

"I saw your note, with the flowers, in the trash."

His breath whooshed out of him. "That was an impulse."

"Picking the flowers and writing the note, or throwing them away?"

"Both?" He let out a shaky laugh and eased me off his lap to stand. Whatever he was about to say, he didn't want to do it with me on top of him. "I meant what I said on the note, but then I saw the picture of your date. Or whatever it was. It looked cozy. I guess I didn't want to get in the way. If you didn't feel the same way about me."

I would never eat salmon again for as long as I lived. "That date was not really a date."

"What was it then?" he asked.

"It was more of a . . ." I twirled my hand, trying to figure out how to explain Eric. Especially if we kept playing this game online. "A business arrangement."

"What?" Paxton had gone still. So still.

Until tonight, I hadn't told anyone about my and Eric's plans to use each other to meet our own ends. Maybe before dinner part of me questioned if it could be real between us after all. Maybe a bigger part of me was ashamed of the levels I'd stooped to for YouTube subscribers.

"Eric wants to be a big-deal sports blogger." I toed at the browning grass under my feet, refusing to meet Paxton's eyes. "All this media attention, it's giving him an edge. His blog hits are through the roof, the Royals gave him locker room access, and I'm helping that along."

Paxton crossed his arms over his chest. "What's in it for you?"

"My YouTube channel just passed two hundred thousand subscribers. Once I post the video of us at dinner, it could go even higher." I glanced up at his tense face. Not at all like the boy who'd been kissing me breathless minutes ago.

"You're dating him for views? Does your ego need that big of a boost?"

His words were like a punch to my gut. "It's not about ego. My videos are monetized, and my other videos are getting clicks too. I've always wanted to build my platform enough to maybe make a living at this, and for the first time, it might be a reality."

"And what happens when this wears off? When a piano-playing cat or an elaborate gender reveal party steals the attention away? Will you go on vacations together? Film an engagement special? Let CBS pay for your dream wedding? How far does it go?"

Every question hammered against me. Every insecurity I felt about playing this game with Eric laid out bare. I knew it was wrong. So wrong that I'd lied to everyone I cared about. The shame of what I'd been willing to do to get out of this town, the shame of wanting to leave in the first place, all hounded me. I didn't even know myself anymore. Still . . .

"Why are you pissed?" I asked. "It has nothing to do with how I feel about you."

He ran a hand through his hair. "I'm not pissed."

I gave him a bland stare.

"Okay, I'm a little pissed. But I'm pissed because I'm worried. Why are you inviting this into your life? Is it worth having voyeurs on your front lawn and people picking apart every word you say, just waiting for a chance to drag you until you bleed?"

"What do you know about it?" I choked down the urge to yell. Lisbeth and Gigi would probably not appreciate my presence at this hour. "You aren't online. You don't even have Facebook. Half the Bees have Facebook."

"I know enough about it." The hard edge in his voice made me pause.

I dared a step forward and peered up at him. Underneath the hardness held an incredible amount of hurt. I wouldn't let it go this time. Even if he kept pushing his past away, I needed to know. "What happened to you?"

"Why do you want to know?" His tone was hollow. "So you have something else to exploit when all this baseball stuff goes away?"

I reeled back, putting more physical distance between us. "That's a bullshit thing to say to me, and you know it." All the anger I felt toward him, toward myself, I flung outward. "I get that my sudden fame is an issue for you, though you won't bother to tell me why, but I'm going to keep doing what I need to do to grow my subscribers. It's my life and you have no say in it. You're not even my boyfriend."

I couldn't read him and it scared me. I'd always been able to get a feel for his moods. The distance between us widened. "You're right. I'm definitely not your boyfriend."

That was all we had left to say. Scraping up the small amount of pride I had left, I turned on my heel and marched toward my car. He didn't follow me or try to stop me.

I waited until I pulled into my driveway to let the tears fall.

CHAPTER
SEVENTEEN

THE NEXT AFTERNOON I hung out with Mom in the Hamptons. I picked at the dead grass and moped. She wore the gaudiest floppy hat adorned with plastic roses, and had a blush to her cheeks that didn't have anything to do with the summer sun. She must've had a good time with cradle-robbing Roger. I wondered if I'd ever meet him, and if I'd be able to keep myself from calling him cradle-robbing Roger.

"You look happy." I nudged her foot with mine. "Did your date go well?"

"Hmm?" Mom looked up from the book she'd been staring at for ten minutes without turning a page. "Oh, yes. We went out on the lake."

"You went out on the lake after the park closed?" I narrowed my eyes. "How?"

"You think Paxton is the only who knows how to break into that shed and snag a boat?" She laughed at my scandalized expression.

"Oh my God. My mom. The rebel teenager." I did not want to know how she knew Paxton stole boats for our movies on the lake. I'd never told her about those nights, but I supposed moms had a sixth sense about those kinds of things.

She went back to her book, and I opened the YouTube app to post the dinner video. First I wanted to check on my *Dirty Dancing* video. It still had a lot of thumbs-downs, way more than my other videos, and while I could admit it had been a rush job, I didn't think it was that bad. I took a peek at the comments.

EmilyChase: *Boring*

MargHenry: *Less movie talk, more Baseball Babe please*

AllySheridan: *what does dirty dancing have to do with baseball babe?*

LincolnDunn: *I'm only here for the porn*

KellyConner: *wake me up when she talks about baseball babe again*

At least they had a running theme. Even Lincoln, in his own trollish way. The more I scrolled through the comments, the more they started to prove Paxton right—they wouldn't care about my videos once the novelty of Fly Ball Girl wore off—which just pissed me off even more. I shut down the app and threw my phone into the grass.

"How did your date go last night?" Mom asked.

I wanted to ask which one, but I wasn't in the mood to be cheeky or to talk about Paxton. "I don't know. It feels icky. Like I'm playing into what other people want for me, not really what I want for myself. I wonder if it would be better if I left it alone."

It was one thing to play up this fauxmance online, but once I'd seen Eric in person, I'd crossed a very fundamental line. I kept telling myself it was worth it, long term, but now I wasn't so sure. Elise didn't seem to think so. Paxton definitely didn't think so. I didn't want to text him, because then I'd just look desperate, so I did the totally reasonable and normal thing by letting it eat away at me instead.

Mom laid a hand on my arm. "For what it's worth, I think Eric genuinely likes you. I got that sense at the stadium, and you both got caught up in an unfortunate circumstance that you can now make the best of."

She was too much of a romantic and a softie to see all the games people played online for their fifteen minutes. We weren't two teenagers in love who'd met by chance at a baseball game. This ultimately wouldn't be a story written in the stars. We'd gotten what many people tried for and only a few attained. Instant, viral fame. And playing it up, stretching it out, to meet our own ends didn't make us good or right, but we did it anyway.

"I still can't believe you let me drive to St. Joseph on my own."

Mom set her book aside. "Are you saying that because you didn't really want to go?"

"No."

She gave me the Look.

"Maybe a little," I said sheepishly. "I don't think it's a good idea to see Eric again." He was way worse off than me, anxiety and nightmares included. His obsession with likes and retweets bordered on masochistic.

Mom tipped her sunglasses down. "Oh?"

"There's no story. It just wasn't a love connection."

"I'm sorry, sweetie. He seemed like a nice boy."

They all seemed like nice boys, until they weren't. I did my best to smile, if only to ease that worry crease between her brows. "It wasn't a total bust. I did get a free meal at Pellegrino's."

Mom brushed her hand over my cheek. "I worry about you."

"You shouldn't. I'm fine." Besides all the lying I'd been doing, the stress over my Twitter mentions and subscribers, the fight I'd had with Paxton, and everything I'd given up to chase something I wasn't even sure I could hold on to.

"Sorry, kiddo, I'm a mom. Worrying is what I do best."

"I know." I slumped in my beach recliner. "Maybe Paxton was right."

"What was Paxton right about?"

"Um." I was five again and learning how to skate. The ice was so cold and slippery. "He wasn't exactly thrilled about my date with Eric."

Mom pinched her lips until they were nothing more than a grim line. "I see."

My ankles wobbled in my skates. "You see what?"

Her back stiffened and she'd become calm. Like eye-of-the-storm calm. "I don't see why who you date is any of his concern, since you work with him."

And I fell through the ice.

"Oh my God." I threw my hands in the air. "He's my friend, Mom. And who even cares if we work together? What if I did date him? I know how you feel about pregnancy— trust me, I know—but do you really think on the first day of work they hand all the guys a time card and a jar of sperm with a slap on the back and say, 'Use it wisely, boys'?"

As soon as the words were out of my mouth, I wanted to

stuff them all back in. I'd never taken that tone with my mom. It's not like we'd never been mad at each other, but we didn't scream at each other. We always walked away to cool down before we got to that point. Or we'd go pick a fight with Gram, who lived to argue, just to burn off some of that frustration.

"That's enough, Macy." Mom's complexion had gone paper white. "You know pregnancy isn't my main concern when it comes to dating your coworkers. You're so headstrong and passionate. You wouldn't have an amicable breakup, and an ugly breakup could cost you your job. There aren't enough jobs to go around this town as it is."

"You're right. It is enough. Because none of this means anything. I'm not dating Paxton, he's not even talking to me, this conversation is asinine, and I have to get ready for work." I stormed into the house and slammed the door behind me.

Days where Paxton and I worked different shifts dragged. Days where I hadn't spoken to him since our fight lasted an eternity. I had no idea what was going on inside his head, and the not knowing was the worst part. I couldn't begin to sort through my feelings, and not really knowing his just exacerbated everything.

Elise leaned against the counter and pursed her lips. Oil stains covered her gray work overalls and she had a streak of grease across her cheekbone. "You look like shit."

"Says the Goodwill version of the Tin Man."

"Yeah, I wanted the Total Bitch costume, but they said you took the last one."

"Sorry." I gave her a light shove. "I'm having a day."

"Anything you want to talk about?" She gave me the same feline grin as the day after the lake. "Like how you keep looking over at Paxton's work space."

I buried my face in my hands. "Anything but that, please."

Her expression went from mischievous to concerned in a flash. "What happened?"

I told her about the kiss and the disaster that happened when I told him the truth about Eric. "Now he's not talking to me."

"Give him a minute to cool down." She patted my hand. "Watching you go viral and knowing you're playing into it isn't easy for him."

"You know what his deal is?"

"I do, and I can't say." She mimed zipping her lips. "It's not my story to tell."

"But I'm your best friend." Elise and Paxton were close, I knew that, but it was always a small gut punch when I realized the two people I considered my closest friends might've been closer to each other than to me.

"And as your best friend, who knows you once had a very riveting sex dream about Mr. Caldwell in which you rode him like Seabiscuit on a lab table, aren't you glad I'm the kind of person who keeps secrets?"

I shuddered. Our chemistry teacher had sallow skin and a nose like a hawk's beak. I could barely stand to look at him the next day in class. "Point taken."

Elise went back to the repair side, while I stewed. Paxton had issues with viral fame, but I had no idea why. I'd already googled him and turned up nothing. He didn't drive, but I had no idea if that was connected. Maybe he'd just sucked at the road test and didn't tell anyone. Though from the small bits of information I'd been able to pick up from Gigi, he wouldn't sit on the driver's side at all, not even when he was younger and rode in the back.

Most of all, I stewed about what he'd said last night. About how far I'd be willing to go to stretch out my fauxmance for views and subscribers. The words he'd flung at me stung, but in the way it'd stung when Elise yelled at me for purposefully taking a dive on our animal science exam last year so I could have an excuse to stop by Lance's farm to study his cows. Like part of me knew he was right. Like I knew all along why my *Dirty Dancing* video had been getting thumbed down. And maybe part of me knew it was going to make him mad, but I'd spent the last week hating myself so much, it was a relief to have someone else do it for me.

I didn't have a ton of time to dwell on it though. Thursday was one of our busiest nights, and as VCRs rentals flew off the shelves, I tried my best to keep that customer service smile plastered to my face. Even with my personal life in a knot I couldn't untangle, and my YouTube channel going from dissecting and discussing eighties movies to becoming a bad eighties movie, I still had a job to do. I still needed that paycheck. And somehow, in the middle of it all, I had to figure out how to accept the choices I'd made.

CHAPTER

EIGHTEEN

WITH TEN MINUTES TO go until we locked up for the night, we finally ushered the last customers out the door. I was supposed to have left a half hour ago, but we got a last-minute rush from a group out of Iowa on their way down to Branson. I turned to Midnight, who stood at the register alone. The rest of the store had a quiet, unused feel to it, like a bedroom no one slept in.

"Where's Elise?" I asked.

"She headed out to the Brewsters' to fix their garbage disposal, and she's going to head straight home after that. She said to tell you bye."

"You're closing alone?"

"Wouldn't be the first time. Butch was supposed to close with me, but you know."

"Butch is an asshole, and he can deal with the overtime. I'm staying."

The bell above the door dinged, and we both turned toward it. Horror curled in my gut as Jared strolled in, with Brett close behind. Jared smirked at me as he stuck his hand in his pocket and jiggled the change in there. All the blood drained from my face.

"You're not allowed in here," Midnight said behind me, her voice smaller than mine had been that time Gram busted me six months ago for trying to sneak out to meet Lance. "You know you're not. Leave now."

Jared lifted his gaze to Midnight, and he reminded me of a shark. Cold and totally devoid of emotion. "You gonna call the police on me, Lexi?" His lip curled in a vicious snarl. "Wait. That's not your name anymore, is it?"

My head whipped around, and I stared hard at Midnight. Beneath the heavy eye makeup, the pale powder that made her skin appear near translucent, and the short, spiked black hair, I had a faint memory overlapping the girl before me. A different girl, with golden curls down to her waist. A farm girl who wore cute skirts and bright shirts. Alexis Peterson. We didn't know her family well because we didn't barter with them. They had a soybean farm, and Gram always said soybeans were for brain-dead vegans with vitamin B12 deficiencies. Alexis had been a grade ahead of me, but I still knew her the way everyone in town knew each other.

I knew her as Jared's girlfriend.

"The restraining order says—" Midnight flinched as Jared clenched a fist.

"I don't give a shit about the restraining order." He bared his teeth, like those wild dogs Gram liked to evoke when she was pissed. "Did you think I'd want to touch you again after you decided to jump off the ugly tree and hit every branch on the way down?"

I backed up a step, closer to the register. If Midnight

could slide me the wrench, I'd use it on him. I'd pound the sneer off his lips and make him crawl out the door, the way he'd made me crawl on the sidewalk.

My movement caught his attention, and he focused on me again. "Famous Macy Evans. You still work here? I thought you'd be on your way to Hollywood by now."

I lifted my chin, refusing to cower before him, even when my bones rattled against my skin. "Get. Out. Or I'll call the police myself."

Jared circled me, and I tracked him, keeping him at my front at all times. He stepped up to the DVD rack and gave it a spin. "I just want to rent a movie."

"We don't want your business," I said.

He got in my face, and the stench of sour milk and beer hit me like a wave. "Why not? Are you too good for my business? You were nothing until you fucked that guy for a fly ball, and next week you'll be nothing again."

Brett had approached me from behind, and I didn't notice him until he'd plucked my phone out of my back pocket. "No one is calling the police. We're just here to rent a movie."

I lunged for him, but he held my phone above his head, laughing like we were just fooling around. He swayed a bit. They were drunk as all hell, which made them ten times meaner than the day they'd glued those quarters to the sidewalk.

We needed to get them out of the store before it got worse, but Midnight had frozen with fear. If I made a run for the door, maybe they'd chase me out and she could call the police.

I darted around Jared, and Brett caught my arm, not hard enough to hurt, but the threat was there. He could hurt me if he wanted. "We're not here to cause a ruckus," he said. "You don't have to run from us. We'll get a movie, then be on our way."

It happened in a blink—I didn't see Midnight move until the wrench went flying from her hand, smacking the side of Jared's head. He stumbled to the side, clutching his temple, and fell against the Action section, knocking the whole shelf over. Movies broke free from their boxes and skittered across the floor.

I used the distraction to rip my arm away from Brett, grab my phone, and run behind the counter. Jared got to his feet and wiped his mouth with the back of his hand. He'd turned beet red and an angry vein throbbed at his temple. He took one step forward. I shoved Midnight behind me, and she was trembling so bad, she didn't even fight it.

With shaky fingers, I unlocked my phone and dialed 9-1-1. The operator answered on the first ring. "We're being attacked by two drunk guys at the Honeyfield Video and Repair on Main." I didn't let Jared out of my sight, daring him to take another step in our direction.

"Dude." Brett's eyes grew as big as Eric's had when I'd faked my allergy. He looked between me and the ruined Action section of the store. "Let's go."

He grabbed Jared, who seemed intent on staying put,

hate etching hard lines in his face. Brett finally managed to haul Jared out the door, and Midnight ran to lock it before they could change their minds and come back.

I stayed on the phone until the lock clicked into place.

I called Mom and Gram to let them know what had happened and explain why it would be a while before I'd be home. Mom wanted to come right away, but I had the car, and no way would I let her walk the streets at night alone when I had no clue where Jared and Brett had gone. I assured her over and over again that the police were on their way, no one had hurt me, she could go to bed, and I'd be home when I finished cleaning up. It took twenty minutes just to get her off the phone.

Sheriff Mulder and Deputy Jeff Harrington, Lance's older brother, came and took our statements. They couldn't do much to Brett, but they'd bring in Jared for violating the restraining order. Jeff almost looked giddy at the idea of charging Jared. Or maybe he was just giddy he'd get to play a real cop in a town that didn't see a lot of action outside the drunk tank. Midnight called Elise and reassured her that she didn't need to come, the same way I'd reassured my mom. Then she called her brother Travis.

After Midnight gave her brother the details and hung up, she turned to me. "Since the sheriff can't do anything about Brett, Travis and his friends will."

I shivered. Farm boys had their own brand of justice.

With the police gone, the store had gone quiet again. I went into the closet/break room and rifled around in the drawers until I found the bottle of peach schnapps.

I set the bottle in front of Midnight. "We could both use a shot."

She unscrewed the top and took a deep swallow. "You probably have a lot of questions."

"Only if you feel like sharing." I had a million questions, but after what she'd gone through, there wasn't a chance in hell I'd put any pressure on her to provide answers.

She sat in front of the counter, facing the ruin of the Action section we'd have to clean up before we left. After taking another sip from the bottle, she passed it to me, and motioned for me to sit beside her. "I used to date Jared in high school."

"I know," I said. When she gave me a sharp look, I shook my head. "I didn't know before tonight, but when he called you Lexi, I remembered you, sort of, from school."

She tilted her head back until it rested against the counter. "His parents' farm is about a mile down the road from my parents' farm. They're not friends. My parents are gentle and Jared's daddy is hard, and they were always like oil and water. I think that's probably why I paid Jared any mind. The whole Romeo and Juliet thing at sixteen is a powerful lure."

"I can see that," I said, twirling the bottle of schnapps between my hands.

"Anyway, we started dating, and he was something else. All the guys in our grade were afraid of him, even Brett, and as much as I hate myself for it now, it felt good to be with the kind of guy who made other people afraid."

"Why?" I'd never gotten the alpha male appeal. My mom sometimes liked them in her romance novels, but in real life they were a total nightmare.

Midnight shrugged. "Big strong man playing the protector. No other guys would go near me. I was Jared's girl, and that scared them enough to keep away. I guess I felt special. Being a farm girl in a house with seven other kids, I didn't get to feel special too often."

"I'm sorry." When I was little, I desperately wanted to be part of a big rowdy family like the farm kids had. To be surrounded by people close to my age, instead of a bunch of old quilting Bee ladies. I'd never considered the downsides of that.

"It is what it is." Midnight waved it away like it was no big deal. "Jared's daddy, he had a temper when he drank, and he knew how to leave bruises on Jared's momma where no one else could see them. Sometimes I'd be at their house for supper, and I'd see his momma wincing in pain when she bent down to take the chicken from the oven."

"Jesus." She hadn't been kidding when she said Jared learned his mean at his daddy's knee. "Did . . ." I clenched my fists. "Did Jared ever leave bruises on you?"

"No." Her eyes darkened.

I blew out a breath of relief. Jared was all muscle from working on the farm his whole life, and Midnight was barely bigger than Gram. If he had hit her, he would've broken bones.

"How did you get out of the relationship?" I didn't ask why they broke up. With the way things had gone down earlier, the pure terror that shook her to her feet when she saw him walk in, I knew it hadn't been a breakup. She'd escaped.

"It started after we'd just eaten supper and his daddy was in a bad mood. Drunk, of course." Midnight's expression hardened. Not like when she and I got into it over dumb work pranks, but absolute, unfiltered rage. "He and Jared got into an argument, don't even remember over what, and his daddy backhanded him. Right there at the table while he was sitting next to me. I froze, scared out of my mind. I still see his split lip and feel his shame from that night. He dropped me off at home, said he'd call me later, didn't want to talk about it."

I grabbed her hand and found it sweat-slicked. "His dad deserves to burn in hell."

"Without a doubt," she said. "Jared never brought it up again. Then one night we were all drinking at the Brewster farm. Jared and Brett had one too many beers and started throwing their weight around. Jeff Harrington got mouthy and Jared coldcocked him. Laid him right out on the barn floor."

"Deputy Jeff?" Holy shit. No wonder he looked happy about hauling in Jared.

She nodded. "I'd been drinking too, and everyone wanted to leave after that. I was pissed he ruined our night, so I said . . ." She swallowed. "I didn't even mean it seriously, but I said he was just as bad as his daddy. He turned on me then, and I swear to God, I saw his daddy in his eyes. I backed away, but he grabbed my hair and wrapped it around his wrist, like he was about to drag me out of the barn and do God knows what."

"That was not your fault." I squeezed her hand. "No matter what you said to him, no matter how much you were both drinking, it wasn't your fault."

"I thought he was going to kill me," she said, her voice a whisper on the air. "Travis came up behind him and hit him over the head with a manure shovel. Jared fell to the ground and Travis grabbed me and took me straight home to tell our parents what happened. They made me call the police and file a restraining order."

"I'm glad they did," I said.

"I was so scared he was going to break into our house and drag me out by my hair to finish what he'd started. I cut it all off that night."

I understood then why she'd given me that look the day I came to work all done up after my *Dirty Dancing* video. Like she'd recognized my chosen armor, because it was hers, too. The short black hair, so different from her golden waves, the heavy powder and eyeliner, the general bite in her voice. All perfectly constructed to keep people an arm's length away. Never letting anyone look too closely, forgetting all about Lexi until Lexi ceased to exist.

"Is this why you and Elise had trouble the last time you were together?" I asked.

"Relationships are hard for me." She picked at the black

nail polish on her thumb. "I'm trying to get better at them. I told Travis I was bi when I was fifteen, so he's the only one in my family who knows about Elise. She probably should've been done with me a long time ago, but for some reason she thinks I'm worth it."

"Because you are worth it." I gave her a shoulder bump because I knew she wasn't the hugging type. "I'm sorry I never considered you might have your own stuff going on. I only saw my best friend hurting, but you also make her really happy, so I guess it evens out."

"Thank you." She stood and offered me her hand. "I'm sorry I put liquid laxatives in your Dr Pepper after you removed the *F* from my shift supervisor sign."

"I take back my sorry."

She laughed. The sound surprised me as much as it had the day I pulled the wrench out to scare that hipster. It wasn't one I heard often. "Too late."

"I sat on the toilet for two days!"

"Trust me, I'm aware." She gave me an evil grin.

I sighed, shaking my head at the mess spread out before us. "We really have to stop brawling in the store. We'll both be fired if we keep this up."

"Who's going to fire us?" She smirked. "Butch?"

"Fair point." Lucky for us, none of our fights occurred during those two hours a month when Butch remembered he had a job and actually attempted to do it. "Should we get started?"

We tipped the shelf back up, and it took us half an

hour to hunt down all the tapes that had broken out of their boxes. Another two hours to put them back in alphabetical order. We finished and locked up, and out in the parking lot, Midnight stopped me.

"I know you're in the middle of some stuff right now," she said.

Understatement of the year. "Yeah?"

"Now that you know my situation, I hope you'll believe me when I say you'll be okay. Sometimes you just have to get through it before you can see it, but on the other side? You'll figure out who you are and what you're really made of."

"Promise?"

She nodded and gave me a genuine smile before climbing into her car. Huh. I think I just became friends with Midnight. This week kept getting stranger.

And the next time Butch bothered to show up, I'd chew him five new assholes, and I didn't care if he was the manager. He'd probably fire me and then forget he'd done it the next day anyway. He never should've left Midnight to close by herself, and if those people from Iowa hadn't come in, I wouldn't have been there with her when Jared showed up. I rubbed my arms against the chill, wishing I'd brought a hoodie to tug on over my clothes.

CHAPTER
NINETEEN

I WENT STRAIGHT HOME. It had been a hell of a night, and all that sleepless scrolling had finally caught up with me. Peg's car still sat in our drive, which meant Gram and Peg had both waited up for me. Probably because Mom had to work in the morning. It was way past both of their regular bedtimes. Or maybe they'd already slept for the night, and were now up for the day. It was after one in the morning. All I wanted to do was peel off my dress, bury myself under the covers, and forget this whole day had ever happened.

My phone buzzed on the passenger seat. Eric: *Why haven't you been online today?*

Ugh. Me: *Leave me alone. I was almost assaulted tonight.*

A minute later. Eric: *Are you okay?*

Me: *Don't insult my intelligence by acting like you care.*

Eric: *Fine. You can upload the video tomorrow.*

I rolled my eyes and resisted the urge to toss my phone out the window and run over it a few times. I went inside, threw my keys on the kitchen counter, and followed the porch light out to the Hamptons. Gram and Peg sat on the beach recliners, howling like the alley cats behind the Video and Repair. An earthy scent wafted on the breeze.

They passed a crumpled Pepsi can back and forth, with smoke curling around them.

It had been a while since they'd gotten into Peg's medicinal marijuana. She'd gotten the prescription for her rheumatoid arthritis years ago, and every once in a while, usually after a really bad day, they'd get higher than kites. They never invited Donna. Probably because she had her own stash, and not of the medical variety.

I stopped in front of them and put my hands on my hips. "Aren't you two up late?"

"Macy!" Gram's red-rimmed eyes were half closed, but she sounded nearly as chipper as Mom. She had her raptor foot in the kiddie pool. Mom would have to bleach the entire thing tomorrow. "Look, Peg. Macy's home."

Peg slowly turned her head to me. "You look like a cupcake."

"I want a cupcake," Gram said.

Amusement quirked my lips. "You two stoners can go to bed now. I'm home and safe."

"Come sit down." Gram motioned to me with her hand, then paused to watch the motion. "We're too buzzed to sleep yet."

Sighing, I grabbed a lawn chair from behind the shed and sat between them. "If you want to know how things went with Jared, Lance's brother is bringing him in."

"What we really want to know is: Pat Sajak, Bob Barker, or Alex Trebek?" Peg's glazed eyes had tears of laughter in them.

"Fuck, marry, kill," Gram said with absolute seriousness.

"Jesus." I looked between them. "How high are you two?"

"Marry Alex Trebek," Peg said. "I like 'em smart. Though he'd probably make us say our vows in the form of a question. Fuck Bob Barker, and kill Pat Sajak because he's utterly useless." I had a feeling she only added Pat Sajak to the kill list to get a rise out of Gram.

"You would pick those." Gram frowned. "Marry Pat Sajak, only because I'd get to spend time with the Queen. Kill Bob Barker. He looks like a sex maniac."

"Why do you think I wanted to fuck him?" Peg laughed.

"Fuck Alex Trebek, because that's my only option left," Gram said.

"I'll take: Macy is horrified and grossed out by this whole conversation for two hundred." I rose to my feet and stretched my arms above my head. It had been a long day, and this was just the cherry on top of a bizarre series of events.

"You never did tell me about your big date with the baseball boy. Did you have a nice time?" Gram asked.

"No." I hadn't. Eric was a complete tool, and while entering into an alliance with him benefited me, it also made me feel like whatever fungus had grown beneath Gram's rotten toenail. "He's not a nice or honest boy, Gram."

"Did he hurt you?" She gripped my arm through the smoky haze.

"No." I patted her hand, which was dry and wrinkled and spotted with age, but steady. She'd always been the steady one in our family. "I just don't like him all that much."

"Then don't see him again," Peg said. "There are plenty of nice and honest boys right here in Honeyfield. Some of them live up the hill on the other side of the woods."

I did not want to talk about Paxton with Peg and Gram. Not under normal circumstances, and definitely not while they were high. "Good night."

I left them to their Pepsi can, and as I shut the screen door, they started debating which daytime TV hosts they'd fuck, marry, or kill. My bedroom was warm, even with the window open and the soft summer air drifting in. I pulled off the dress, hung it in my closet, and grabbed a wrinkled T-shirt and cotton shorts from the laundry basket of clean clothes.

I kicked off the quilt, but kept the sheet over my legs. Ever since I was a little girl, I had this notion that if my legs were uncovered in bed, the Vanna dolls would eat them in my sleep. It remained enough of a fear to become a habit.

As I drifted off, I decided I'd talk to Paxton tomorrow. I didn't care if he was mad at me, or I was mad at him. I didn't want to throw away what we could possibly be for a bunch of subscribers who might not even stay loyal after the Baseball Babe hype died down.

Then I'd have to figure out what to do about Eric.

I woke up to my phone buzzing at seven. The first time in days where nightmares hadn't woken me up in the middle of the night, and I had to get texts when I'd barely gotten five hours of sleep. Someone had better be on fire or dead.

I yanked my phone out of the charger and scowled at it.

Eric: *Are you asleep?*

Eric: *Why haven't you uploaded the video yet?*

Eric: *Everyone on Twitter is asking where it is*

How could he be awake already when he'd been texting me at one last night? Vampire. That was the only explanation for his ridiculous schedule and even more ridiculous good looks.

Me: *Go away. I'll upload it when I'm awake*

Eric: *But if you're not awake, how could you be texting me right now?*

Asshole. I uploaded the video so he'd leave me alone, and I tried to go back to sleep, but it was too late. I rolled out of bed and shuffled into the dining room. Gram and Peg both had enormous mugs of coffee on their side tables, looking as if they'd been out all night partying like teenagers. Even if their voices were lively, their bodies hadn't gotten the message. Donna kept eyeing them like she knew they'd gotten high without her, but she kept her full lips pressed together as she concentrated on her quilt square.

"What are you doing up so early?" Gram asked.

"I could ask you the same thing, considering—"

"Macy, be a dear and put on another pot of coffee," Peg cut in.

Fine. What happens in the Hamptons stays in the Hamptons. I got the second pot going and leaned against the counter, turning a toaster pastry over in my hands as I debated if my stomach could handle breakfast. Mom came into the kitchen a moment later, her hair tied up and apron already on. She had the seven-thirty-to-four shift today.

She immediately pulled me into a bone-crushing hug.

"I'm going to murder Jared and that other idiot. They're going to learn what happens when they mess with my daughter."

"No need." I patted her back. "Midnight's brother supposedly took care of it."

She pulled back, her mouth set in a grim line. "Good."

Our fight yesterday hung heavy between us. The words had been bottled up for so long, they'd just spewed out in the worst way possible. I'd already apologized, but I wasn't sorry for what I'd said; I was just sorry for the way I'd said it. Still, she hadn't backed down on her misguided "no coworkers" mantra. Not that it mattered. Paxton and I weren't even talking.

Mom brushed my cheek. "Listen, Macy—"

"Don't you have to get to work?" I didn't want to get into it again. There were a lot of unfinished words between us, and I had a feeling she'd taken on an extra dose of worry after the Jared incident, which only would've made me want to reassure her when I didn't know if that was the role I still wanted to play in our relationship.

She bit her lip and looked at the clock again. "Yes. But we'll talk more tonight, okay?"

As she rushed out the door, I poured myself a cup of coffee. Nasty stuff, but my eyelids felt like lead. I checked YouTube to see how my video with Eric was faring. Ten thousand views already. Who were these sleepless monsters? I closed the app and stared out at the Hamptons.

CHAPTER
TWENTY

THAT EVENING, I WENT into work for my shift. Friday nights were always busy, but twice a month we pushed the shelves against the walls to open up the store and pull down the giant projection screen. Honeyfield didn't have a movie theater, so like with a lot of other things, we made our own. We charged five dollars at the door, first come, first served until we were at full capacity. Old folks lined up camp chairs in the back, while younger people and families took up the floor with blankets and coolers like Movie in the Park, minus the park. Tourists who regularly passed through our town loved it, and locals didn't have much else to do, so we filled up fast. Some people even dressed up as characters from our features. It was a whole thing.

I loved dressing up for movie night—especially because it often allowed me to recycle some of those costumes Gram had helped me with for my reviews—but between my fight with Paxton and my run-in with Jared, I'd forgotten all about it. And *Mean Girls* had so many iconic outfits too, damn it. Brady gave me a shy wave from behind the register. Even he'd worn a pink polo in an easy nod to Cady Heron.

"Hey, look, Batman—Robin is here," Elise said to

Midnight as she jumped off the counter where they'd been talking. Elise's long dark hair and big eyes were hidden behind a blue hoodie and sunglasses. "You two had one hell of a night."

"Why am I Robin?" I asked. "I want to be Batman."

Elise gave me an incredulous look. "Are you serious? Our Midnight is literally the Dark Knight of Honeyfield, and she's the one who has done the actual ass-kicking."

Okay. Solid points. I still wanted to be Batman.

Midnight smiled at Elise. "Thank you, love."

"Where's your costume?" Elise asked me. "Don't you live for these nights?"

I glanced down at my short-sleeved yellow sweater and jeans. "I'm the extra who shoves another girl against the lockers during the big fight scene. You only see the back of her head, but I was going for understated."

"Deep," Brady said.

Indeed.

Midnight had the night off, but she stuck around so she and Elise could have a date night of sorts. Even though they wouldn't so much as hold hands in public, and Elise was on call and could leave at any moment. It was still sweet. And so much more than Midnight had been willing to do even six months ago. She'd really meant it when she said things would be different this time around.

Brady and I were responsible for running movie night, but once we dealt with the initial rush of people trying to get in the door, it pretty much ran itself. I set up the rickety wooden table and metal box for the entry fee. Brady got the projector and DVD set up.

"Ready?" I asked him. He gave me a thumbs-up, and I unlocked the door.

Lenny Jackson, formerly of the Jackson farm before he sold it to his son and moved into town, hobbled in with his camp chair under his arm. "Don't know why you kids can't show a good, old-fashioned shoot-'em-up once in a while."

"I hear your cries, Mr. Jackson." I took his five and he set up his chair at the back of the store. He bitched about every movie we featured, but it didn't stop him from being first through the door every other Friday.

A steady stream of people flowed in off the sidewalk for the next half hour. Brady gave me a nod to let me know we were almost at capacity—just enough room left for one more small family or a couple. I turned back around to let the people coming in next know they were last, and froze on the spot. Paxton stood before me.

With his arm draped over the shoulders of Strawberry Sinclair.

My heart dropped to my stomach. Paxton brought a date to movie night, when he knew damn well I'd be working. Strawberry—who had been cursed with an incredibly awful name, but made up for it by being all sweetness and sunshine—shifted uncomfortably at Paxton's side. With his goofy face that was somehow cute even when it shouldn't have been, and her miles of golden-brown hair and her heart-shaped face, they made a perfect little picture. The boy who raised bunnies was out on a date with the farmer's daughter who was active in 4-H and loved animals more than people. She'd be perfect for Paxton. Just perfect.

He had the nerve to smile when he handed me a ten.

"I . . . uh . . ." *Am dying? Want to punch you in your solar plexus?* Oh God. Tears gathered under my lids. I couldn't do this. I couldn't let him think this upset me. I had to play this casual. No big deal. "What the fuck do you think you're doing?"

Nailed it.

The Brewsters shuffled their grandkids to the far end of the store, shooting me dirty looks over their shoulders. Like they wouldn't be learning worse words from the movie. Strawberry bit her lip while Brady glared at us, his arms crossed over his broad chest. Awesome. I'd somehow managed to piss off the nicest guy in town. But seriously, who hasn't dropped an f-bomb or two at a family-friendly function?

"Come on, Macy." Paxton lowered his voice. "That's not fair and you know it."

I swallowed the lump in my throat. Of course it wasn't fair. He was free to date whoever he wanted. We'd both said some ugly things to each other we probably couldn't ever take back, and where else was he supposed to take a date in this town? I put his ten in the metal box and slammed the lid shut a little harder than intended.

"You're right." I tried to plaster on a smile and it hurt; it hurt so bad, I thought my whole face might crack. "I hope you fall in love and make lots of pretty babies together."

Jealousy was such a gross emotion. If it were a color, it would be chartreuse.

Strawberry choked and took a noticeable step away from Paxton, unhooking his arm from her shoulder in the process. "I didn't really sign up for marriage and babies."

"Who said anything about marriage?" I asked.

A long shadow fell over the three of us, and I glanced up at Brady. I hadn't seen him so visibly pissed since the day he'd stood up to Jared. "Is this how it's going to be?" Brady asked.

Huh. He hadn't been glaring at me after all. I looked back over at Strawberry. She cringed for a brief second before snuggling back up to Paxton. I knew that game. And I had the likes, retweets, and subscribers to prove it.

I pointed between Paxton and Strawberry. "I see what's going on here. Well played, you two. You had me there for a moment."

Strawberry rolled her eyes and grabbed Paxton's hand. "Let's go find some seats."

She bumped into Brady as she passed, and not in a friendly way. For some reason it made me like her more. Even though she was technically helping Paxton in his Make Macy Feel Like Shit campaign, I appreciated the reason why she'd done it.

I jumped off my seat to hang the At Capacity sign on the door, really more of an excuse to get my feelings under control. By the time I turned back around, Brady still stood in the same place, slack-jawed.

I rested my elbow on his shoulder, which I had to raise over my head at an odd angle. "Looks like we've got the same problem. Want to be my pathetic pity date for the night?"

A low, humorless chuckle rumbled in Brady's chest. "We're working."

"Hey, Midnight!" one of the Brewster boys yelled. "Nice Janis Ian costume."

Midnight hadn't dressed up.

"I think you better start that movie before a murder is committed," I whispered to Brady.

He nodded and dimmed the lights before Midnight could launch herself across the store. She had an amazing amount of velocity for someone so tiny. Like a scary Wes Craven–esque hummingbird.

I hadn't watched where Paxton had gone, but it didn't stop my eyes from seeking him out anyway. He and Strawberry had laid out a blanket and put their backs against the counter, right underneath the register. I had a strong urge to drop the wrench on Paxton's head and see how accidental I could make it look. They didn't act like two people on a date, though. They were both job interview levels of stiff and formal. In fact, I'd shown more affection for the salmon Eric had tried to shove down my throat.

Paxton caught me staring, and before I could look away, he leaned toward Strawberry and whispered in her ear. Whatever the two of them were up to, they both sucked at faking it. It would've been comical if it hadn't been done in part to get a rise out of me. I stuck my nose in the air and hopped up on my stool behind the register. It didn't bother me that Paxton had purposely tried to hurt me. Not at all. Because the first rule of professional-level faking: you had to convince yourself before you had a chance of convincing anyone else.

I zoned out during the first half of the movie, keeping my ears trained in the direction of the not-so-happy couple on the other side of the counter, and my eyes on Brady's expressions. He loomed in the back, his face illuminated by the projector, and he had a clear line of sight of the two people who had us both on edge. Every time he frowned, I had the urge to lean over the counter until I could see for myself what was going on.

Strawberry got up to use the bathroom, and because I had no shame, I took the opportunity to claim her seat next to Paxton. "Date going well?" I asked.

He shook his head and turned back toward the movie. "It's fine."

"I get what you're doing. I even get why." I reached across him and took some of his M&M's because again, no shame. Goose bumps peppered my arm when I brushed his. "But do you have to torture Brady, too? He has nothing to do with why you're pissed at me."

Paxton gave me a cold stare. "Contrary to what you believe, the world doesn't revolve around you."

"I never said it did." I popped an M&M into my mouth. "I only pointed out your obvious sham, and just because I'm ninety-nine percent sure it has something to do with me, doesn't mean I'm a narcissist."

We both turned at the sound of the bell dinging above the entrance. Just in time to see Strawberry's golden-brown hair flying out the door, Brady not far behind. I gave him a mental fist bump.

"Oh darn," I said. "Looks like you lost your date."

"Looks like it," Paxton said without much heat. He stood and dusted off his jeans. "Enjoy your movie, Macy Mae."

The bell dinged again as Paxton walked out of the store, and I only half pretended I'd sat through the credits hoping he'd eventually come back.

CHAPTER
TWENTY-ONE

SUNDAY MORNING I SAT in bed with my quilt pulled over my head like a floral cave. After the Friday night movie disaster, Saturday had been a blur of suckage I'd rather not remember. Work had kept me busy, and Paxton had taken the on-call shift and spent it at the Jackson farm repairing their leaky garage freezer. He really went above and beyond to avoid me. Which not only annoyed me on a me level, but it also validated my mom's stance on not complicating work with romance. Or, in my case, not-romance. Elise and Midnight had offered to take me out and get me grossly drunk after work, but I had big plans to stay in and scroll through Twitter until I passed out in a puddle of my own misery. Good times.

Since the Bees chattering away had pulled me out of sleep at seven, I decided to open YouTube and see how my dinner video with Eric was doing. We'd passed half a million views. I tried to muster some kind of excitement, at the very least a Judd Nelson fist pump, but I had nothing. It was as if all those things I wanted were happening to someone else, and I was just a spectator on the outside. I was numb, underwhelmed, and uninspired. I didn't even want to do another movie review, since my *Dirty Dancing* one had gotten so many thumbs-downs.

If I left the video alone, it would easily reach a million views. My golden ticket. The magic number I'd been waiting years for. But it would also send a clear message about the kind of person I'd chosen to be. About what I'd be willing to do for clickbait.

Having a video hit a million didn't mean anything if I didn't come by it honestly. It would never be my accomplishment. And if I couldn't get a million views on my own with my regular content, what was the point?

If I deleted the video, my YouTube channel might suffer, my business arrangement with Eric would definitely suffer, but I'd still have my soul. That had to be worth something.

I logged on to Video Manager, and my finger hovered over the delete button. One click and it would be gone. A few more clicks and my Twitter would go with it. Gritting my teeth, I shut down the app and left my phone on my bed while I went to get ready for the day. I couldn't delete the video. I wanted to. Just like I wanted to quit scrolling through Twitter in the middle of the night, but in the end, I couldn't do that, either. I'd built my entire world and every plan for my future around YouTube, and I wasn't ready to test who I'd be without it.

After I took a shower and dried my hair, I headed into the dining room. Peg and Donna were already taking swipes at each other, and no wonder. They didn't have their usual peacekeeper to sit between them.

"Where's Gigi?" I asked.

The three Bees looked at each other, then back at their patterns. Weird.

"She'll be along later," Gram said.

I didn't stick around. They'd gotten far enough into their quilt where they wouldn't want me peeking at it before the big show. With Mom already gone to work, I curled up on the recliner in the living room. Eric tweeted about making plans with me for next weekend (he hadn't), and I didn't have enough energy to do more than like it.

I closed Twitter and went into my saved photos, pulling up the one Elise had sent me of Paxton messing with Midnight last week. A tight fist wrapped around my heart and squeezed. I missed him. Not just the kissing, though that had been excellent. I missed his lopsided smile and his late-night texts and his self-deprecating sense of humor and the ridiculous way he let Gigi dress him and the way he looked when he held one of his bunnies. I missed all of him. And I couldn't stand to go another day with all this nothingness between us.

We needed a grand gesture. The tropiest of tropes. The heart and soul of every eighties rom-com. The very thing I'm pretty sure had turned my mom into a lifelong romantic. And I had the best/worst idea on what to do.

I went down to the basement and dug out Gram's old boom box from the 1980s, and blessed her for never throwing anything away. It probably didn't work since it had been rotting in the basement for at least twenty years, but it didn't matter. I had Peter Gabriel's "In Your Eyes" already downloaded on my phone. It would have to do. I'd stand in front of Paxton's bedroom window like Lloyd stood outside Diane's in *Say Anything*, and it would be cheesy and sweet and awful enough that he would have to talk to me.

I went out the front, around the house, and cut through the woods to Paxton's. Bumblebees hummed over wildflowers as the morning sun cast a greenish glow through the canopy of leaves. The world still rolled on peacefully, while my insides twisted worse than the summer storms that would blow our kiddie pool into the next neighborhood. This had to work. I wanted him, I missed my friend, and I was tired of waiting for him to figure out how much he missed me too. Besides, I'd already been humiliated, shamed, lost all sense of right and honesty, so it wasn't like I had a whole lot more to lose. Like Midnight had said, sometimes you just had to go through it before you figured out what you were really made of.

I'd just reached the top of the hill, when I spotted an unfamiliar car in the driveway. Lisbeth stood on the front porch in her nursing home uniform. Loose tendrils of gray hair had come undone from her bun. Gigi was next to Lisbeth, her arm around Paxton, who kept his head down, as if waiting for the ground to swallow him up. The three of them stood before a middle-aged couple. The woman had soft brown hair, the same shade as Paxton's, and she was crying. The man next to her frowned, and the familiar expression stirred something in me. Even though the man was years older, I'd seen the same look on Paxton's face the night I'd told him about my arrangement with Eric. Same nose, same jawline, same downward tilt of his mouth.

A lead weight dropped in my stomach as the realization set in. I was looking at Paxton's parents. The ones everyone assumed were dead.

A twig snapped under my foot and everyone turned to look at me standing at the edge of the property line. Paxton lifted his head, and when he caught my gaze, the fear pouring out of him nearly knocked me over. It was a million times worse than the day he'd shown up at my house when the bloggers were there. A worry line creased across Gigi's forehead as she looked between the two of us. My palms were sweating so bad, I nearly dropped the boom box. Then I hurled the boom box into the woods, because I suddenly realized how immensely ridiculous I must've looked. I didn't know what to say or what to do with my body.

"Sorry to interrupt," I choked out. "I'm not really here. You didn't see me. I'm so sorry."

Without waiting for anyone to respond, I backed away and disappeared into the trees.

CHAPTER
TWENTY-TWO

PAXTON'S PARENTS WERE ALIVE. I had no idea what that meant. He'd been living with Lisbeth and Gigi for nine years, wouldn't drive, wouldn't talk about why. Everyone in town assumed his parents had died in a car accident and he had some kind of survivor's guilt.

Maybe his parents were drug addicts, even though they didn't really look like it, but Eric hadn't looked like a vampire, and Midnight certainly didn't look like the fresh-faced farm girl I knew from school either. Looks were super-deceiving. Or maybe they were horrific abusers. The thought of that made my heart ache. Whatever had happened when Paxton was nine was bad enough that he still didn't want to talk about it, and I'd just interrupted a very intense family meeting with my boy drama.

I flopped onto a beach recliner in the Hamptons and nearly took off my sandal to dip my feet in the water, when I remembered that Gram had had her raptor foot in there and Mom hadn't gotten the chance to bleach the pool yet. My next movie review was due to be uploaded tomorrow, but I didn't have anything prepared, and I didn't care. I had no energy.

"Hey." Paxton stood at the edge of the Hamptons, his

hands in his pockets.

I nearly fell off my beach recliner. "Hi."

We stared at each other for what felt like a full minute, not saying anything. I didn't know if he was waiting for an invitation into the Hamptons. It's not like I'd ever bothered to ask permission before I'd wandered into his backyard.

"You can sit down," I said. "Don't put your feet in the pool."

"Okay." He took the lawn chair I'd sat in when Gram and Peg had gotten high. "Do I want to know why you showed up at my house at eight in the morning with a boom box?"

"I was trying to be cute." I hit play on the Peter Gabriel song on my phone and held my arms over my head where the boom box would've been if I hadn't thrown it into the woods. When he cracked a smile, I shut the song off. "An important moment in cinematic history."

"You don't need gimmicks to be cute." He stared at his hands. "I think you're cute all the time, just the way you are."

My face heated. "You do still?"

"I'm sorry." He knotted his fingers together with his head bent low, as if in prayer. "I've been a complete asshole. I know you saw right through my date with Strawberry, but I still shouldn't have brought her to movie night. Seeing you go viral triggered a lot of things for me, and seeing you embrace it is hard. But you were right. It is your life, and your decision, and my personal issues shouldn't get in the way of the things you're trying to do."

All the lingering doubt I had about keeping things going with Eric vanished. I didn't need gimmicks or the Fly Ball Girl persona. I just needed to be me. And if that wasn't good enough for the Twitter masses and my recent subscribers, then I didn't need their approval anyway. The people I knew, the ones I cared about, liked me just fine.

They were the only ones who mattered.

"I miss you," I said.

Paxton's gaze was blazing. "I miss you more than you can possibly know."

"I'm going to do a thing, and I want you to watch." And wow, inuendo. Judging by Paxton's smirk, he hadn't missed it either. I fumbled with my phone as I strived to recover from my awkward wording. "I'm shutting down the Baseball Babe stuff."

"You don't have to do that."

"I want to. It's not good for my mental health." The constant scrolling, the sleepless nights, the anxiety, the nightmares . . . I couldn't do it anymore. Twitter was slowly eating me alive, and the more I engaged, the hungrier it became.

I proceeded to delete every tweet I'd sent in the last week. Next I flipped over to the Video Manager in YouTube. With only a small pang for the lost revenue, I deleted both of my Eric videos. I also deleted the *Dirty Dancing* video for good measure. The movie my mom had used to teach me about reproductive rights deserved better. And so did the subscribers who'd been with me before Baseball Babe.

"I'm done with all of it." I stood and Paxton watched me with increasing intensity as I sat on his lap and wrapped my arms around his neck. "I don't want to be the person who gives away their entire sense of self for clicks. I never wanted to be that person."

His hand skimmed my bare thigh, which I'd taken the time to shave this morning. "Are you sure that's what you want? If you need to play the part for YouTube, I'd understand."

He wouldn't like it, but he'd understand, because he understood me. The real me. "I'm very sure. Eric is going to be furious, but whatever."

Speak of the devil and he shall appear. My phone buzzed with a series of texts and I barely glanced at it.

Eric: *Macy*

Eric: *Macy, why are you deleting tweets???*

Eric: *You BITCH! YOU FUCKING BITCH!!!*

Oops. Someone just checked YouTube.

Eric: *Macy, I'm sorry. I didn't mean that. Please text me back. I want to help you. I want to give you the life you've always dreamed of, the life we both want.*

I shut my phone off and threw it into the grass.

Paxton wrapped his arms around my waist and held me tighter. "I'm so sorry. For everything. You had to put up with so much shit this week."

"Karma will take care of Eric. I hope he gets uncurable anal fleas and has to spend the rest of his days dragging his ass across the floor like the dog he is."

"Wow." Paxton's hands roamed up my back in a gentle stroking motion, and I shivered in response. "You really are Bizzy's granddaughter."

I caught his mouth with my own and kissed him. His arms tightened around me, like he was afraid I'd blow away if he didn't hold on. I nipped his bottom lip, and he tilted my head back, kissing me so deep that my entire body shuddered in response.

"It's about damn time!" Peg hollered.

We instantly broke apart and looked at the kitchen window, where Peg, Gram, and Donna had their faces pressed against the screen. Grinning like fools, all three of them.

"Don't you have a quilt to make?" I asked.

"We're retired. We've got nothing but time," Donna said. "Go on back to your kissing."

"Sorry, you three ruined the moment. There will be no more kissing today." I waved them away, and they left the window, grumbling the whole time. I glanced at Paxton and even his ears had gone red. "If you're going to date me, you might as well get used to this. The Bees are part of the package."

"I live with a Bee; I know how they are. I'd just prefer not to make out in front of them, if that's okay with you."

I laughed and hugged him, wanting that closeness, even if we weren't kissing. "I'd rather not make out in front of them either, the old pervs. Just wait until I tell you about the conversation Peg and Gram had the other night. I will never be able to scrub it from my brain, and I'm now going to subject you to it so I don't have to suffer alone."

He kissed my neck. "There's no one else I'd rather suffer with more than you."

I pulled back, skimming my fingers over his cheek. I didn't want to do anything to dim the light and easiness between us, but . . . "Do you want to talk about this morning?" I paused. "About your parents?"

"No." He buried his face in my shoulder. "But I probably should."

"You don't have to." I rubbed his arms.

"I need to." He lifted his head. "If we're going to do this me and you thing, I think you need to know some things about me, and decide . . ." He gulped. "And decide if this is something you still want to do."

No matter what he said, I wouldn't walk away from him. It had taken me way too much to get here in the first place. But if he needed to get it off his chest, then I'd be there for him, the way I knew he'd be there for me.

"I'm listening," I said.

"I had a sister." He turned his head, like he couldn't stand to look at me while he talked. "Her name was Daisy. She was five and loved art. Her fingers were always covered in chalk dust and no matter how many times my mom washed her hair, she always had streaks of paint in it."

"She sounds really sweet," I said. I hadn't missed the past tense reference.

"She was, and I was her hero, even though I mostly thought she was a pain in the ass when she'd paint on my walls." He gave a pain-laced smile at the memory, and I'd never seen anything more heartbreaking in my life. "She loved to draw me pictures. Of baseballs and bats and diamonds, and sometimes stick figures of me in uniform."

My grip on his arm tightened a fraction. "You played baseball?"

"Little League. My dad was the coach."

"Is that why all this fly ball stuff—"

"No." He blew out a breath. "Baseball is a smaller trigger, one I can usually handle. Social media, especially the viral stuff, that's what I have trouble with. And driving."

"Okay." I grabbed his hand, in case he needed something to hold on to.

"We had to get to a game. My dad started the car, and then remembered he'd left his wallet on the kitchen table. So he ran back inside to get it. He said he'd be right back." He choked on the last word and I squeezed his hand.

"You don't have to tell me any more if this is too much," I said. Tears hovered in his eyes. Even though I wanted to know what had happened, and wanted him to feel comfortable enough with me to tell me, I would've done anything to keep them from falling.

"I'm okay." He squeezed my hand back. "I just need a second." He took several deep breaths, like it was a technique he was used to, like he'd had to calm and center himself countless times in the past. "I was restless and horsing around in the car. Normal behavior for nine-year-old boys, according to my therapist."

"That *is* normal." I'd babysat enough a few years ago to know how fidgety and energetic kids at that age could be.

"I'm not there yet. Sometimes I can look back and say I was just being a kid, but those days are few and far between. I'm trying. Therapy helps."

I'd had no idea he was in therapy. "I'm glad it helps."

"I found one of my mom's cloth headbands she wore at

the gym, in a cup holder." He took another deep breath. "I thought it would make a good slingshot. I looped it over the gear shift and pulled it back, and put the car in reverse. We had a steep driveway."

I could see him then, a nine-year-old boy in his Little League uniform, messing around in the car while his dad ran inside. The fear he must've felt when the car shifted into reverse and started rolling backward. He wouldn't have understood how to stop it.

"I didn't know." He paused, his breath coming out faster, more panicked. The tears hovering in his eyes broke free. "I didn't know Daisy had snuck out of the house with her chalk. That she wanted to draw a picture on the sidewalk, of me winning the game, for good luck."

I stopped breathing. Stopped hearing sound or seeing anything around me. The pieces of what had happened that day came together. A car rolling backward on a steep drive, a five-year-old girl so caught up in her chalk drawing that she didn't see it coming toward her. The horror of it crashed into me, and I wanted to scream a warning to that long-ago girl to run, to get out of the way, but she couldn't hear me. She wasn't here anymore.

I wrapped my arms around him, and he was shaking so bad. "It was an accident. A horrible, tragic accident. You were just a little boy."

His tears soaked into my shirt as I held him, rocking from side to side, trying to calm the tremors racking his body. "I still feel it, the impact. The bump of the tires as they ran her over. Sometimes I wake up in the middle of the night and I don't know where I am, and I think I'm back in that car, and my dad is running out of the house, but it's too late. She's gone. And I'm the one who killed her. I killed my baby sister, who loved me enough to draw baseballs in every room in our house. I was her hero, and she's dead because of me."

"It was an accident." I held him while he sobbed, murmuring the words over and over again. It was an accident, an accident, an accident. Every beat of my heart hurt for that little boy forced to endure the kind of nightmare most adults couldn't survive.

I had no idea how much time had passed while I rubbed his back, holding him through it until the tears on my shoulder began to dry. When he finally looked up, his face was bleak and swollen. I brushed away the last of his tears and kissed him gently.

"The days following the accident were hard on my parents." He had a faraway look in his eyes, but his voice sounded steadier. Like he had to talk his way through the worst of it before he could face the other side. "The media had parked out on our lawn, and they still had to bury their daughter and grieve. They were dragged all over social media. It became a viral story, a cautionary tale about parental neglect. Even though it was my fault." He stopped, breathed, and started again. "Strangers on Facebook and Twitter took hard swings at my dad for leaving me alone in a running car."

I didn't want to tell him that if a story like that had crossed my timeline, I probably would've had the same reaction. It was so easy, too easy, to judge people you didn't know online. To see a tiny slip of their worst moment and make assumptions about them as a whole. And to deal with that while also trying to grieve a lost child . . . I couldn't comprehend the toll that would take on a family.

"My parents sent me to live with my grandma and Gigi," he said. "Just for a little bit, they said. Until the media circus calmed down. My dad was a quality control engineer down in Kansas City. He lost his job over what happened."

"I'm sorry," I said. They felt like useless words, but I was at a loss.

"The boss he'd worked under for ten years told him that if he couldn't even keep an eye on his own children, then he probably couldn't be trusted to keep an eye on the parts in the shop. He said that to my dad three days after we buried Daisy."

"What the fuck?" I didn't mean to yell that out loud, but what kind of a monster would say something like that to a grieving father?

"My dad was a villain online; the hate was so strong, it spilled over onto everything. Their friends stopped talking to them because they didn't want to be associated and catch even an ember of the heat directed my parents' way."

"I'm so, so sorry. None of you deserved that."

"My dad couldn't get another job. Every time a prospective employer googled him, it was all over. They eventually changed our family name." That was why I hadn't been able to find anything on him when I googled. "My parents left KC and moved to St. Louis. My dad got a job, and eventually the Internet moved on to their next scandal. They didn't bring me home, though, and after a year or two, I stopped expecting them to."

"Why not?" My heart broke all over again for Paxton, left alone to deal with what had happened. What it must've felt like to know he'd been abandoned.

"Part of it was because, with Gigi, I'd started to get better. She introduced me to raising rabbits for show, and having something small and innocent to care for, to know the rabbits depended on me, it was like a different sort of therapy. One I desperately needed. If she hadn't done that, I would've taken my own life years ago."

My hand clenched his on instinct. He always said raising rabbits saved him. I didn't know he meant that literally. "You're not thinking of doing that anymore, are you?"

He shook his head. "I've had a lot of therapy, both clinical and with the rabbits. I still have bad days, but they aren't nearly as bad as they used to be, or nearly as often. I'm learning how to live with it. I'm learning how to live."

"Do your parents visit often?" I hadn't spent a ton of time over at Paxton's house, but they couldn't have come to visit that often if everyone in town thought they were dead.

"They don't. I think it's easier for them to stay away. Because part of them . . . even though they don't want to admit it, part of them blames me still. And I can't do anything about that. They love me, but it's hard. All of it is hard for all of us."

That even a part of them could blame him for an

accident like that made a fierce anger roll within me, but I checked it for his sake. "Why did they come today?"

He turned his head away from me. "My mom is pregnant. They're going to try to start a family again, and they wanted to tell me in person."

"Are you okay?" I placed my hands on his cheeks. "I keep saying I'm sorry because I don't know what else to say, but if there is anything I can do, I'll do it."

"You don't have to do anything. Being here, not running from me, is more than I could've hoped for." He took my hands and kissed both of them. "I'm fine with my mom's pregnancy, or as fine as I can be, I guess. To be honest, they haven't felt like my parents in a really long time. I'm not angry at them for shutting me out. I'm not expecting to be part of their new family. I wish them well, but my feelings for them are very distant and healed over. Like watching someone else's life from a telescope."

I understood why he'd tried to warn me when I first went viral, the kind of fear he felt for me. I even understood why he'd gotten so angry when I played into it. The kind of memories it dredged up for him turned my veins ice-cold. What his family had faced, what he had faced, once the wolves of the Internet had sunk their teeth in was unimaginable. They already had to live through the worst, but to have it used against them day after day was nothing short of hell. Paxton had already lived through it, knew what it had done to his family, and he saw the same thing happening to me.

For the first time since I'd gone viral, I had no desire to check Twitter.

CHAPTER
TWENTY-THREE

PAXTON AND I SAT on that lawn chair until he needed to get ready for work. I didn't want to leave the Hamptons, but he assured me he was okay. I offered to walk him home, and we only made it as far as the woods before we fell on each other again. We made out against a tree, behind some bushes, and had a near miss with a patch of poison ivy. Paxton told me he'd wanted to kiss me since the first day we'd started working together, so we had a lot of lost time to make up for. I couldn't get enough of touching him, kissing him, just being near him.

I didn't turn my phone back on. I had no idea what people were saying about me, and I didn't care. It was so freeing not to care.

We finally pulled away from each other when Paxton had to do the responsible thing and show up to work. I offered to drive because I wanted to go in and see Elise, but when we reached the door outside Video and Repair, it was locked. Paxton and I looked at each other. Elise, Brady, and Midnight were all supposed to be there.

"Should I text Midnight?" I asked.

Before Paxton could open his mouth to respond, Midnight flung open the door, Brady and Elise behind her.

"Guess what day it is."

"Sunday," Paxton said.

"Correct," Elise said. "It's also Cleaning Day."

"Already?" I asked.

"We tried to text you, but didn't get a response," Midnight said.

"Sorry, my phone's been off all day."

Cleaning Day was a Video and Repair tradition. Once a quarter a company came in and did a full-scale clean on the store: carpet scrubbing, shelf washing, a total detox of the place. Those of us who worked here, minus Butch, took advantage of the store being closed to go camping. Midnight's uncle had a small patch of land up north he'd bought for hunting. We'd all gone camping up there on the last Cleaning Day, and would probably go again on the next one. Part of her would always be the farm girl who loved the outdoors.

"Is it okay if I bring my girlfriend?" Brady asked. I had a feeling I knew his girlfriend, and I couldn't hide my smile. But we'd never allowed outsiders for Cleaning Day before, usually because we spent most of the night drinking and bitching about work, and it would've bored anyone else present. "It's just, with everyone else coupled up, I don't want to be alone in my tent while you're all banging."

Oh my God. I tried to swallow my laugh and failed miserably. "Did shy and quiet Brady just use the word *banging* in a sentence?"

"Shut up." He grinned at me, and his cheeks turned pink.

"One of us! One of us!" Elise chanted.

"Hold on." Midnight held up a hand. "Who else is coupled up?"

Elise, Brady, and Midnight all turned to me and Paxton. Paxton just raised an eyebrow, like it would be up to me when and where to reveal our new status.

"We're a thing." There was no point in hiding it. It's not like we'd do a great job of keeping it quiet once we got up to the campsite.

"What kind of thing?" Midnight smiled as sweetly as venom.

"A thing. You know." I pointed between her and Elise. "That kind of thing."

"Like, you both finally set your bullshit aside, because it's obvious to anyone with eyes you both have a huge thing for each other? That kind of thing?" Elise asked.

"As much as it does wonders for my ego to hear you talk about my huge thing"—Paxton poked Elise on the nose and she smacked his hand—"you can quit torturing my girlfriend now."

"I knew it!" Elise punched the air. "I can't believe you two kept this from me. How long has this been going on? Tell me everything."

"It just started." Though, if I were being completely honest, it had been going on for a while; we'd just now gotten around to figuring it out. I said to Brady, "It's fine if you bring your girlfriend, but she's probably going to find us boring at best and annoying at worst."

"I think she'll have fun. She knows you all." Brady winked at me. "And she still wanted to come for some reason."

"Who is your girlfriend?" Midnight asked.

"Strawberry Sinclair," Brady said, more to Paxton than any of us.

Everyone besides me froze.

"Awkward," Elise mumbled.

Paxton cleared his throat. "How long has she been your girlfriend?"

"Most recently, since Friday night." Brady held Paxton's stare, as if considering if he should elaborate. "She broke up with me a few weeks ago to focus on 4-H, and only agreed to your date because she thought she'd see me there. Is it still cool if she comes?"

"I don't mind," I said. I found the whole thing more amusing than I should've.

"I don't mind if she comes along either," Paxton said. "But do me a favor and tell her I'm sorry for the sucky date before we all get there."

"She knows." Brady let out a laugh. "The whole damn town knows you've been in love with Macy for the last year."

Paxton stiffened beside me as that one word hung in the air between us. *Love.* It rattled around in my system like a pinball. I knew Paxton liked me, and he really liked kissing me, but love? Was he in love with me?

"We should get going. Me and Macy have to pick up our tents," Paxton said, with an emphasis on tent*s*, as in two, as in we weren't sleeping together. "Do you know how to get there, Brady?" When Brady nodded, he took my hand. "We'll see you then."

I got in the driver side of my car, and Paxton got in the passenger side. I put the key in the ignition, but waited a beat before starting it. "So, about that love thing?"

"Oh, you heard that?" Paxton gave me a half grin.

"Do you?" I turned to him. "Love me?"

"I guess it depends."

I pursed my lips. "On what?"

"If it freaks you out," he said softly. "Then definitely not."

"And if it doesn't freak me out?"

"Then I'd tell you I've been in love with you since our first day at work. When Midnight tried to put on her shift supervisor face and terrorize you like she did Brady, but you weren't having any of it. I watched you wait until she went into the break room, then you put a wad of gum in the receipt paper so it would get all stuck and messy with the next customer she rang up. And the first thing that popped into my head when you did that was *Damn, I think I love that girl*."

I laughed. "That's a terrible reason to fall in love with someone."

"What can I say? I'm a sucker for girls who can hold their own and aren't afraid to pull out a wrench and scare the shit out of some hipsters every now and again."

I leaned over the console, until I was close enough to feel the warmth of him. "Lucky for you, I'm a sucker for boys who know how to break into community sheds and who love old movies as much as I do and who raise rabbits for show."

"That is a very specific set of desires. How fortunate for me indeed."

"I love you too." I pressed my lips against his, cursing the console for being so boxy and in the way when all I wanted to do was crawl onto his lap.

A tap on the roof of the car had us breaking apart.

Elise bent down, waving the air in front of her. "The hormones. I can't take it. I'm choking on the fumes."

I wrinkled my nose at her. "Did you need something?"

"Bring a jar of your grandma's blackberry jam for breakfast. Momma made us a loaf of bread, and she ate all the jam we got for fixing your dryer already."

"Will do." I started cranking up the window to make her go away.

"Save it for the campsite!" she hollered as she climbed into her truck.

I sighed and turned the ignition. "We probably should go or we'll never make it there."

Paxton was grinning at me.

"What?" I rubbed my cheeks. "Do I have something on my face?"

"You love me," he said.

I thought we'd already established that. "And? You love me too."

He settled back in his seat. "I just like saying it out loud."

"You are such a dork." I took his hand and threaded his fingers through mine.

I drove to the end of Main Street and turned down my road. We planned to grab my tent first and then stop at his house on the way to our campsite. An unfamiliar car sat in the drive. A new car. The kind that probably had heated seats and a rearview camera.

I glanced at Paxton. "Wait here."

If another reporter had shown up, I didn't want them anywhere near Paxton. Though I couldn't imagine Gram letting anyone in the house, and I didn't see anyone skulking around the Hamptons. My heart thudded as I approached the screen door. The sound of laughter floated outside. Definitely not a reporter.

The first thing I noticed was Mom sitting on the plastic-covered couch. She never sat on the couch. Neither of us could stand the feel of it. The second thing I noticed was the man sitting beside her. They both stood as the door slammed behind me. He had warm brown eyes and the beginnings of gray hair around his temples.

"Macy, I want you to meet Roger." Mom held his hand. She looked as happy as she had at the Royals game, and I decided right then not to hate him on sight.

"Hi. It's so nice to meet you"—*don't call him cradle-robbing Roger, don't call him cradle-robbing Roger*—"Cr-oger."

"Croger is my stage name." He had a gleam in his eye. "You can call me Roger."

Mom chuckled as she hooked her arm through his. "I think Macy was trying really hard not to call you her grandma's preferred nickname."

"He's closer to my age than he is to yours," Gram called from the dining room.

I cringed. "Sorry."

"No worries." Roger waved a hand. "I'll win her over eventually."

"Don't count on it!" Gram yelled.

"Quit being rude!" Mom yelled back. She turned to me. "We're heading out in a few minutes, but I'm glad you got a chance to say hello."

"Me too." I glanced at Roger and he was looking at Mom like she held the world. I decided I definitely didn't hate him. "Is it okay if I keep the car then? It's Cleaning Day."

"Ah, are you headed out to the campsite then?"

"Yeah." Even though I should've told Mom about Paxton before we went camping, I really didn't want to have that conversation in front of Roger. "How did you two meet?"

"Roger stopped in for lunch at the diner after checking in on a few of his businesses. He came in during a lull, so he was the only customer, and he invited me to sit with him. At first, I was just hoping to get a bigger tip, but he won me over by the end of it."

"You have businesses in Honeyfield?" I asked. There weren't a lot of businesses to have in town. "Which ones?"

"The diner," he said, giving Mom a sly smile.

"Dipping your pen in the company ink!" Gram yelled.

"Go back to your quilting!" I yelled at her. "She's in a mood."

"Despite what your grandma thinks," Mom raised her voice loud enough for Gram to hear, "Roger didn't tell me he owned the diner until our third date. He thought I wouldn't want to go out with him."

"I thought you wouldn't sit with me if you knew I was the boss." His whole face filled with awe when he looked at my mom. It was weird, but not entirely unpleasant, to see.

"And rightly so," Mom said.

They'd gotten so caught up in their own meet-cute, I was 99 percent certain they'd forgotten I was standing there. "So, you just own the diner?"

"And the repair shop," he said.

"Wait. What?" I couldn't have heard him correctly. "The Video and Repair?"

"I technically own both, but I'm only in charge of the repair side. It's my business partner's job to take care of the video side."

"I work there," I said, for lack of a better thing to say. This completely threw me for a loop. "Does your business partner live in Shelbyville too?"

"No, he lives here in Honeyfield." Roger gave me an amused grin, like he knew how much this was twisting my sense of reality. "I believe you all know him as Butch."

"Butch is your business partner?" Midnight would absolutely lose it. She still hadn't forgiven him for the Unholy Mistress nickname. "Jesus. No wonder it's basically falling apart."

Roger laughed. "Why do you think I split the responsibility down the middle?"

"I'm going to—" I pointed at the door. "It was super-nice to meet you, Roger."

"Likewise." He gave me a firm handshake.

I grabbed our tent from the shed out back and packed an overnight bag. All this new information swam in my head as I walked back to the car, barely aware of my feet moving. I slid into the driver's side. I fumbled for my keys and tried to focus on Paxton, even though I was still reeling.

"What's wrong?" he asked.

"My mom is dating your boss." So weird. "Who is also her boss. Is that, like, an ethical thing, or no? Because he didn't tell her he was the boss until after they went out, so it's not like he was trying to use his position to manipulate her, and he's totally into her."

Paxton held up his hands. "I think you need to backtrack about five thousand steps so I can catch up. Your mom is dating Butch?"

"No." I shook my head, but I couldn't clear out all the noise. "His name is Roger."

"Butch's name is Roger?"

"I'll explain it on the way. And as an early birthday present, I'll let you be the one who breaks the news to Midnight."

I started up the car and backed out of my drive. As I threaded my fingers with Paxton's, I tried to keep my mind off the impending tantrum Eric was sure to have once he realized I was done being Fly Ball Girl. I had no idea how deep his obsession with Internet fame ran, and I really didn't want to find out.

CHAPTER
TWENTY-FOUR

WE MADE IT TO the campsite, where Midnight and Elise had one tent. Brady and Strawberry had one tent. I glanced at Paxton. Even though I had no problem sharing a tent with him, he'd been very clear in front of the store that we'd have separate tents.

I dumped my stuff on a patch of open ground near the trees and pulled my tent out of the vinyl bag. It reeked like death and was covered in black patches. I flung it away from me and shook my hands in the air. "Ew. Ew. Ew."

"What's wrong?" Paxton asked.

"My tent is covered in mold. It must've happened when I threw it in the shed after the last time we went camping. But I can ask Elise and Midnight if I can bunk with them, if you're not comfortable sleeping with me yet," I said. "They won't be happy, but they'll be all right."

"Why do you think I wouldn't be comfortable sleeping with you?"

"At the store, you said two tents."

Paxton tilted my chin up and kissed me. "I only said that to get them off your back. I was hoping you'd just sneak into my tent in the middle of the night."

My mouth had gone dry. "I guess that settles that."

"We don't have to—" Paxton rubbed the back of his neck. "If you want to sleep, and not do other things, I'm totally fine with that. I'm not expecting anything just because we're sharing a tent."

Sleeping with Paxton would be way different from sleeping with Lance. My feelings for Lance had been like candlelight, soft and gentle. My feelings for Paxton were a forest fire that could consume me. The old fear of getting in too deep with a boy attached to a town I was determined to escape rose up in me again, but instead of running from it, I faced the irrationality of it. My mom's history wasn't my future. My life belonged to me.

I rubbed my hands over his chest. "I like sleep."

"Sleep is nice." He swallowed.

"But then again, I really don't want all those condoms in my backpack to go to waste."

A really terrible pun about pitching a tent was on the tip of my tongue, but I left Paxton to pick his jaw back up from the ground as I went over to help Elise and Midnight set up the lawn chairs around the fire. Elise and I went into the woods to look for fallen logs for our fire, and I told her about Mom and Roger, leaving out the news about Butch. I'd already promised Paxton he'd get to drop that little gem at a time and place of his choosing.

The air felt fresher than back home. Like this little slice of nature had truly been left untouched. The earthy scent of the forest was so much stronger out here. If I could've bottled that smell and kept it with me forever, I would've done it in a heartbeat. By the time we got back, Paxton, Brady, and Strawberry were already laughing over Paxton and Strawberry's awful date. Even Midnight managed to crack a smile.

We passed around a bottle of peach schnapps, Midnight's new preferred drink, but both Paxton and I only took a few sips. We wanted to be sober for what we had planned after everyone went to bed. Midnight let us all know Jared had been picked up, and refused to post bail, deciding he'd rather sit in jail and await his hearing than deal with Midnight's brother.

"I heard Travis and his friends took care of Brett and he hasn't dared to leave his house since," Strawberry said. "I always did like your brother."

"It'll be a long while before Brett shows his face anywhere around town. Which is fine by me," Midnight said. "Even though I sometimes wonder if he would've been decent if not for Jared. I like his parents and siblings."

"How exactly did Travis take care of Brett?" I asked. I had visions of broken kneecaps and shoving his fingers into a corn shucker, or however else they did things on the farm.

"Travis and his friends stripped Brett down to his briefs and tied him to that big tree outside the feedstore so every farmer in the county would see him before someone cut him loose." Midnight grinned with wicked delight. "It was really cold that morning."

"Oh my God." I didn't know whether to be pleased or horrified.

Midnight shrugged. "He's lucky he got to keep his briefs. Travis just wanted to give him a taste of what it felt like to be helpless, so maybe he'd think twice before using his muscles to intimidate anyone smaller than him again."

"Serves him right." Strawberry lifted the bottle of schnapps in a silent toast to Travis. "Last summer Jared and Brett thought it would be real funny to open our stables in the middle of the night and let our horses run loose. My brother caught them and they beat the hell out of him for it."

Strawberry's brother was only sixteen. I didn't feel the slightest bit horrified anymore. Brett got exactly what he deserved. It was only a shame that Jared hid in jail, but I had a feeling he'd be getting a visit from Midnight's brother the moment he got out.

After we did a significant amount of bitching about work, ate two packages of hot dogs grilled over the open fire, and did more bitching, the liquor started to set in for everyone. Paxton still hadn't revealed the Butch news, and I wondered if he felt bad for Midnight about Jared, or if he just wanted a more advantageous time to drop that bomb. The sun finally set, which meant the mosquitos came out in full force. We had a dozen citronella candles burning, but it didn't keep those little bloodsuckers from feasting.

Everyone else weaved and swayed toward their tents, while Paxton and I, the only sober ones present, stayed behind to put out the fire. Once the last ember had been snuffed out with a bucket of sand, we went back to our tent.

Paxton laid out his bedroll and covered it with his

sleeping bag. One of the camping battery lanterns was half open, illuminating the tent in a low and subtle light. He took off his shirt and pants, leaving his boxers on. My toes tingled as my gaze wandered over the lean muscles in his arms and chest. I'd never seen him in so few clothes. I could get very, very used to the sight of Paxton without any clothes.

I walked over to him on my knees, rubbing my hands over his chest and down his arms. Every plane of his body was firm from doing repairs in the shop and whatever Gigi needed done around the house. He kept his hands to himself while he let me explore him and get used to the feel of his skin, already warm from anticipation. I caught his mouth with my own, gently tugging on his bottom lip with my teeth, and that was all it took for him to pull me against him.

His fingers played with the hem of my tank top as his thumbs dipped under and grazed my bare skin. I shivered. Too many clothes. I had way too many clothes on. I pulled my tank top off and threw it into the corner of the tent, followed immediately by my shorts, until I wore only my nonmatching bra and underwear.

A soft glow lit Paxton's eyes as I kneeled before him. "You're gorgeous."

If the wonder in his voice hadn't convinced me, the bulge in his boxers certainly did. Keeping my gaze on him, I unhooked my bra and let it fall to the ground. A near animal sound escaped his lips as I approached him.

"I think you're gorgeous too." I was already breathless. "How lucky for both of us."

I kissed him hard and deep, the skin-to-skin contact undoing any amount of restraint I might've shown. He lowered us to the ground until I was straddling him, rocking against him with our underwear still between us. His hands touched me everywhere, and a soft sound rose up in my throat as the friction between us built right down the center of me. I cried out as the orgasm hit me fast. I buried my face in his shoulder as the tremors spread to my toes and fingertips. I'd never had one so quickly before, not even on those nights when I gave them to myself.

When I lifted my head, he was smiling up at me. His touch trailed up and down my arms. "That noise you made at the end might be the most beautiful sound in the world."

I kissed his chest. "We're not done yet."

My fingers ran down his stomach, lower, until I pushed his boxers down and took him in my hand. He groaned as I moved my hand up and down, and he was kind enough to return the favor to me. Our gazes locked as we touched each other. It was the most intimate moment in my life. As the heat began to build in me again, I rolled over to my backpack and grabbed a condom out of the side pocket.

Paxton took his boxers all the way off and paused. "Are you sure?"

"Very sure." I slid my underwear off and threw them next to my tank top. His gaze trailed over me, half glazed, as if he were dreaming while awake. It gave me enough confidence to forget whatever awkwardness I would've felt about being wholly naked.

CHAPTER
TWENTY-FIVE

I WOKE TO THE sound of Paxton breathing deeply beside me, still asleep. If he got to pick a favorite sound of mine, then I'd get one too, and this was definitely it. His hair had fallen over his forehead in the night, and I brushed it back. He stirred awake. His lips parted as his eyes went in and out of focus, like he couldn't quite believe he was there. We were there. Together.

"How did you sleep?" I whispered.

"Amazingly." He cupped my cheek. "I haven't slept that good in nine years."

Elise tapped on our tent. "Are you decent?"

"No. Go away." I snuggled against Paxton, and his arms wrapped around me as he tucked my head under his chin.

"Get decent then, and come out," she said. "We need to talk."

My stomach dropped. I hated it when people said "we need to talk" without saying what they wanted to talk about. It always left me running over a million scenarios in my mind, asking myself if I'd done anything to piss them off, or if something had happened to someone I loved. It was the worst way to wake up.

"I'll be back in a minute," I said to Paxton.

He mumbled something and put his pillow over his head, like it could block out the light. The sight of his bare chest and the slight soreness between my legs had me smiling all over again. Once I found out what Elise wanted to talk about, I'd put another one of those condoms in my backpack to good use.

I got dressed, brushed my teeth, and stumbled out of the tent. Elise sat in one of the lawn chairs by the firepit. A cool morning mist snaked across the ground. Drops of dew clung to the clover and leaves as the sun barely crested the horizon.

"It's so early," I whined. Everyone else was still in their tents. "What did you want to talk about that couldn't have waited another two hours?"

"You're my best friend." Elise stared at the firepit, and my anxiety spiked. "I love you, and will always take your side no matter what. But Paxton is my friend too, and he's grossly, desperately in love with you. If you're still going to play Twitter games with Eric, you have to let Paxton know what's going on. Please don't string him along."

I dropped into the seat beside her. I had no idea where this had come from. Never mind the fact that I was equally as grossly in love with Paxton as he was with me. "What the hell are you talking about? What makes you think I'd ever string him along?"

"I checked Jessica Banks's Instagram this morning. Since you said you were done with that whole Baseball Babe fiasco, I wanted to let you know if she tried anything."

She handed me her phone. I unlocked the screen with her birth date and she had Jessica Banks's Instagram video open. My stomach rolled before I even hit play. Ever since Paxton had told me about what had happened with his sister, I had no desire to go online. I hadn't been keeping tabs on Eric or Jessica, and that was a huge mistake on my part.

"I got the inside scoop from Eric, y'all." Jessica's face was so smug, so proud of the wrecking ball she'd smashed through my life. I hated her with the fire of a thousand suns. "He's still going strong with Macy. Neither of them were online yesterday, because they've taken things to a more private level. If you know what I mean." She winked at the camera and I wanted to reach through the screen and choke her. "But I talked to Eric this morning, and he wanted me to give a shout-out to his new YouTube channel. I'll be driving up to the Shelby County Fair for the exclusive, and I'll have a live Instagram stream going for the reunion you've all been waiting for. See you beauties on Tuesday at two."

The screen went black and I let out a scream so loud, birds took off out of the trees, and once-silent tents unzipped. "I hope she does drive up here. I'm going to rip her to shreds and send her dismembered parts in a box to Eric."

"Okay, so you're not still playing along with the Baseball Babe stuff." The relief pouring off Elise made me want to cry.

"You thought I was lying when I said I was done with all that?" Paxton's dad flashed through my mind, how all his friends thought the worst of him and ditched him, what his boss had said to him. "How could you think for one second I'd lie about that?"

At least Elise had the good sense to look ashamed. "I don't know. You didn't tell me about it the first time, and I guess it was just easy to think you'd do it again. And you didn't tell me you'd gotten together with Paxton until you both showed up at work together. It just feels like lately I'm finding out everything about you after the fact."

As much as I hated what she was saying, I was also kind of relieved I wasn't the only one who felt like we'd been drifting recently. But she was still my best friend, and she should've known better. "For the millionth time, I'm sorry I didn't tell you about Eric, but the only reason I didn't tell you about Paxton is because it literally just happened. And we were so busy making out before we had to go into work, I wouldn't have had time to tell you before then."

Paxton laid a hand on my shoulder. "It's true. She's insatiable."

I looked up at him, pleased to see he hadn't bothered to put his shirt on before he came out of the tent. "I didn't hear any complaints out of you."

"Okay. Fine. I can accept that," Elise said. "But I'm still confused. If you told Eric you don't want to see him anymore, why is he posting YouTube videos like you two are a couple?"

Paxton's hand tightened on my shoulder. I hoped not because he doubted me. He knew all too well how the Internet fame game worked.

"I have no idea what Eric is doing or why," I said. "And I couldn't care less. I haven't even looked at my phone since yesterday."

"Um . . ." Elise took her phone back and opened the YouTube app. Eric's face flooded the screen, and it turned out there was someone I hated more than Jessica Banks. "Hey, Macy. I miss you already, but yesterday was so fun. No pictures though, people, sorry. NSFW. Can't wait to see you at the fair on Tuesday. I'll win you one of those big bears at the milk jug toss. It'll be just like the first time we met."

The screen faded to black, and I would've screamed again if my voice hadn't gone hoarse. I'd kill him. I would literally murder him on sight. Paxton had gone eerily still as his free hand curled into a fist. I glanced up at him and a muscle ticked in his jaw. I'd kill Eric dead for all the stuff he was bringing up for Paxton alone.

"I'm sorry." Elise rubbed my arm. "I never should've doubted you. It's just—"

"I get it. You don't have to explain." It was so easy, too easy, to believe anything people said online. To make monsters out of ordinary people just trying to do their best. "I don't know how to make this go away. If I'd left it alone, none of this would be happening."

"Maybe he's lying about the fair," Elise said. "Like he lied about this past weekend."

"Maybe." He had to know I'd punch him in the face as soon as he set foot in my town. That wouldn't flow well with this narrative he was trying to concoct. "Just in case, though, I better text him and tell him not to bother showing up."

I went back to the tent and rummaged around in my backpack until I found my phone. I brought it back out to the firepit. Elise and Paxton peered over my shoulder as I unlocked my phone and opened my texts. I had sixteen unread messages—all from Eric.

Eric: *Macy. Talk to me. Don't do this.*

Eric: *I'll do whatever you want. Do you want me to be your boyfriend for real? I can be your boyfriend. We could spend a few weeks at my family's lake house.*

Eric: *Macy*

Eric: *Don't shut me out. I thought we had a deal*

A dozen variations of the same message followed, where he occasionally broke to call me a fucking bitch again. He was a real charmer. His texts came in at all different times during the night. Because vampire. I only had one from him this morning.

Eric: *If you don't show up to the shelby county fair on tuesday, I'll make you the villain. I'll shred your YouTube channel apart. I'll tell the world you used me and broke my heart. Two o'clock, by the milk jug toss.*

Eric had gone full mustache-twirling, railroad-track-tying villain. I would've laughed if a cold rope of fear hadn't squeezed around my chest. While I'd distanced myself from the Fly Ball Girl persona, I still wanted to do movie reviews and grow my YouTube channel with the kind of content I wanted to post. Not to mention whatever he said about me online would follow me for the rest of my life. One Google search could kill job opportunities, personal relationships, the way people viewed me until the end of time. Just like it had with Paxton's dad.

And it would be so easy for him to vilify me, so easy for everyone to believe the worst. If I'd learned anything from spending so much time online, it was this: People reacted with a lot more passion to negativity. Happy, shiny couples were boring. They wanted scandal and drama and someone to hate, and if Eric had his way, I'd be that person.

I blocked Eric's number and powered off my phone.

"He's on minute fourteen. His time is almost up and he's getting desperate. This will blow over," I said. Paxton didn't look so sure. I gave him a confident smile, but I didn't know if it was more for him or myself.

Paxton was quiet the entire ride home, and I tried not to let it freak me out. He just needed to process. Knowing what I knew now, I could understand how hard all this had hit him. When I dropped him off, he said he'd text me later—in a faraway voice that sounded like he only half meant it—but at least he wasn't running this time. Progress.

The Bees were in full quilting mode; with the county fair starting up, they were down to the wire. They didn't even glance up as I passed through the dining room on my way to the Hamptons. I hadn't taken a close look at their quilt in the last week, per tradition. Gram covered it with a tablecloth when they weren't working on it, and we'd gotten so used to having Bees and quilts going at different times of the year, we eventually tuned it out.

Mom hung out in the Hamptons with a Susan Elizabeth

Phillips novel, one foot dipped in the freshly bleached kiddie pool. She had the day off too, and would likely spend most of it out here. Unless she and Roger had plans.

"Permission to enter the Hamptons?" I asked.

Mom looked up and smiled. "Permission granted."

I took a seat on the lawn chair where Paxton had told me his story. It felt like a lifetime ago. So much had happened since then, and Mom knew none of it. While I didn't fill her in on everything, or a lot of things really, I couldn't lie to her about Paxton. He'd become too important to me.

"How was camping?" Mom asked.

"Fine." Okay, I could lie about some Paxton-related things. "Can I ask you some questions about Roger?"

She set her book down and sat up. "Ask away."

"Do you think it's okay to bend your stance on coworkers because you like him?"

"I wouldn't call him my coworker, since I didn't even know he owned the diner until he told me, and he doesn't actively work there." She gave me a piercing look. The kind only moms could give. Like they had X-ray vision, but instead of bones, they saw their children's secrets and lies. "But you're not really asking about me and Roger, are you?"

"No." I stared at my joined hands. "I'm in love with Paxton, and he's in love with me, and I'm sorry if that hurts you, but we're together now."

She rubbed her temples. "Did Paxton go camping too?"

"Umm . . ." I couldn't risk the lie. Too many people knew about the Cleaning Day tradition, and Gigi would know that

Paxton hadn't been home last night. "Yes?"

"Is that why I didn't see you come home with the tent?"

Oh shit. Shit, shit, shit.

"No," I said. Very slowly. "The tent was covered in mold and I threw it out. And by the way, thanks for springing that whole 'Mom's new boyfriend owns half of Honeyfield' thing on me. How could you keep that a secret?"

She rolled her eyes. "Roger owns the diner and the repair shop, not half of Honeyfield."

"Have you been on Main Street? That is literally half of Honeyfield."

"Don't use that tone with me, and don't try to change the subject." She crossed her arms, and it was like looking at a younger version of Gram. "Did you or did you not share a tent with Paxton Croft last night?"

"So what if I did?" I hadn't intended to confess that part—Elise would've covered for me on the tent front—but I was so sick of having my life dictated by her choices.

"Goddamn it, Macy." She stood and paced in front of me. "You are supposed to be smarter than this. You are supposed to get the hell out of this town and have a better life and never have to know what it feels like to work until you're dead."

"I can still do those things." I hated this. I hated this entire conversation. "I'm not going to be tied down and pregnant just because I had sex with a boy. I know what a condom is. I'm not you."

Her head snapped back as if I'd slapped her. I'd said

too much, struck too deep. I opened my mouth to tell her I was sorry and that I didn't mean it, but she cut me off with a single raised hand. "You think I didn't know what a condom was? How do you think I felt being one of the lucky two percent it failed on?"

I'd had no idea. She'd never said anything like that before. I'd just assumed she'd had unprotected sex, and that was how I came to be. But still, her words hit me as hard as I'd hit her, and we'd reached a point where we were just one-upping who could hurt who more.

"I bet you felt awful," I said. "I bet having me was the worst thing that ever happened to you."

She sat with a heavy thump on the beach recliner. As if all the fight had been knocked clean out of her. "That's not what I said."

"You didn't have to say it." I already knew. Just like I knew I'd done everything in my power to be the perfect daughter. Because my entire life I'd been trying to apologize for existing.

"That's enough." Gram stood on the back porch, her hands on her hips. "I've got twelve hours left to get a quilt ready enough to win, and I'm not going to sit inside and listen to another minute of this nonsense."

"Then go back to your quilt and mind your own business," Mom said.

"Don't take that tone with me, young lady. I don't give a good goddamn if you are grown; I will whip your ass from here until Sunday." Gram stalked across the yard and stared

Mom down until we both shrunk to the size of the ants crawling among the brown grass.

"Sorry," Mom mumbled.

"How much did you hear?" I winced, knowing Gigi was inside.

"Everything." Gram turned on me, and I flinched from her fire. "The entire neighborhood could hear the way you two were screaming at each other, and we're going to settle this now so I can get back to quilting in peace."

"You don't need to settle anything," Mom said, with significantly less tone. "This is between me and Macy."

"Like hell it is. I'm not going to sit back while you throw knives at each other until you're both nothing but bloody ribbons. Gracie"—Gram turned to Mom, and she flinched just the way I had—"Paxton is as fine a boy as there ever was, he's got a soft heart, and I *know* you've seen the way he looks at Macy. He's not that piece of shit college boy who abandoned you; he could never be that boy. You need to let it go."

"Don't talk to her like that," I said. Even though I fully agreed with her, and she was taking my side, the need to protect Mom ran so bone-deep, I couldn't help myself.

"You'd do well to shut your mouth when I'm defending you," Gram said.

"Yes, ma'am," I said to my feet.

"And you." Gram flung her pointed finger at me. "You didn't tell your momma about Paxton before you went camping, and you know that's wrong. We expect better of you."

"I know." I toed at the anthill hidden in the grass. "I'm sorry."

"Another thing you need to know." Gram grasped my chin and tilted my face up. "You have been a joy and a blessing in our lives. It was tough when your momma found out she was pregnant, tough on all of us, but don't think for one second that we regret you being here. We love you, Macy. You're the brightest bit of sunshine we have in this dark world."

I knew they loved me. Of course I did, but it was so hard to look at the life Mom had and know it could've been easier without me, to not feel selfish and ungrateful that I wanted something different. But just like Mom needed to let go of her past, I needed to let go too. My family meant the world to me—I never wanted them to think they weren't enough—but I'd graduated. Next year I'd be moving on. And I had to accept that I couldn't fix or change something I wasn't responsible for, or I'd never stand on my own.

"I love you too. Both of you. Nothing will ever change that." I stood and turned to my mom. "But I'm not going to stop seeing Paxton. I need you to let me make my own choices. And maybe I'll screw it up, but for me, it's a risk worth taking."

Mom didn't speak, and I quietly died inside while she sat silent. I wouldn't take back a single word though. This confrontation had been a long time coming. If we hadn't dealt with it now, all the guilt I carried around would've turned to bitter resentment, and the damage to our relationship would've been catastrophic.

"Gracie." Gram's voice turned softer. "Are you going to talk to your daughter, or are you just going to keep sitting there like a stiff?"

"Mom." I had to explain this in a way she'd understand. It always came back to *Say Anything.* "He's my Lloyd Dobler."

Her eyes widened a fraction, but she still didn't make a sound.

"And I'm not saying I'm Diane, or you're trying to put me in a box, but maybe . . ." If I didn't say what was on my mind now, this would pass, and we'd go on as we had been with her worrying all the time and me feeling guilty all the time, and I couldn't do it anymore. "Maybe sometimes you do, without meaning to. I know life got hard, and I know you don't want the same for me, but at what point will you believe that you've done enough?"

"I don't know what you're talking about." Her nose wrinkled the way mine sometimes did when I knew I'd been busted at something.

"Yes, you do." My voice had gone so quiet, Gram had to come closer to act like she wasn't hanging on every word. "My life is good. It's full of people I love who love me back because you made sure I'd always have that. You gave me everything I'd ever need, choices and guidance and roots, and I'm so grateful for it all. It's because of those things that I love Paxton. Because of those things, he loves me too. Because of who you raised me to be."

She stood and I braced myself for her to keep up this fight she'd been having with herself and projecting onto me, but she wrapped me in her arms and held me tight as she stroked my hair. "I love you, baby girl. And I'm so proud of the woman you've become."

"Even with Paxton?" I couldn't let this part go. I needed her to be okay with us.

"I know I've been a hard-ass about the coworker thing, but I can admit Paxton is good, and anyone can see how he loves you. I promise I won't get in the way of that."

"Thank you." I squeezed her back.

Mom gently rocked side to side as she held me, pouring every ounce of love she had for me into that hug. When we both started getting weepy, we opened up our arms and pulled Gram into our fold until the three of us became a single unit. We were Evanses. We were forged of fire and steel, and we would not bend for anyone.

Except each other.

CHAPTER
TWENTY-SIX

TUESDAY, THE FIRST OFFICIAL day of the county fair, had arrived, and the Bees were in a tizzy. They'd finished their quilt under the wire the night before, and had it wrapped up and on the way to the craft hall before Mom or I got a look at it. They fluttered around the living room, checking each other's hair, pointing out who had lipstick on their teeth (Donna) and who had a coffee stain on their blouse (Peg). After fussing and changing outfits twice, the Queens of the Shelby County Fair were ready to make their grand entrance.

Mom and Roger waved them off from the driveway. Gram couldn't resist giving Roger the middle finger before she piled into Peg's car, but she did it with a smile. It seemed he was winning her over after all. Slowly. Then he got into his car with Mom and followed the Bees. After they helped them get everything set in the craft hall, they planned to make a day of the fair, like a couple of gross and in-love teenagers. It made me ridiculously happy.

Me: *The adults are gone. Want to come over and get me naked?*

Paxton: *Would love nothing more, but I'm already at the fair. Needed to get here early for Matilda. Rain check?*

Me: *No problem.*

I'd just seen him yesterday morning, but he'd already asked for two rain checks when I'd suggested we get together. I tried not to let that worry me. He had to get Matilda ready, and the Shelby County Fair was the biggest rabbit show of the season. But still. The timing of it all with Eric's threats had left me with a certain amount of unease.

I hadn't gone online since Elise had shown me Eric's YouTube video, but she'd been keeping tabs on him. His likes and retweets had dropped significantly in the last week, and that worried me more than anything. Desperation made people do terrible things. He wasn't willing to let the Baseball Babe thing go, and since I'd gone dark, I had to assume the public had either lost interest or turned against him. But apparently he and Jessica still intended to show up today around two. Elise said it looked like he was trying to get more coverage, tagging various news organizations daily for our big appearance together.

Maybe it was better for Paxton to keep his distance right now. I didn't want him anywhere near Eric and Jessica, not when Jessica planned on live streaming for Instagram. If they ended up filming him, if people got curious, it could bring up everything that had happened with his sister all over again. The long-dead story—buried by years of People of Walmart, Tan Mom, and Yanny or Laurel—would be dragged out again. Though Paxton's family had broken under the strain, and healed again in the only ways they knew how, I would not be part of ripping open that wound again.

I had a lot of hard decisions to make before I met up with Eric and Jessica, but one thing was certain: I was no longer willing to do whatever it took to boost my numbers. I had other options if I dared to explore them.

Millions of people who didn't go to college had decent jobs and good lives. Maybe one day I could open my own store. I'd sell movies and cosplay costumes to go with them, and host watching parties, and have movie club discussions with fancy wine and cheese, and have birthday parties with Disney movies and princess dresses. I could make it a whole experience. Something to get people out of their homes and away from streaming services.

I didn't have to keep giving away pieces of myself to survive. Maybe it had been that way for Gram and Mom, but I could break the cycle. It wasn't too late. I could still be who I chose to be, not who Twitter wanted me to be.

With nothing better to do than sit around the house and stress, I grabbed the car keys and headed out to the fair. By the time I arrived, the parking lot was overflowing. Everyone and their dog had come out for the first day. Most of the businesses in the surrounding towns shut down.

The scents reminded me of a combination of the Royals game and Paxton's backyard—fried bread and grilled sausages mixed with barnyard hay. Little kids with balloon animals and lemonade ran through the crowds. The whoosh of mechanical rides and the screams of terrified riders filled the air. A giant Ferris wheel loomed over the crowd, and just looking at it made my stomach pitch. I'd gone through a weird carnival horror stories phase after renting one of the *Final Destination* movies a few years ago, and there were now maybe five rides I didn't think of as pretty little death traps.

I had exactly three dollars, mostly in dimes and nickels I'd picked out of various drawers in the house, and I was starving. I wandered around the concession stands, debating between cotton candy and candy apples, when I caught sight of Midnight and Elise. They sat at a picnic table sharing a half-grape–half-strawberry snow cone like a 1950s ad for a malt shop.

I sat at their table. "Aren't you two love birds sickeningly cute?"

Elise flipped me off. "You're just jealous we won't share our snow cone."

True. It looked delicious.

"Is Paxton showing Matilda today?" Elise asked.

I nodded. "At five. He's with Gigi at the 4-H barn, if you want to stop over and see them. I guess they bring her in early so she gets accustomed to the crowd."

At three, she'd be weighed, measured, and checked in. Then Paxton would groom her again before the posing. The rabbit shows weren't really a spectator sport, but I planned on watching anyway. There were few things in this world cuter than a boy and his bunny.

A little girl with ribbons in her hair walked by, one hand in her mom's and the other clutching a candy apple. My mouth watered. "I'm getting a candy apple."

"Hey, you," Paxton said.

I spun and threw my arms around him. My pockets jingled with all my change. He hugged me back, and I could feel the tension in his arms. Probably because of Matilda's show and the prospect of Eric lurking around. At least that was what I kept telling myself.

"I'm surprised to see you," I said. "Aren't you prepping Matilda?"

"Gigi wanted cotton candy." He smiled, but it didn't quite reach his eyes. "I can't talk right now. I really shouldn't even be out here."

My heart twisted into a knot. "Oh. Okay. I have stuff to do too."

I turned away before he could see how much his distance affected me, and made it five steps before I caught sight of a familiar profile: a ridiculously hot guy with a manipulative streak and a thirst for fame. And next to him, bobbing through the crowds, a perky woman with a pink bow in her hair.

Eric and Jessica had their backs to me. They didn't notice as I weaved between people by the packed concession stands. Instinct had me pulling my phone out of my back pocket. I wasn't close enough to hear them yet, but I started recording anyway. They veered to the right, toward the games on the midway. Maybe they planned on setting up a camera or meeting up with a news crew early? But they passed right by the milk jug toss, and there were no cameras, no one who looked like a reporter or blogger, and no one who took any interest in Eric and Jessica. Huh.

Still, I kept pace with them, far enough back so they wouldn't see me, until they got to the end of the games row.

When they turned and went behind the tents, I crept to the side. The air vents and generators masked my steps, but they also made it hard to hear. I risked peeking around the corner, where they had their backs to me, both looking down. I held my phone, still recording, and thanks to all the background noise, they had no idea.

"Are you sure she's even going to show?" Jessica asked.

"If she doesn't come by 2:05, text this to her," Eric said. They must've had their heads bent to look at his phone. I couldn't see what it was she was supposed to text me. "I'll send you the picture and her number. She has me blocked, so I can't do it."

"I'm worried this is going to make things worse for us," Jessica said.

"It can't get any worse." The bite in Eric's voice nearly made me take a step back. "Listen, I just need to see her, and I can get her back on track. I had Macy eating out of my hand before; I can do it again."

"If I threaten her though?" Jessica's voice got lower, and I chanced another step closer to make sure my phone picked up every word. "People already hate us. If she posts that text—"

"Don't text anything but the pictures," Eric said. "What is she going to do with those?"

My blood boiled, making the very air around me hot and tight. I'd heard enough. I didn't even care whether I had enough ammunition recorded. This was going to end now.

"Aren't you two just the cozy couple?" My voice had gone as soft as death. "What pictures are you planning to share without my consent this time?"

CHAPTER
TWENTY-SEVEN

JESSICA AND ERIC SPUN around, both with their eyes bulging in a cartoonish way.

"We're not a couple," Jessica sputtered. "He's young enough to be my son." Which hadn't stopped her from adding a bunch of heart-eye emojis to his shirtless picture. "We're friends, and we're both here to see you."

"Macy, you're a little early." Eric smiled, smoothly transitioning into game mode, like he hadn't just been plotting to threaten me. "I've really missed you."

"You can drop the act," I said. "I have you blocked. This isn't a happy reunion."

Eric's earnest expression flipped to vicious in an instant, like he could turn his looks on and off at will. "Do you have any idea what you've done to us?"

It hit me then, how little I knew about Eric outside his interest in baseball. I had no idea about his state of mind or what he could be capable of. He was just some guy I'd sat next to at a baseball game. If he'd bought his ticket a day later, maybe he would've had a different seat. If Jessica had possessed a shred of decency, she wouldn't have tweeted those pictures. The three of us didn't belong in each other's orbits, but here we were, and the collision was about to get ugly.

"There is no us. Please tell me you haven't become that delusional," I said.

"Not you and me. I mean us." Eric pointed between him and Jessica. "Ever since you deleted your tweets and videos, we've been going through hell. The entire Internet thinks I did something to you to make you shut down our interactions, and Jessica is being dragged harder than ever for creating that thread. We're both getting death threats."

"Spare me your tears," I said. "Where were either of you when I got dragged for supposedly having sex in a bathroom? When strangers showed up at my house?"

Eric narrowed his eyes. "I set the record straight on that. Twice."

"How much later?" I asked. Eric looked away, dismissing me completely. "That's exactly what I thought." I turned to Jessica. "Are you proud of all this? Did you feel good when you followed us to the bathroom after you encouraged us to go together? Did those likes and retweets fill that empty place where your soul should be? Why did you do it?"

Jessica's lip trembled. "I didn't mean for it to get so out of hand. At first I just meant to take that picture of you spilling your food and drink on him for laughs, but then I saw the way you looked at him when he took off his shirt, and—"

I held up my hand to cut her off. "Don't you dare put this on me. Back up and think really hard about how you want to frame this story."

"I screwed up, okay?" Her nostrils flared slightly. "I thought it would be a cute and fun thread, and I thought blurring out your faces would keep you anonymous. I was wrong."

"When did you decide you were wrong?" I asked. "Just now? When Twitter turned on you? At any point when you took pictures of strangers and lied about them?"

Jessica opened her mouth and Eric put a hand on her shoulder to stop her. "We can go around and around on this all day," he said. "It's not like you're innocent either. We all got caught up in the fame game and we lost. We just want you to help us make it right. If you log back onto Twitter, say things are going great with us, you're not mad at Jessica, you're just more of a private person and that's why you deleted everything, this will all go away."

"You can't be serious." Every single tweet I'd read in a cold sweat in the middle of the night boiled inside me. "I'm not doing either of you any favors."

"I told everyone we didn't have sex in the bathroom so they'd leave you alone," he said. "Why can't you do this so they stop harassing me?"

"Because I didn't have sex with you in the bathroom!" I threw my hands in the air, careful to keep my grip on my phone. "You don't get a fucking cookie for telling the truth."

"We don't want to start the Baseball Babe stuff again," Jessica said. "We just want it to die. If you make it clear that you're not a victim, then people will stop treating us like perpetrators and it ends there."

"I'm not doing it." I held my phone tighter, praying it was still recording, and that Eric and Jessica could be heard over the generators. "You made your bed. Lie in it."

"Macy, please. We need you." Eric switched back to sad dog. He had so many masks, I had no idea which was real. Forget blogging. He really should've gone into acting.

He reached for my hand. It happened so fast, I barely had time to flinch away from him.

Paxton stepped up beside me. Rage rolled off him like a relentless summer storm. He grabbed Eric's wrist, and Eric's fear tinged the air as he tried to yank his arm away.

"She didn't give you permission to touch her," Paxton said. He released Eric and shoved him back a step. "Don't try that again."

Half of my heart soared. Paxton had shown up for me. The other half was terrified. I didn't want him anywhere near Eric and Jessica. What if they were lying and didn't plan to let their viral fame go anytime soon?

"You can't be here." I reached for Paxton's hand, prepared to drag him away, but he just shook his head. He wouldn't budge.

"I'm not leaving you alone with them." He bent closer to me so only I could hear him above the generators. "You're a risk worth taking."

"I really didn't want to do this," Eric said quietly. "But if you're not going to help us, then we're out of options."

Eric opened his screen and turned it to me. Two pictures of me and Paxton popped up. One of me hugging him, from when I'd seen him earlier, and the other where I looked up at him with my heart in my eyes. I had no doubt in my mind what Eric planned to do with those pictures.

Horror slammed into my gut, and vomit threatened to climb in my throat. I gritted my teeth, willing it back down, mentally soothing the sickness. If Eric saw what those pictures did to me, I'd never get the upper hand. Paxton breathed in deep through his nose.

"If you don't tweet what I asked, then I'm going to make you the villain. I'm going to tell the entire world you screwed me over." Eric tried to look remorseful. Tried, and failed miserably. He thought he had me again. I wanted to smack that smug undercoating off his face so bad, my entire arm was already vibrating from the impending contact. "If you thought the shaming was bad when everyone tweeted about you fucking me in the bathroom, wait until I tell them I only said you didn't do it to protect you. Poor me. I was so in love. Until I found out you had a boyfriend the entire time. They will burn you alive."

And they'd believe him. No matter what I said or did, they would believe him. The word of a sun-kissed boy with a pretty smile would always be worth more than that of a teenage girl.

Just like Eric and Jessica had brought every bit of hate down on themselves, I'd done this too. If I hadn't played along, if I hadn't wanted those YouTube subscribers so bad, Eric wouldn't have anything to hold over me. I didn't care what anyone said about me on Twitter. Not anymore. But if he posted those pictures, Paxton would be all over the Internet again. He'd go viral again. Amateur sleuths would uncover his real name and his entire past would be rehashed and chewed on by wolves again. Because of me. Because of the decisions I'd made when I'd been scared and hurt and worn down.

Eric put his phone away. "What's it going to be, Macy?"

I still had one card left to play. And I prayed it would be enough. "Go ahead and do it."

Paxton whipped his head toward me, and I silently begged him not to say anything. I couldn't let Eric think those pictures had any weight. If he knew what I'd be willing to give to make sure Paxton never appeared on the Internet again, I'd never escape. Eric would never let those pictures go. He'd never let Fly Ball Girl go.

"But if you do that, then this is going up on YouTube." I stopped recording, turned my own phone toward him and Jessica, and hit play. "It sucks when people invade your privacy and film you without your consent, doesn't it?"

Paxton relaxed beside me as Eric and Jessica both paled at the sound of their voices, their threats to use those pictures against me, which could be heard loud and clear above the generator. Bless modern technology. And as we glared at each other over my phone, we entered into a new game. One with bigger stakes. It was only a matter of who would fold first.

Eric had his blog and I had YouTube. Desperation to grow our numbers had brought us both to this point. Eric was right about one thing: I wasn't innocent either. I'd hurt and lied to people I genuinely cared about who genuinely cared about me, because I didn't believe in myself enough to think I could be anything other than Internet famous. While I couldn't go back and change my mistakes, I could still make better choices going forward.

Those tough decisions were now my only option if I wanted a clean break. I held up my phone so Eric could get a front-row view, opened up Twitter, and shut the whole thing down. Bye-bye thirty-five thousand followers. I never knew you, and you certainly never knew me. Next, I flipped over to YouTube. This one was way harder, but I needed all the leverage I could get. With a few clicks, they were gone. Every single one of my reviews.

"There. It's done. I have nothing to lose if you post those pictures," I said. "Sure, strangers will drag me, but it'll be like a tree falling in the forest, and I won't be around to hear it. But you will be."

"If you don't care, then you won't mind if I upload these pictures so people will leave me alone." Eric sneered, but his lip wobbled too much for it to be anything other than comical.

"I care about strangers showing up at my house again. I care about my grandma having to change our number again." I also cared about keeping Paxton out of this mess. "But you care a whole lot more about online hate than I do. I wonder if the Royals will still let you into the locker room? Don't they revoke press credentials for manipulative, abusive assholes?"

"You wouldn't dare." Eric turned so red, if he'd been a cartoon, steam would've poured out of his ears. "I will fucking ruin you."

"True." I gave him my sweetest smile, the one where I showed all my teeth. I could practically taste his blood on them. "But not nearly as bad as I'll ruin you."

"What do you want?" Jessica asked.

"I want your phones," I said. "Both of them."

They looked at each other. The pleading in Jessica's pouty lip met with Eric's stubborn ego. I had her. Now I just needed to get him. "What are you going to do?" Eric asked me.

"I'm going to delete your pictures, then I'm going to hop on Twitter and delete every thread and mention of Baseball Babe."

"We can do that ourselves," Jessica said.

"No." I knew how deleting worked. How they'd be saved in the trash for thirty days. I wouldn't be taking any chances with this. "I want to do it. I need to make sure they are really wiped clean." I handed my phone to Paxton, who held it with a white-knuckle grip.

"How do we know you won't wipe away our photos, the only leverage we have, and then load that video anyway?" Eric asked.

I tapped a finger to my lips. "I suppose you'll just have to trust me."

And I hoped it haunted them. I hoped they'd wake up in the middle of the night, frantically scrolling through YouTube to see if I'd uploaded that video after all. I hoped they felt a fraction of the terror I'd gone through. But most of all, I hoped Jessica would learn how to keep her camera to herself from now on.

Jessica handed me her phone first, grinding her jaw the entire time. "Just do it."

She nudged Eric, shooting daggers at him, until he finally relented and gave me his phone too. I deleted the pictures of me and Paxton first, in case they changed their minds and tried to snatch their phones back, then I went in and deleted the photos permanently from the trash, making sure they hadn't downloaded from the Cloud yet. I even checked their emails and texts too. I deleted every tweet, every Instagram video, every YouTube video until every interaction, every mention of that day at the Royals game, disappeared. With every click, that black hole in my heart healed over. I couldn't do anything about the hashtags or screenshots, but it was enough for me.

Once I finished, I handed them their phones. "Change your Twitter handles, bios, and profile pictures. You'll both be forgotten by the end of the week when someone new goes viral. And if you so much as think my name again, I'll lawyer up."

I linked my arm through Paxton's and we left them behind the game tents among the generators. Jessica and Eric, who had come into my life by chance, left again just as quickly. The damage Jessica had caused with those photos would linger in some ways for a long time, for all of us, but even if the Internet was forever, attention spans generally weren't.

CHAPTER
TWENTY-EIGHT

AS SOON AS WE walked back to the midway, Paxton tugged me against him and kissed me deeply. The carnival worker at the milk jug toss game whistled and tried to encourage Paxton to win me a giant stuffed banana, but we ignored him.

"You were brilliant." He held my shoulders as he kissed my forehead. "Utterly." He kissed my cheek. "Completely." He kissed my other cheek. "Brilliant." He kissed my lips again. "As soon as Eric showed those pictures, I thought it was all over for us. How did you know to record them?"

"I'm a fast learner." I pulled back and looked him over. "How did you find us?"

He rubbed his jaw. "I followed you. I'm sorry it took me so long to really get there."

"You didn't have to show up at all, you know. I had it handled."

"I know." He blew out a breath. "I'm sorry about being distant the past two days. It's still a lot for me, and I kept my distance so I could get a grip on it all. But I'll always stand by you."

"That's why I love you." I took his hand. We still had

another hour before he had to get back to Matilda for her show. "Let's go ride something that won't kill us."

I texted Elise to meet us by the Tilt-A-Whirl. She was already there with Midnight by the time we got to the other side of the fair. Elise wore a pirate hat made out of balloons and looked deliriously happy about it, while Midnight stood beside her, glaring at the ride.

I nudged Midnight. "You do know there are children here, Unholy Mistress. Maybe try not to look like you'll eat their souls?"

She turned her glare on me. "Who in their right mind would pay money to purposefully make themselves sick?"

Elise cocked her head, and the balloon feather in her balloon pirate hat bounced with the movement. "Are you afraid of the Tilt-A-Whirl?"

"No." Midnight kicked at the ground. "Okay, maybe."

I couldn't believe it. The girl who'd faced her demons by becoming one was afraid of the tamest ride outside the merry-go-round. Even I'd ride the Tilt-A-Whirl, and I was terrified of nearly every other ride at the fair.

"We are definitely going on it now," I said.

"I will definitely puke on you," Midnight shot back. "If you force me on that thing, I'm sitting with you."

"Okay, you win." I held up my hands in surrender. "No rides. Promise."

"Did you find Jessica and Eric?" Elise asked.

I took out my phone and showed her the video, just to give her the full effect. Midnight and Elise swore and cursed

Eric and Jessica the whole time, and when they'd reached the point where I'd stopped recording, I filled them in on the rest.

"My best friend." Elise hugged me. "The badass."

I squeezed her tight. "Does this mean I get to be Batman now?"

"Hell no." Elise pulled back and shook her head. "You're still Robin, but, like, a really buffed-up, cool version of Robin."

"I'll take it, I guess." I glanced at the time on my phone and turned to Paxton. "If you want to go get Matilda checked in, I'll stop by the craft hall to see the Bees' quilt and meet you over there in time for the judging."

"That works for me." He kissed me again before disappearing into the crowds.

"Did you two want to come with me?" I asked Elise and Midnight.

They looked at each other. "Nah," Elise said. "We're going to go make out in my truck before the rabbit show. My girlfriend has a thing for pirates."

"Arrr," Midnight said, her face turning the color of the red shells over the Tilt-A-Whirl.

I waved them off and made my way over to the craft hall, which was really just a huge white barn that didn't have any animals in it. Crowds and flies filtered in and out of the wide-open doors. Booths holding paintings, pottery, beadwork, photography, pies, cookies, and handwoven rugs filled the aisles. Anything considered an art or a hobby could be judged at the Shelby County Fair. Though nothing else created the same buzz as the quilts. They took up the entire back wall of the barn, all hung up on hooks to show their full detail.

As soon as I spotted the Bees—minus Gigi, who was assisting Paxton—at their table, I looked up and put a hand over my chest. There on the wall, the Bees hadn't just embroidered Defining Moments in Recent History, but Defining Moments in *their* histories.

I recognized each square by their signature stitches. Peg's depicted two women seated at a table with needle and thread. The first time she and Gram had sewn together, when Gram started the Bees and Peg became as much a part of my family as a certified Evans. Donna's showed a woman with flowing blond hair, dancing in a field of flowers and surrounded by five boys. Gigi's square took my breath away. A young boy, age nine if I had to guess, holding a rabbit in a yard bordered by daffodils. And Gram's. She'd sewn a teenage girl and her mom, with both of their hands holding a heart over the pregnant belly of the girl.

I approached the table and managed not to turn into a sobbing mess. "I think this is your best work yet."

"It certainly turned out well." Gram rested her arm on my shoulder.

The pride radiating off her was thicker than the flies hovering around the animal barns, but she kept it reined in. Like she did every year, knowing the quilt would go to beef. Not this year though. Not this quilt. Even if I had to dig into my savings, I'd make sure the Bees got to keep this one.

"It's nice and coherent, too." Donna gave a nod to Peg.

All wars went into cease-fire mode during fair days.

"Who are all those boys?" I asked Donna.

"I had fun in the sixties." She glanced up at her square. "I couldn't remember which one I liked the most, so I went ahead and sewed them all up there."

"It's perfect."

Strangers lingered at their table, drawn in by the lovely needlework. They'd take first place again this year for sure.

"You just missed your momma and Roger," Gram said.

I raised my eyebrows. "Oh, he's just Roger now?"

"He's okay." She huffed, as if it pained her to say so. "Still old."

That was damned near a seal of approval from Gram. "I have to get over to Matilda's show, but I wanted to stop by and see what all the screaming and fights produced this year."

Gram patted my cheek and grinned. "Such a smart mouth on you."

It was true. I'd learned it from the best.

Matilda was officially a blue-ribbon bunny. She'd posed like a pro, and Paxton had handled her with all the skill and grace of someone with his experience. He lifted her over his head and planted soft kisses on her nose, like that day I'd wandered into his backyard and changed everything between us. The Bees left the fair to have dinner. Their quilt would be judged tomorrow, but I had no doubt they'd win. Gigi packed up Matilda and took her home.

I wrapped an arm around Paxton's waist. "How does it feel to be a blue-ribbon owner?"

"Pretty damn amazing." He grinned at me. "Do you want to hang around here some more, or do you want to get out of here?"

"Let's go."

Midnight and Elise had left right after the rabbit show, with Elise still wearing her balloon pirate hat. We waved to Strawberry and Brady, who was carrying around a giant stuffed banana, and a few other people we knew from town. I wanted to come back later for the fireworks show, but that wouldn't be for hours.

I drove us back to town, parked beside the lake, and took a blanket out of my trunk. The park was closed, the lake and playground empty. Everyone in town was either at the fair or taking a break from the fair before they went back for the fireworks. Within minutes, Paxton had broken into the shed, and we were out on the water with another boat. This time while Paxton rowed, I let myself enjoy the view.

Once he got to the center of the lake, he rested the oars in their metal holders. "Tell me something I don't know about you, Macy Mae."

"That night when we first hung out alone, I wanted to kiss you. And I almost did." I linked our fingers. "That's why I flung myself into the water."

Amusement sparked in his hazel eyes. "I said tell me something I *don't* know."

I shoved him, and the whole boat rocked.

"Careful," he said. "You know how easy it is to go overboard in one of these."

"All right. You want something you don't know?" I leaned in closer, and whispered in his ear about that night when the house was quiet and I imagined his lips were my fingers.

"That." His voice cracked, and he cleared his throat. "That's definitely something I didn't know. Feel free to tell me about those things more often."

"I think you should tell me something I don't know about you," I said. "Why am I always the one revealing my secrets out here?"

"Mine aren't as fun as yours." He took my hands, his expression going serious. "I want to learn how to drive, and I want you to be the one to teach me."

My breathing stilled. "Are you sure?"

He nodded. "It's time. I can't keep relying on Gigi, and if I ever want to leave this town one day, it's a thing I'll need to know how to do."

"You want to leave Honeyfield too?" I'd always thought of Paxton as a permanent fixture in town, or maybe I hadn't considered that he'd ever leave because of the driving thing. The old fear of being stuck here lessened even more.

"I've been talking to Elise about maybe going in for half of the shop she wants to open in Chicago, and we can't make anything of ourselves if we stay here. Teaching me won't be easy." He tucked a lock of hair behind my ear. "I'll be a terrible student, and I might freak out a few times, but I'm not comfortable dealing with that in front of anyone else but you."

I cupped his face and kissed him. "I'd be happy to teach you."

He rowed us to the other side of the lake, to a grassy bank surrounded by raspberry bushes. I spread out the blanket I'd brought and I laid my head in the crook of his arm while we watched *Say Anything* on his phone. His favorite movie and my favorite movie had unintentionally, or maybe intentionally, become our movie.

As the credits rolled, I sat up. "I want you to film me."

His eyebrows practically touched his hairline.

"Not like that." I laughed. "I mean, I want to make one last YouTube video. A goodbye to my Misty Morning persona. It'll be the only video left on my channel."

I wouldn't be starting a new channel to continue the reviews. Jessica Banks had taken YouTube from me. Even if I eventually forgave her for everything else, that was one thing I would never forgive. Paxton took my phone and I showed him where to hold the camera. As soon as he gave me the thumbs-up, I let everything go.

"Hi, all, my name is Macy, but you might also know me as Fly Ball Girl or Misty. I have a final video, a little different from my previous content. This one is for me."

I told the camera everything about what I'd gone through in the past few weeks. What it had been like to have my every move documented without my consent, what it did to my mental health to scroll through Twitter in the middle of the night, how being trampled on and slut-shamed by strangers made me feel. I didn't reveal what Eric and I had done to play into that, since I intended to stay true to my word and not expose either of us to further harm, but I couldn't go completely dark without having my say. It was one thing if Jessica learned her lesson, but regular people just trying to live got captioned or tweeted or turned into memes every day without anyone thinking about the consequences. If I could convince even one person with a phone to think twice before turning their camera on a stranger, it would be worth it.

When I finished talking, I took my phone back and uploaded the video to YouTube, then deleted the app. Tomorrow, I'd start a new Instagram account. A private one, where only people I allowed could follow me and view my pictures. I'd still post movie reviews for my friends. I wouldn't let Jessica take everything I loved.

Paxton gathered the blanket, and as we rowed back across the lake, he asked me, "What are you going to do, now that you're done with YouTube?"

I tilted my head and let the last rays of the sinking sun warm my face. "Anything."

The idea of opening my own store had started to take root in me. Not right away. First I'd get a job at a media store, work my way up, and learn all the ropes of how to run that kind of a business. Then I'd strike out on my own. I didn't need to check YouTube to see how many views I'd gotten. I didn't need to depend on the approval of a fickle audience. I already had everything I wanted in the present.

The future would be completely up to me.

ACKNOWLEDGMENTS

I'M SO THANKFUL FOR my readers, and I hope you enjoyed spending a little time with Macy.

To my agent, Rebecca Podos, I'm eternally grateful for your wisdom and guidance over the years. You truly epitomize that agent meme with the drowning kid holding the rope, until the adult comes along and shows them that they can stand.

To my editor, Ashley Hearn, working with you has been a dream come true. Your incredible insight into Macy and the people she loves and the world she lives in has been invaluable. Thank you for helping me dig deeper into the heart of this story.

To my copy editor, Kaitlin Severini, I so appreciate how you never fail to catch my slip-ups, and do so with humor and fun.

Huge thank you to my publicists Lizzy Mason (I'm so glad we got to hang out!) and Lauren Cepero, editorial intern Hanna Mathews, editorial assistants Tamara Grasty and Franny Donington, managing editor Hayley Gundlach, production manager Meg Palmer, editorial director Marissa Giambelluca, designer Kylie Alexander for once again knocking it out of the park with a cover I love beyond words, publisher Will Kiester, and the wonderful sales team at Macmillan.

Jen Hawkins, my literary soulmate, my ambassador to the TPF, I love you. I'm so grateful you're in my life, my writing wouldn't be the same without you.

Kellye Garrett and Roselle Lim, we're still dancing.

Coven: Kelsey Rodkey, Annette Christie, Andrea Contos, Auriane Desombre, Rachel Lynn Solomon, Susan Lee, I don't know where I'd be without all of you. Endless hugs and gratitude for your friendship, laughs, and giving me a reason to keep Twitter on my phone.

Jenny Howe, Diana Urban, Laurie Dennison thank you so much for your incredible feedback and kind words. I'm so lucky to have you in my life.

To my husband and my girls, every day with you is an adventure.

ABOUT THE AUTHOR

SONIA HARTL IS THE author of *Have a Little Faith in Me* (Page Street), which received a starred review in *BookPage* and earned nominations for the Georgia Peach Book Award, YALSA's Quick Picks for Reluctant Readers, and ALA's Rise: A Feminist Book Project List. When she's not writing or reading, she's enjoying pub trivia, marathoning Disney movies, or taking a walk outside in the fall. She's a member of SCBWI and the Managing Director for Pitch Wars 2020. She lives in Grand Rapids with her husband and two daughters. Follow her on Twitter @SoniaHartl1.

Have a Little Faith in Me

Sonia Hartl

**AVAILABLE WHEREVER BOOKS
ARE SOLD**